OFF T

A NOVEL

*To Joseph S. Micallef and partners
With much gratitude
LPMaya*

OFF THE VILLAGE MAT
A NOVEL

Love P. Maya

VANTAGE PRESS
New York

FIRST EDITION

All rights reserved, including the right of
reproduction in whole or in part in any form.

Copyright © 1998 by Love P. Maya

Published by Vantage Press, Inc.
516 West 34th Street, New York, New York 10001

Manufactured in the United States of America
ISBN: 0-533-12548-0

Library of Congress Catalog Card No.: 97-91048

0 9 8 7 6 5 4 3 2 1

Contents

Acknowledgments   vii

1.	Late News	1
2.	The Fertile Seed	12
3.	The Stranger	21
4.	Motor Mouth	40
5.	Tidings	66
6.	Disposition	76
7.	Transition	83
8.	The Interview	103
9.	Friend Everlasting	112
10.	The Professor	121
11.	Stepping Out	140
12.	The Dove	160
13.	Outcast	173
14.	Wild Cat	190
15.	The Messengers	199
16.	White Chief	218
17.	The Wedding	235
18.	Recantation	242

Acknowledgments

To my deceased parents, who would have been proud; my dearest daughter, whose love, loyalty, and support inspired me throughout the writing of this book; my sisters, Muriel Abisogun and Maud Meyer, and my cousin, Chief Robert Walters; my loving and loyal friends, Angelika and Ernst Pawlitshek, Bisi Ajayi, and Mark and Ann Scarcella; Donovan Hohn, for his ingenious feedback; Jim Weiner, Hugh Hohn, Maureen Costello, and Walter Clark, for their time and technical assistance; and my landlord, Vincent Denietolis, for his genuine interest in this project and his persistent efforts to ensure my comfort.

OFF THE VILLAGE MAT
A NOVEL

1
Late News

There was every indication the celebrations would continue until dawn. It was already 3:00 A.M. and guests were still arriving; no one was leaving. Music blared rhythmically to the High Life and Juju music. Guests swayed, gyrated, or hopped about to the compelling sounds of the thumping music; others sat, balancing the plates of jollof rice and fried plantain on their laps, while others pranced about eating out of the plates they held in their hands. There were still others, who, not because of a shortage of chairs or sitting space, were leaning against either a chair, a door, or a table, as they raked jollof rice or jabbed their forks into slices of plantain. Thus, in the midst of this activity, I confided my intention to Helen Balogun, to escape to a hotel in Ikoyi or Victoria Island where I could sleep peacefully for a long time. Helen and Bola Balogun had organized a surprise party to greet me on my arrival from Paris. The celebrations were already in progress when I arrived at the Baloguns' from Murtala Muhammed International Airport in Ikeja. No one realized I was near collapse both mentally and physically. I was still in extreme turmoil from my ordeal in France and had not slept in two nights. Giving up my joyous and contented life in France was like cutting off my arms and legs. My life had literally crumbled before me. It took all the energy I could muster to pretend I was having a good time along with the guests. I faked the smiles and laughter, and danced as though it was the happiest day of my life; but my heart and the inner core of my belly seemed as if they were being sandpapered and rubbed with the hottest of Nigerian dried red pepper.

At Ikoyi Hotel where I had fled, I was faced with yet another incontestable menace—the vibrating and steady buzzing of the air conditioner which summoned my attention to its incessant and irritating sound. For the one hundredth time, it seemed, I rolled from one side to the other. Several hours had tolled by, yet sleep eluded me. It is said that one's entire life flashes before one's eyes when death is near. How could I have being dying? I was young, vibrant, and had never been ill a single day in my life. Nevertheless, as I rolled for that one hundredth time, remaining on my back and focusing my eyes on the dreamy painting of Badagary Beach on the wall in front of me, my entire life did unfold before my eyes like the unrolling of a long, tightly folded mat.

As I gazed at the painting, my life began during the stampede into the bush, which turned out to be home for me and my family for some time. I was thirteen. The news that the civil war between the Federal troops and the Biafran army had ended had not reached us. We were still in hiding in a dense and isolated bush, several miles from our village, Uzoakoli. On this particular day, the blinding sun had retreated into the sky. For us, the day had passed like most of the other days in the bush. We had huddled together in sleep underneath a mahogany tree after a fruitless search for food throughout the day, but I could not sleep. My hunger pains were now excruciating. I had to eat something, I told myself, anything—insects, lizard, roots. So, I decided to try again for the last time before nightfall in search of something to eat. I chose to go in a direction my family had never taken. Easing my body slowly, weakly, away from the huddle, I looked about me.

As I stood over my family observing the sleepy faces of my parents and nine brothers and sisters, I thanked the gods of my ancestors that my family had stuck together during the stampede. How we had remained together as we fled our village had been a mystery to me over the years. Thousands of people had fled aimlessly when the Federal troops advanced into our area. In the panic and confusion that ensued, hundreds of people became separated from their families. Petrified and pathetic looking children could be seen running aimlessly, screaming, and calling out for their parents. Likewise, panic-stricken parents searched in vain for their children. Yet, my family had remained together. I was certain this was possible, because I had prayed to the God the nuns at the village school taught me about, and to my deceased relatives and the other gods I had learned about from my family.

As I continued to observe my sleeping family, I noticed the tiny, bony, patched face of Comfort, the youngest of the family now since the death of Esther there in the bush. I had always believed that Esther would not have died if there had been food to eat. I did not want Comfort to be the next victim to hunger. I wanted to do all I could to prevent another death from occurring. I felt a great urge to do something spectacular to surprise my miserable and starving family. Before starting on my mission, I took one last look at the distended bellies and green hair of each of my siblings. I could see also that my own belly was distended, but I could only suspect that my hair had also turned green. I observed my surroundings as I ran my fingers through my knotted hair and imagined in horror what shade of green it had become. I felt around my waist and hips which had once filled my navy blue pinafore school uniform, and was alarmed to feel a structure that felt like a dried-up sugarcane. I brushed my face with the palm of my hand; it was all nose and chin. With both hands, I slapped the dust off my once beige-and-pink floral organza dress which had now being transformed into dangling, solid brown rags. I took a few steps backward, my eyes still travelling from one family member to the other. Then, with only a fleeting doubt as to whether my proposed mission would be fruitful, coupled with the intense desire to help my family in some way, I swung around and scuttled into the bush.

I walked for what seemed like miles in an unfamiliar section of the bush. Suddenly, as if by a wave of the wand of an ancestral spirit, wild fruit trees with succulent looking fruits of various sorts exploded before my tired eyes. At first, I was afraid my eyes were playing a cruel trick on me. To test my eyes, I stood for a second, closed them tightly and rubbed them vigorously with my forefingers. When I finally opened them, I was astonished to find that the fruit trees were still standing, and I was also able to see something I had not observed earlier. Very near the fruit trees was a silver sheet of a small, luminous stream. *This cannot be real*, I thought, *but perhaps the gods and my deceased ancestors have finally answered our prayers.* Since my family came into hiding in the bush, we had never failed to pray to all the gods and spirits to deliver us from our ravaging ordeal. We prayed in the morning and we prayed at night before we tried to sleep amidst the sounds of crickets and the flashing of fireflies.

From where I stood, the fruits were indistinguishable, but that was my least worry. Whatever they were, they were going to be food for my starving family. Suddenly, my limbs developed an uncanny vigor, and I began to run. Moving swiftly toward the fruit trees, I observed the area as I whisked by. At times in my excitement, I would twirl around and run backward. There were luxuriant patches of dew-covered, bottle-green shrubbery, and a mosaic of blooming tropical flowers in red, yellow, violet, purple, and various shades of pink, some of which I had never seen. At the village school, I had been taught about the Garden of Eden in the Roman Catholic catechism, and now I wondered whether the biblical garden was any match for what was now before my eyes.

Finally, I reached the spot where the miracle garden stood, and hurried first to the stream. I threw myself on my belly beside it, stuck out my dry, patchy tongue, and began lapping up the water like a thirsty animal. I felt as though I could continue to drink forever; however, the thought of my mission caused me to choke. I jumped to my feet as I began to cough. Feeling light-headed, I sat on the ground to regain my composure and gather my thoughts. When things began to make sense, I proceeded to think of strategies for transporting fruits and water to where my family was. I gazed at all the fruits and wondered which ones to start on first. There were mangoes, breadfruit, soursop, bananas, pears, guava, oranges, limes, cashews, grapefruit, pink bell-shaped apples, and other fruits that were not familiar to me. I decided I would start with the bananas so I could eat a few as I gathered them. I approached a banana plant and removed a ripe bunch off the center of the cluster. The thought of food finally going into my mouth caused my hands to tremble. Quickly, I tore off the ripest banana from the bunch, peeled it in only two layers, and ate it in two gulps. As I reached for another one, I was stopped by a sudden biting pain in my stomach which caused me to lose my appetite. So, I decided to devote my attention to the task at hand. I turned around in order to start climbing a mango tree to get to its fruit when I fell into the arms of a man clad in military attire. My heart seemed to stop beating. I glared at the man.

"No fear, no fear, titi,* stan' still," the soldier grabbed my shoulders to steady me. Then, I heard another voice behind me,

"Titi where you come from? Where your people dem?" I swung all the way around to see who had just spoken. It was another soldier. Both men were carrying rifles, with revolvers tucked in their belts. I parted my lips to let out a scream, but no sound escaped. I brushed past the soldiers in an attempt to get away, and they simultaneously blocked my path.

The first soldier held my hand gently, "Titi, ah say, make you no fear. We don' come because war don' finish. We de tell people make dem go home. War don' finish."

"You insigh' bush all by yousef? Where you mama an' you papa day?" inquired the second soldier.

I was still speechless and did not answer. I searched the eyes of both men, and then eyed their rifles and revolvers. Suddenly, a deathly fright racked my body, and I felt my whole being trembling.

"You no fit talk?" the first soldier asked, looking about him, "You by yousef? What village you don' come from?" Still petrified, I did not answer. My eyes felt strained for having to open them as wide as I could as they moved mechanically from one soldier to the other.

"Talk!" the first soldier barked, squinting his eyes, creasing his forehead, and pointing at me. "Ah say, where you from? Where you mama an' you papa day?"

I was still frozen with fear. Instead of answering, I was contemplating a way to escape. I fell on my knees and attempted to dash off between the second soldier's legs. Again, both soldiers blocked my path with their bodies, while the first soldier dug his fingers into my knotted hair

*titi—a young girl

with one hand, and with the other hand, lifted me off my feet and slammed me onto the ground on my back.

"Stay dere and no make me vex for you," he said through his teeth, "you betta behave yousef."

"So, if she day lost, den, she no get mama an' she no get papa. She don' stay for bush all by herself," the second soldier remarked, smiling triumphantly and winking at his partner.

"Den, we-e no for worry for notin, make you go fest my broda. I go fest yestaday with dat fest gal wee fin' in dee bush, rememba?" the first soldier replied.

I began to whimper. I sensed trouble, but I had no idea what it might be. "Ah beg you," I pleaded, "Ah get mama, an' papa, an' brodas an' sistas. Ah come find food for dem. Na dat ah day do before you don' come," I rattled off, "Ah beg, make you no kill me."

"Oh, hoh!" the second soldier exclaimed. "She fit talk! an' she get family!"

"Where you family day?" the first soldier asked, looking almost fearful.

"Den day far, far, over dere insigh' bush. Den don' hungry so tay, den no fit walk. Ah beg, make ah take fruit go give dem for chop. Ah beg you, make ah getup," I replied looking up at the towering, uniformed figures who reminded me of giant Alakoko who had passed through our village the previous planting season.

"Look, titi," the second soldier cautioned, getting on one knee beside me, "you listen me good good. No make me an' dis my broda vex for you, you hear? Make you stay jus' like dat, an' you go make me an' my broda here very very happy. You make we happy, we no go shoot you, kill you, or anyting like dat. You undastan' me?"

I nodded frantically. "Yesa, ah undastan', sa."

"Good gal," he replied.

"You an' you family no know say war don' finish?" the first soldier inquired in a somewhat kindly voice.

"No sa, we no know sa," I replied, puzzled at the revelation.

"Make you no fear, titi, dee war don' finish. Na-im make wee day come tell people say make dem go back to dere village. You undastan' what ah say?"

I nodded although I was terribly confused. *If the war was over, why hadn't someone found us before now?* I thought.

The soldier continued, "So, you make me an' my broda happy, an' jus' do waytin wee say make you do, wee go follow you go where you moda, you fada, an' all you sistas an' brodas day, an' carry you all back to you village. You see? You undastan'?"

"Yesa, yesa," I replied, raising my head.

"Ah, ah, ah, ah," the soldier uttered, forcing my head back, "you day forget say wee don' tell you say make you stay like dat an' do waytin wee say do?"

"No sa, ah no forget sa. I'm sorry sa. Ah go do anytin way you say, sa. Ah want make me an' my family go back to Uzoakoli."

With that, the second soldier rose to his feet while the first soldier stepped backward and stood a few feet away. Quickly, the second soldier placed his rifle and revolver on the ground, unbuckled his belt, unzipped his pants, and slowly lowered himself to the ground as though to sit beside me. Suddenly, he swung himself over, with his knees astride my body and mounted me, pushing back my dress.

Seconds later, I was screeching in pain. I had never experienced such an agonizing pain. Even the hunger pains I had experienced from time to time in the bush, had not seemed severe enough to bring tears to my eyes as this agonizing pain did.

"Shutup!" he said. "Or wee no go carry you an' you family go back to Uzoakoli."

That was what I wanted more than anything in the world—a normal life once again in Uzoakoli with my family. So, I decided to conceal my pain and do nothing to irritate the soldiers. I closed my eyes tightly and clenched my fists, hoping that would ease the pain; but the pain got progressively worse. I then tried to stuff my mouth with one fist and clamp my teeth down on it. Nothing seemed to help. Just when I felt some relief as the second soldier got off me, the dreadful pain returned when the first soldier took his place. And that was all I could remember.

"Wake up, titi," someone was saying in a kindly voice and stroking my cheeks softly, "Get up, titi, make we carry you and you family go to you village. You say you village be Uzoakoli, right?"

I raised my head and nodded. 'Yes sa, my village be Uzoakoli, sa."

The sound of the name of my village was like inhaling the pungent smell of smelling salts. I was revived immediately. I sprang to my feet although they were unsteady. The first soldier quickly interrupted the buckling of his belt to put his arm about my shoulder to prevent me from falling.

I observed my brutal attackers almost lovingly now since they seemed sincere in bringing my family and me back to our village. I also felt grateful to them that I had not died from my ordeal; that the lives of my family members would also be saved; and that we would finally be returning to our village to live a normal life. To me, that was of much greater concern than the brutal assault on me. I felt something streaming down my legs and thought

I had lost control of my bladder. I looked down at my legs, and when I saw that it was blood, I thought I would still die; that I would bleed to death. I looked over at where I had lain. Patches of bright, red blood marked the spot, so I had a fairly good idea why I was bleeding. I examined my dress. It was not soiled since it had been raised up to my neck.

"Titi," the first soldier finally said, as he also noticed my bloody legs, "go take wata over dere and wash blood comot for you leg. Go quick quick make we de go carry fruit go for you family, an' den we go go get you family an' take you all go back for you village."

When I emerged from the stream, both soldiers stood waiting with every pocket bulging with fruits. Their caps had even become fruit baskets.

"Hold dee rest of dee fruit in you dress make we go," the second soldier commanded.

"Titi, you happy war don' finish?" the first soldier asked, probably in an attempt to get my mind off what they had just done to me, as he sensed that I must have been experiencing some kind of physical pain, resentment, and anger. It must have been obvious also that I was forcing myself to walk normally in spite of the persistent pain. I had determined not to say or do anything that would jeopardize my chances of staying alive and getting food back to my family.

"Yesa, ah happy sa," I replied, forcing a smile, "but ah fear one ting, sa."

"Waytin be dat?" both men replied almost simultaneously.

"Sa, ah fear say, when we go meet my family, you go do waytin you do me on my moda an' my sistas."

"Oho! Na dat day worry you?" the second soldier laughed, patting me on the head. "Make you no worry, titi, we de happy wit' you. You don' make me an' dis my broda here very very happy. So, we go treat you nice, an' you family too. We no go toush you moda an' you sistas. You hear? We promise you dat."

"Ah hear, sa. Tank you sa," I replied quickly.

"But, na one more ting you go do for me and dis my broda here."

"Waytin be dat, sa? Ah go do anyting you say, sa," I offered.

"Oooh! Now, you listen good good. You no for tell nobody waytin we do you. If ah find out say you don' tell somebody, we go come back an' kill you, kill you moda, kill you fada, an' kill all you family. You undastan'?"

"Ah undastan', sa. Ah no go tell nobody, sa. Ah swear for my granmoda in dee grave, ah no go talk. Until ah die, sa, ah no go talk."

2
The Fertile Seed

The dazzling sun hung high over the steaming white clouds, as it beat down on the bare backs of the farm hands working in the nearby farms. Not one male farm worker had a shirt on. Most wore khaki shorts; some wore colorful rubber thongs, and others went barefoot. The bright, multicolored outfits of the female workers which were either short cotton dresses or lappas,* formed a brilliant play of colors in the rays of the sun. Some of these women wore wide-brimmed straw hats secured firmly with strings tied securely under their chins. Some went hatless, displaying intricately braided hair in ostentatious designs. Also emerging from the greenish shallow streams were other barefooted women; some also barechested, with babies secured firmly to their backs with bright multicolored lappas. Each woman carried a bucket of water or a bundle of freshly laundered clothing on her head. Some walked briskly with both hands swinging systematically by their sides, while others seemed to flounce laboriously up the steep incline with one hand balancing the load on their heads and the other hand either cradling a baby tied to their backs or placed on the hip for support. Finally, in a single file, the women reached the narrow pathway which led to their respective compounds.

Along the main road which separated one village from the other, yet other women could be seen, also waddling, carrying heavy bundles of firewood on their care-

*lappa—the traditional wrap-around worn by Nigerian women

fully constructed katas.* The frolicking sounds of children, barking dogs, and the faint sounds of distant drums presented a cacophonous, yet exciting, combination of sounds. In the compounds, and in front of the roadside huts, older men sat idly under shady trees in rustic wooden easy chairs puffing avidly on crudely carved bone pipes. This was the sleepy village of Uzoakoli, in the Bendel area of Imo State, on the Southeastern section of Nigeria where I grew up. Uzoakoli was a strategic point in one of the battle zones during the bloody civil war between the Nigerian Federal Government and the former Biafrans who wished to secede from the central government.

Approximately a year and a half had passed since the Biafran war ended, and the return of my family was a particularly joyful and emotional reunion for the villagers of Uzoakoli, since they had already given up hope of ever seeing us again. Besides having much regard for my family, the villagers missed our services to the village and the surrounding area. Our farm had been a reputable place to buy produce and livestock before the civil war broke out. It was not surprising, therefore, that the welcome-home celebrations for my family continued for days. In the months that followed, the relatives of our family, in conjunction with dozens of villagers, assisted in rebuilding and renovating various sections of our compound and farm. Soon, our farm began to flourish once again with succulent crops, enabling us to resume our once thriving produce business.

It was another planting season. The wind blew lightly, but the air was heavy and hot. Dark gray skies had cast a dense shadow over Uzoakoli and the surrounding area,

*kata—a handmade pad placed on the head to ease the weight of a heavy object carried on one's head

foreshadowing the type of torrential rains which could persist for days. In the village school nearby, the school bell signaled the end of the school day. Scurrying about like a swarm of bees, and screeching at the top of their lungs, children ran recklessly out of the schoolhouse into the large, dusty school compound. Some children remained in the yard to play, while others ran through the gates of the low school fence into the various footpaths which led to their respective compounds. I was one of the first children to emerge from the school grounds. After running a short distance with my schoolmates, I noticed that the belt to my uniform was missing. My heart sank as I thought about the serious reprimand I would receive from the nuns if I appeared in school the following day without a complete uniform, a navy blue pinafore over a white, cotton, short-sleeved blouse. I had to get back into the schoolhouse to search for my belt.

Balancing my multicolored raffia* schoolbag on my head, I swung around and gazed at the schoolhouse, but was discouraged by the sight of the frantic mob of children forcing their way out through the narrow wooden door. Besides, I reasoned that my task at hand was, after all, more important than finding that belt. Also, the nuns' punishment for not wearing a belt was, invariably, "I WILL ALWAYS WEAR MY COMPLETE UNIFORM, AND I WILL ALWAYS BE CLEAN, NEAT AND TIDY," written fifty times in one's exercise book, after school. I had never found that to be much of a punishment, since I loved to read and write and I invariably welcomed, willingly, every opportunity to practice those skills.

So, pivoting back around, I proceeded to run along the footpath which led directly to my family farm. This

---

*raffia—the fibre of the raffia palm used for making bags, baskets, and hats

was the day the school report cards were given out. My report card was excellent, according to my teacher, Sister Juliana, and I could hardly wait to show it to my father. I knew just where to find him on the farm at that particular time of day.

School had always been a joyful experience for me; however, there was another important reason I liked school. Once, I had confided in Sister Juliana about my desire to leave the farm some day in search of another life in one of the large and progressive cities in Nigeria. Sister Juliana's advice was that I should first excel in school if I wanted to venture out into the world and make something of myself. I had taken Sister Juliana's advice and directed all my energies toward my education. My hard work was paying off, because I was considered one of the best pupils in the school.

Balancing my schoolbag on my head with one hand, and with the other hand raising my skirt to prevent it from hindering my strides, I raced home. Soon I was at the edge of my family farm, at the section where I thought my father would be. But, he was nowhere to be found. Shading my eyes with both hands, I scanned the entire area of the farm as I called out to him. Then, to my delight, I heard the familiar sound; his voice reverberating in the light afternoon breeze. He had heard me. With much delight, I swung around and advanced toward the sweet melodious voice. Vaguely, I could see him standing amidst the cassava* plants, behind the largest of the pear trees. With both hands down at my sides, leaving the bookbag well balanced on my head, I skipped sportively toward him. However, when I drew closer to the cassava patch, my father had disappeared once again.

*cassava—a tropical plant with edible, starchy roots

I had enjoyed the "hide-and-seek" game, up until now. I became a bit irritated; my patience had suddenly run out. I was no more in the mood for games; I was about some serious business. Showing off an "excellent" report card was more important to me, at this moment, than a silly hide-and-seek game with an adult. With slight irritation in my voice, I called out to my father again, in Igbo, since he spoke no English.

"My father! My father! It's me, Grace. I have something to show you. Stop playing games with me. Come away from behind that tree. I know you're there; I can see you," I lied, "you're hiding from me, but what I have to show you is very important, and it will also please you very much."

Finally, I reached the spot where I had seen him, and jumped quickly behind the pear tree, assuming the position of a frog, as if in readiness to leap forward in an attempt to "frighten" him. However, as I leaped forward, I saw my father's sprawled body lying quite still between two rows of cassava plants.

Mortified, I rushed to his side. After a quick, careful examination of his outstretched body, and discovering a small gash on the side of his neck, I knew immediately what had happened. I recognized the gash to be that of a snake bite. That area had a high incidence of snake bites. Almost everyone in the village, including children, had witnessed several cases of people being bitten by snakes.

Suddenly, I realized my father was dead, and I would never hear that melodious voice again. My eyes felt as if someone had suddenly buried the highest ant hill inside the middle of my head. Quickly, I wrenched the bookbag off my head and flung it wildly in the air. My books, including my report card, came raining down on the cassava plants and onto my father's stilled body. Feeling somewhat crazed, I sat beside my father's body cradling his head on my lap for some time. Then, I straightened his head to take a good look at his eyes, which stared coldly at me, unblinking; and while easing his head off my lap, I stood up slowly, feeling disoriented. I looked all about me wondering where I was; but another look at my father's lifeless body brought me back to my senses, causing my head to explode with my own deafening shriek, which escaped uncontrollably from my throat, summoning whole villages to our farm from every possible direction.

* * *

Shortly after my father's death, my mother's health began to deteriorate. My mother, Clara Nwokeji, who was known affectionately by the villagers as "Mama Grace," sank into deep depression. She had lost all interest in her surroundings and her family. Her condition was the talk of the village. According to the gossip that spread among the villagers, my mother did not possess the strength of an African woman, since she had allowed the evil spirits to take hold of her. Normally, the villagers believed that after the initial shock and trauma resulting from the death of a spouse or close relative, the spirit of the deceased invariably provided the survivor with enough strength to carry on with her life. Therefore, it appeared to the villagers that my mother was resisting help from her husband's spirit; that, instead, she had succumbed to the control of evil spirits who had built a solid, impenetrable wall around her, forcing her to retreat into their world.

I was now fifteen and notably aware of the heavy responsibility I must face, as the eldest child, with my father dead, and my mother unable to function. I was also aware of, and disturbed by, the gossip concerning my mother. So, I decided that soon after the grieving period for my deceased father, I would strive to develop the moral and physical strength of an African woman, so the villagers would praise me. I vowed to take over the running of the farm, with the help of my brothers and sisters. I calculated that when the time came for me to leave the farm and seek my destiny in the outside world, my brothers and sisters would have become mature, more responsible, and most importantly, expert farmers.

I was confident things would work out now, since it was clear to me that my father's spirit had joined the number of good spirits who were watching over me and my family. I also believed that my father would have approved of my leaving the farm life one day, as he was well aware of my conversations with Uncle Jeremiah regarding my burning desire to leave the farm someday in favor of a better life in one of the larger cities in Nigeria. I recalled the times when Uncle Jeremiah made frequent visits to the village from Owerri when I was a little girl. My father used to take pride at the unending questions I asked my uncle during those visits; questions such as:

"Uncle, what dee Civil Savice send you abroad to America and Englan' for?"

"In white man country, who day sweep dee street, an' day do all dee dotty work?"

"White man country get villages an' huts?"

"Waytin white man day chop? Den fit chop gari* an' foofoo† wit soup like okra soup an' egusi soup‡?"

Uncle Jeremiah would let out a big "Ho, ho, ho" laugh, and reply, "My child, I think I understand why

*gari—cassava flour
†foofoo—pounded flour made from yam, cassava, or plantain
‡egusi soup—soup made of the seeds of a type of melon

you're asking these kinds of questions. I'm laughing, my child, because I wondered about all those things myself before I began travelling to Europe. You see, it's natural for people who have not travelled abroad to think that way. Because they see white men here in only managerial positions, people find it difficult to imagine white men doing menial work."

Uncle Jeremiah also talked about his first hours in London as he rode in a taxi to his hotel in the center of the city; that it was a white porter who carried his bags from the airport terminal to his taxi; and that, as the taxi glided through the streets of London, he saw Europeans from all walks of life, some of whom were sanitation workers. Stories such as those never failed to leave me completely spellbound.

I recalled how my father enjoyed observing the way I marveled at Uncle Jeremiah's stories about places he had been on his Civil Service assignments, which included other sections of Nigeria. Regarding whether white people could eat Nigerian dishes, Uncle Jeremiah had one favorite story which he repeated over and over. It was about a British couple who had been invited to have dinner with a Yoruba family in Abeokuta. As they ate, the English gentleman did not appear to have any problem whatsoever. In fact, as he ate, he was professing how much he was enjoying the foofoo and ogbono* soup. However, his wife was not so lucky. She had fled the house with a glass of ice water in hand after her first bite. Uncle Jeremiah and the woman's husband had run after her and found her pouring the ice water on her outstretched tongue as she cried out in pain.

I remembered my father's supportive comments as

*ogbono—large lentil seeds

he listened to the conversation between Uncle Jeremiah and me, and I was confident that his spirit would approve if I left the farm some day.

"I tell you," he would say proudly, "this girl is different from the rest of my children. If you ask me, I don't think she's meant to be a farmer. But, as for my other children? That's a different story altogether."

So, it was Uncle Jeremiah's intriguing stories that fanned my burning desire to live and work in one of those supposedly fascinating cities, like Lagos.

3

The Stranger

Adding to the discomfort of the sun's rays, intense heat hung heavily around the flaming wood-fire outside the doorless, thatched-roof mud hut where I was assiduously preparing the evening meal. The egusi soup in the colossal, charcoal-black, four-legged iron pot, boiled vigorously. Feet spread apart, I stood poised in front of the crude, wooden mortar, ready to prepare the yam* foofoo. My mother had gone over the procedure step by step so many times with me before she became ill that I was now skilled at it. I imitated her every move. I had grown to love yam pounding, and was always proud of the finished product.

Lifting up the weighty pestle, I gradually dropped small pieces of piping hot, boiled yam into the mortar and began pounding. I focused my full attention on the crushed yam in the mortar so that I would not miss the lumps. Tightening my grip on the long-handled wooden pestle, I raised it up and down in steady, deliberate and systematic movements. Soon, beads of perspiration began forming on my forehead, saturating the edge of the bright yellow cotton scarf tied securely around my head. Every now and then, I paused briefly to catch my breath and brush off perspiration from the side of my face with my forearm. Then, I would dry my arm by brushing it against the side of my floral, sky-blue cotton dress and resume pounding.

*yam—a tropical plant with edible tuberous roots

Gradually, some boys and young men from the neighboring compounds began dawdling around observing what I was doing. Obviously, my spectators assumed that the loud thumping sound of the mortar would prevent me from hearing their conversation. Hence, they spoke freely in Igbo.

"Why do you always come around whenever Grace starts pounding yam?" one boy said to another.

"For the same reason you're here. Look at her. Isn't she the most beautiful girl in all of Uzoakoli?"

"She certainly is," came the reply.

"Now, look at that! This is why I come," said an older sounding voice, "She is even more beautiful when she drips in perspiration. Look at how the dampness of her dress, coupled with the continuous motion of her lithe form, accentuates the details of her fresh and youthful body."

The younger voices snickered, and the older voice asked, "How old is she now, by the way?"

Another older voice replied, "She has to be about eighteen now."

"How do you know that?" the first older voice shot back.

"I am twenty-six, and I have been coming to this compound even before she was born."

Although the pounding was almost deafening, I could hear the whole conversation, but pretended I could hear nothing. I was embarrassed by the comments, and the more embarrassed I felt, the harder I pounded.

The lively fire beside my mortar hissed and crackled. I finally let go of the pestle and turned to inspect the wood fire. The flame was much too great for the egusi soup. Quickly, I dropped to my knees and began removing some of the firewood to reduce the impetuous yellow flame. Then I continued the pounding, stopping occasionally to stir the soup gently with a huge, long-handled wooden spoon. Finally, the foofoo and egusi soup were ready. I stopped pounding for a moment to perform a taste test. Leaning the pestle to one side of the mortar, I picked up the spoon, scooped a small portion of the egusi soup, deposited it on the palm of my hand and licked it off, savoring the flavor. A humming sound and the smacking of the lips emitted simultaneously from my spectators. Next, I pinched off a small portion of the yam foofoo to feel its texture, and I nodded, proud of my handiwork. The meal was now ready to be served and I called out to Justine to give me a hand. I continued to ignore my spectators, who finally began to disperse.

I prepared my ailing mother's tray first, which contained a bowl of yam foofoo and a bowl of egusi soup, and handed it to Justine who was already standing by waiting to deliver it to our mother's hut. The remainder of the yam foofoo and egusi soup were put in separate huge bowls which were to be placed on a mat underneath the low-branched, sprawling pear tree, where Chukuemeka, the next eldest sibling, together with the other children, were already waiting patiently for the meal to be served. The younger children knew that before they came to the mat, they were to wash their hands by the water-bucket, and to also leave a bowl of water beside the mat for Chukuemeka and me in which to wash our hands, since we were the eldest. Soon, we were sitting in a circle around the two bowls of food. As our eager fingers began digging into the yam foo-foo and egusi soup, Chukuemeka suddenly noticed that the plates were not resting evenly on the mat.

"Justine," Chukuemeka chided, "why deedn't you clear the ground before you spread dee mat?"

"I deed, my broda, and noting was dere."

"If you deed, my sister, why is sometin dere now?"

"Awright," I said, rising to my knees and signalling wildly. "Everybody! Stop eating! And move away from the mat and let's remove whatever is there. It's that simple."

As we stood around the edge of the mat, I quickly added, "Let's first ask the jokester of the family whether he's pulling one of his pranks again."

No one said a word; however, all eyes stared askance at Ofo, who quickly denied any wrongdoing. So, Patrick picked up the bowl of yam foofoo while Chike picked up the bowl of egusi soup. Both boys quickly stepped away while Chukuemeka whisked the mat to the side. Suddenly, frenzied screams filled the compound. Chike and Patrick aimed the bowls of yam foofoo and egusi soup they were holding, at what they perceived to be a large snake that had curled itself into a neat bundle under the mat and had fallen asleep there. Instinctively, the rest of us had all bolted toward the entrance of the compound. As we viewed our eating place from where we stood, we discovered that Chukuemeka was not with us. He was still standing there, mat in hand, observing the "snake."

"Come back," he called out to us. "It's not a real snake, but it's a bloody good imitation of a boa constrictor."

Feeling much relieved, we ran back to join Chukuemeka. Strangely enough, the more I gazed at the "snake," the more in awe I became of its beauty and its creator.

"Let's give thanks to the gods it's not a real snake," I sighed, "but you must admit it's a beautiful imitation of one. Look at those colors, the eyes, the skin! Is it made of cloth or leather?"

"I don't care about dee beauty of dis snake, I want to know who put it dere to scare us," Justine said haughtily, hands on her hips. "It's not funny, scaring us like dat. It's only one porson in dis family dat would do a ting like dat. Who else, but dee clown an' artist of dee family."

"Ofo! Where Ofo go? Where Ofo go?" everyone chanted, looking around for Ofo.

"I'm like you, Justine, I don't care how dis snake look, an' I don't care wheda Ofo made it or not, I jus' wano eat; I'm hungry. Where our food go?" Obi said impatiently.

"You didn't see Chike and Patrick throw the food at the snake?" I asked.

"No," Obi replied, "I was running."

"Don't worry, Obi," I said, "I know you're hungry. We're all hungry. There's plenty more soup in the pot, but we'll have to settle for gari this time because it'll be quicker to make."

"By the way, where is Ofo?" Chukuemeka asked once again.

"If he know what good for him let him keep running because I'll change him into a snake when I catch him," Justine replied resolutely.

The second meal was eaten in silence, except for the sounds of the smacking of lips and occasional compliments to the "cook." At the end of the meal, not a particle of food was left in the plates. Almost immediately, and without any prodding by anyone, the younger siblings hastened off to clean the soiled plates, while the others made their way to the water-bucket to collect some water for hand-washing.

After the hand-washing, the children returned to the mat once again for their regular relaxation and storytelling session. Ofor, who had once vanished from sight after the incident with the "snake," suddenly appeared as if nothing had happened. He took his place beside Obi, who sat leaning against the bottom of the tree trunk. Patrick and Chike lay on their sides, legs outstretched, leaning on their elbows. Patricia, Isaac, and Comfort lay on their bellies also with legs outstretched, both hands supporting their heads; and Justine sat between Chukuemeka and me.

One after the other, Chukuemeka and I regaled the children with enchanting animal fables until we ran out of stories to tell. Nevertheless, soon no one was listening. All eyes were closed in deep slumber, including Chukuemeka's. I was telling my last story when I realized I had been talking to myself. I continued however, because I liked to hear it. Besides, since Chukuemeka and I decided to tell the stories in standard English, it gave me the opportunity to practice that language.

My last story was about a wolf who hung around the compound of the village nuns in a remote area of Ohafia, in an attempt to get to the twenty goats the pupils in the boarding school were raising. It was impossible for the wolf to jump over the high fence that surrounded the compound. One day, as the wolf roamed the dense bushes, he found the shredded skin of a goat. Suddenly, an ingenious idea came to him. He would put on the shredded goat's skin and wait for an opportunity to sneak into the compound. Each night he waited for that chance. Finally, one night, as the night watchman chatted with another night watchman who happened to be passing by, the wolf's opportunity came. The gate had been left ajar as the two watchmen chatted. The wolf hurried in quickly to mingle with the goats. His scheme worked for a while, until the goat's skin he was wearing began to wear off and the pupils also began to notice that the number of the goats had dwindled to seventeen. The wolf was ultimately detected as the wolf that he was and died by the sword of the night watchman.

Since I was the only one awake, I decided to make an

attempt to go to sleep. I stretched my legs out in front of me and leaned sideways against Chukuemeka who had sprawled out beside me. I knew it would be pointless closing my eyes to try to sleep, because I had not been sleeping well lately, even during the night. Ever since I had become proficient in speaking and writing the English language, I had been corresponding with Uncle Jeremiah in Owerri regarding the possibility of leaving the compound someday and making another life for myself away from the farm. Also, a letter to Uncle Jeremiah gave me another opportunity to practice my writing. Sister Michael, my English teacher at school, had convinced me that if I continued speaking pidgin English, it would interfere with my ability to speak standard English; and that if I was going to leave the farm in search of another life in the world, a good command of the English language would be essential. I never agreed completely with Sister Michael although I took her advice. I often thought that Sister Michael failed to see beyond the professional work force, and was ignoring the fact that masses of the population were uneducated, and many times, had no choice but to communicate with each other in either their indigenous language or pidgin English. I reasoned therefore, that since both the educated and the uneducated interacted on a daily basis, it was essential that educated Nigerians should retain their knowledge of both pidgin English and their indigenous language in order to facilitate communication. So, when I decided to take Sister Michael's advice, it was only partially; which meant that, as long as I was in the process of learning the English language, I would avoid speaking pidgin English; at the same time, I would make a conscious effort to retain my knowledge of both pidgin English and my indigenous language.

Uncle Jeremiah's letters had been a great source of

inspiration and hope to me. He had given me continued support regarding my plan to leave the village after graduating from secondary school. He had also agreed that Owerri should be my first stop and could be used as a stepping stone toward my other goals. But suddenly, Uncle Jeremiah's letters had stopped coming, causing me much anxiety; hence my sleepless nights. I was afraid that if Uncle Jeremiah changed his mind about putting me up in Owerri, I would have no other recourse but to cancel my plans of leaving the farm altogether.

As my siblings slept, I moved away quietly and sat alone facing the path that led to the main road. Pensively, I retrieved the last letter I had received from Uncle Jeremiah—almost a year previously—from the large pocket of my lavender and purple floral cotton dress. Lately, I had been carrying that letter around with me. Flipping the envelope over, I moved my fingers slowly across the sender's name and address, and read softly to myself. Then, I took out the enclosed letter, unfolded it slowly, and proceeded to read only the section right in the middle of the page that gave me the most encouragement:

> Exercise much patience. The two remaining years you have in school will go by very quickly, you'll see. You just learn as much as you can. When you get here, I'll take care of the rest. You won't have to worry about a thing. You can live with us until you decide you want to leave. A job will even be waiting for you in the ministry where I work. I've already discussed you with my immediate superior, and he is also anxiously waiting for you to make the move.

At this point, I stopped reading and asked myself, "But why the silence now, after all these encouraging letters?" I had been receiving at least one letter every month from Uncle Jeremiah for the past several years. Could it be that he had reneged on his promise to be my mentor and my host? To comfort myself, I had to rationalize for my uncle. Perhaps he was on one of those extended government sponsored courses taking place out of the country? Perhaps he was in another city in Nigeria on a departmental conference? But, what about the letters I had written within the past year that had gone unanswered? These questions floated around in my head.

I pondered these things as my siblings slept. I would write Uncle Jeremiah another letter and remind him that I had passed my School Leaving Certificate exam, and that it was time to begin arranging to make the proposed transition possible. In the letter, I would bring him up-to-date regarding the situation on our farm. I would tell him all about my siblings; how they had all grown up both physically and mentally; how Chukuemeka was the one doing the manly chores around the compound and farm since the death of our father, and how he had become a strong and efficient worker. Now seventeen, Chukuemeka was tall, muscular, and strong, just like a grown man. And although a girl of medium height, sixteen-year-old Justine also had the strength of a man. She was in charge of the distribution of the gari made by our family, which was sold to the neighboring villages. Twice a week, with enormous gari bags on their heads, Justine and fifteen-year-old Obi would go from compound to compound and sometimes from village to village, selling gari. There was fourteen-year-old Ofo, the family comic and artist, with a reputation of being able to make even the devil laugh. However, we gave him credit for knowing when to frolic and when to be serious, until that incident with the "boa constrictor." There were thirteen-year-old Patrick and twelve-year-old Chike, all Chukuemeka's helpers around the farm. There were, also, eleven-year-old Patricia, ten-year-old Isaac, and nine-year-old Comfort, who were my helpers around the compound. So it was, that each member of the family contributed efficaciously to the running of the farm.

As I reflected on the contents of what my next letter to Uncle Jeremiah would be, a woman's voice coming from the periphery of the compound jolted me from my thoughts. I jumped to my feet and craned my neck sideways to get a better look at the stranger. She did not appear to be anyone I knew. Indeed, it was immediately obvious to me that the stranger was not even an African; it was a white woman. She could not have been one of the nuns, since the nuns would never have worn attire similar to this stranger's.

The stranger was close enough now for me to observe her more thoroughly. She wore a rose and beige floral halter top which covered only her chest area, leaving her belly bare. She also wore faded baby-blue jeans secured around the hips with a brown leather belt, accentuated with a wooden elephant-head buckle. As I eyed the woman who was now standing in front of me, I noticed that on her feet, she wore a pair of alligator thongs, which revealed bright, ruby-red toenails matching the color of her long, well-trimmed finger nails. I admired the stranger's jeans and thought about the pair of jeans Uncle Jeremiah sent me through a villager who had traveled to Owerri; but I had not had the courage to wear them there in the village for fear of being ridiculed. I had never seen a village girl or woman wearing any type of trousers. In my village, trousers were always considered to be men's attire. So, I had decided to save the jeans for such time that I would have the opportunity to live in a fast-paced cosmopolitan city.

"Hallo! You speak English, yes?" the stranger asked, smiling broadly. *What a friendly woman,* I thought. Usually, when the wives of the expatriates* came to buy vegetables and fruits, they wore serious red faces and looked hot and bothered from the sun. Bringing their drivers with them, they would select what they wanted and leave quickly.

"Yes, madam," I replied, hands behind my back, and curtseying slightly.

"You grow lettuce, yes?" the woman asked.

"Yes, madam."

"Ah, goot," she replied, breathing a sigh of relief, "I been to so many farm in dee area an' nobody grow lettuce."

I was surprised that the woman did not speak standard English. I was under the impression that all white people were born speaking standard English. I looked over my shoulders at my siblings. They were still fast asleep and were not aware of the woman's presence.

I walked passed the woman quickly. "Madam, follow me, I'll show you; we have nice lettuce," I said, leading the way.

The woman followed, trying to keep up with my fast pace. "You speak English vell. Where you learn such goot English?"

"I went to school here in the village, madam," I replied proudly.

"You on holiday?"

"No, madam. I have finished secondary school. I passed the exam last year. I'm so happy for that, madam," I replied, clapping my hands gleefully.

"I'm happy for you too," the woman said, looking over at me as though seeing me for the first time. She suddenly appeared to be intrigued by me. I wondered about

---

*expatriate—a white person who is either visiting or working in Nigeria

that for a moment and came up with an explanation: She probably had never run into an educated village girl, with seemingly high intelligence, I reasoned.

"What you do now you finish school?" she asked.

"I want to go and work in a big city like Lagos, Madam."

"Goot idee-ya! When you go?"

"I don't know yet, madam. I will be going to Owerri first to live with my uncle."

"Oh, goot. I vish you luck. You very smat gal an' you very beautiful too."

"Thank you, madam. Come in, madam." I gestured as we reached the entrance to the fruit and vegetable shed. Inside, I lifted a large plastic bowl containing some lettuce and balanced it against my chest. "You see, madam? We have lettuce, nice fresh lettuce."

The woman fingered the lettuce. "Dis all dee lettuce you have, yes?" she asked, raising her eyebrows.

"You want more, madam?" I replied, anxiously.

"No, no, you have plenty, but dem so small. Why lettuce so small in Nigeria?"

"Small, madam?" I replied, squinting my eyes in confusion. I had never seen larger lettuce. "You sure, Madam, it's lettuce you want? Maybe it's cabbage you want."

"No no no, is lettuce I vant. In Romania, in Europe, lettuce bik bik. Here in Nigeria, lettuce so small. Why dat?"

I shrugged my shoulders, thoroughly confused, but I was consoled by the woman's congenial personality. She looked around at the other vegetables and fruits piled up neatly on large long tables made with large logs of wood. There were paw-paw, mangoes, udala, utum unene (banana), olome (oranges), mmimi ute, ihulubana (grapes), ube (pears), soursop, grapefruit, guavas, pineapple, cabbage, carrots, and cucumbers.

"You still want the lettuce, madam?" I asked, placing the bowl of lettuce on the table.

"Oh yes ofcus I take dee lettuce," the woman replied, fingering the rest of the produce.

"Sorry, madam, that the lettuce is so small, and sorry we don't have more. We don't grow too much here, madam, because the people in the village don't buy it; only the nuns and the expatriates buy it. The same with the cabbage; the villagers don't buy that too; it's for the expatriates."

"Yes, cabbage," the woman replied. "I vant cabbage too, gee me one cabbage." And looking about her, she asked, "Where dee tomatoes an' dee peppas? Dee green one. You have?"

"Yes, madam, in the other shed. The other shed has most of the other things the villagers like, such as ukpeke (plantain), regular yam and cocoa-yam, and Nigerian vegetables like, onugbu, ugu, ahihala, nteoke, and mgbolobu."

Soon, the woman's large blue net shopping bag was full to its capacity. "How much everything cost?" she asked, testing how heavy the bag was.

"Madam, you're a nice customer, so I'll give you a good price. Madam, I will charge you only 10 shillings for everything because I want you to come back and be our regular customer."

"10 shilling! Das goot money," the woman replied as she dug into the back pocket of her tight jeans for a ten-shilling note.

"Don't worry, madam. I will carry your bag to your car," I said, as I put away the ten-shilling note in an empty cigarette tin underneath one of the tables. Then, I lifted the woman's bag and placed it on top of my head.

"Oh, tank you! You goot girl. Wass your name?"

"Grace, madam."

"Grace, you have goot tings here," the woman said as she led the way to her car which was parked by the main road, "I'll come back an' buy vegetables again, Grace; I like you. Grace! Nice name. My name is Mrs. Eva, Mrs. Andrea Eva."

"Mrs. Eva?" I repeated, anxious to get the name right.

"Yes, Eva, E.W.A., Eva," the woman offered. "Is Calabar name. My husband is from Calabar."

Finally recognizing the name to be indeed a Calabar name, I replied, "Oh! Ewa! Thank you, Madam Ewa, for coming to our farm to buy your vegetables."

"Oh! da-sawright, Grace. I mean vat I say, I'll come back. Tank you wery much!"

We reached Madam Ewa's car and I hurried toward the boot* while she tried to open it. Removing Madam Ewa's bag gently off my head, I placed it carefully inside the boot.

"Your parents do goot job here," Madam Ewa said, as she opened the car door and proceeded to get in. "I see you help wery much, yes?"

"Madam, my father is dead and my mother is not well, so, my brothers and sisters and me, we all pitch in and do the work," I replied, moving closer to the window on the driver's side.

"You pitch?" Madam Ewa repeated, creasing her eyebrows.

"Yes, madam, I mean, we all work together as a team." I intertwined my fingers illustrating unity.

"Yes, yes, I understan'," Madam Ewa replied nodding vigorously.

*boot—the trunk of an automobile

"Also, madam, during the planting and harvest seasons, we get plenty of help from the people in other compounds, and some of our relatives from other villages. You see madam, in a way, we are lucky we don't have a father, and that our mother is not well. That means that we belong to all the families in this village. Everybody wants to help and make sure we're all right."

"Das-is so nice. Das-is why I like dee African culture. In Europe and some oda country, people min' deir own business." Then, looking backward, she added, "Dose your brodas and sistas sleeping unda dee tree in your compound, yes?" Madam Ewa added, changing the subject.

"Yes madam."

"You dee old one, yes?"

"Yes madam, I'm the eldest."

"What kind-o-vork you vant in bit city when you leeve dee fam?" Madam Ewa was obviously enjoying talking with me.

"I don't know yet, madam. When I go and live with my uncle in Owerri, he will give me the advice I need."

"I know Owerri. My husband vork in Owerri before," Madam Ewa replied, glancing at her watch, "I must go now, Grace. I like you," she added, as she started the engine. "Grace, I mean vat I say, I vant you come visit me in my house, yes? You vill, yes?"

"I will, madam." I nodded, not actually taking the woman seriously. I suspected that she was merely trying to be friendly and did not actually expect a visit from me. I also suspected that she must have been aware, as I was, that as a young village girl, I could not possibly have anything in common with her.

"Yes? You vill come? Good. I don't leeve far," she was speaking louder now, as she raced the engine of the car.

"Is easy to find. Is prefab* house. Now, let me give you direction."

I listened, although I was convinced that a visit to the woman's house was out of the question.

"You take dis main road as if you go to Ahaba, but you vill go only a few kilometers before you vill find dee road to my house. From here you vill come to a wery small wood bridge. Follow dee small road by dee bridge and go straight until you see big construction. Go to dee oda side to dee back on your right an' you vill see many small prefab house. My house is number eleven."

I squinted my eyes wondering what prefab meant.

"Wass wrong? You don't know prefab house, yes?"

I shook my head, slightly embarrassed, hoping it was not something that everyone should be knowledgeable about.

"Vell, I tell you. Prefab house you can put togeda, quick quick, an' den you can take dem down, quick quick, any time you vant to leeve dee place. You see?"

I nodded, although I did not quite understand the concept.

"Goot. Anyway, don' worry. When you come visit me and you see all dee prefab house, you vill understan'. Ven you come, you vill see Mallam, dee watchman. Jus say to him you van to see Madam Eva, dee white woman who marry dee Calabar man."

"Yes, madam," I nodded repeating the instruction. "I will ask for the white woman who is married to a Calabar man."

"Goot. You vill come den, yes?"

"Yes, madam, I will come."

"Goot. I vill look for you. Come now, you hear? I vill

---

*prefab—prefabricated houses or other buildings that can be assembled or disassembled tell my husban' about you. He vill like you too."

"Thank you madam; good-bye madam," I said, moving away from the car. Then, I watched as Madam Ewa manipulated the stick shift and put the car in "drive."

"Goodbye now, Grace, see you ven you come visit me, yes?"

"Yes madam," I lied again, still convinced that I would never pay this stranger a visit. Yet, I found myself glued to the same spot for several minutes, long after I had watched Madam Ewa's car take off and disappear. Finally, dropping my hands wearily down at my sides, I sauntered back toward the compound, preoccupied with thoughts about the stranger and her unusual invitation which I had perceived as being utterly ludicrous. I tried to come up with a list of what she and I might have in common, and I found the task impossible. Worse yet, Madam Ewa was married to a Nigerian. *What an awkward match*, I thought. *What could they possibly have in common as husband and wife?* Yet, despite all of these odds, I was actually developing a liking for the woman. I wondered why I was fascinated by a woman who was so profoundly different from me. As I contemplated, I came up with at least one answer. I sensed her warmth, honesty, sensibility, open spirit, and a caring nature. For some reason, I felt comfortable with her and could trust her. Conversely, my traditional upbringing made it difficult for me to reconcile my incongruous emotions. As a result, the whole incident put me in a muddled state of mind.

The cries of the children broke my concentration. I stopped walking and raised my head to investigate; and there, running along the path outside the compound to meet me, were five of my siblings—Patrick, Chike, Patricia, Isaac, and Comfort. Fearing that something dreadful might have occurred, I hurried to meet them halfway. I dropped to my knees as I reached them and arched my back to allow Comfort to ride my back. Then, with the help of the other children, I rose slowly.

"What's wrong? Where are the others?" I asked anxiously, standing on my toes and craning my neck as my eyes searched the compound.

"Nothing happened," the children replied in unison, and in Igbo.

"Speak English, and correct English," I cautioned. "Remember our agreement? That, for my sake, we'll all speak proper English amongst ourselves until I leave the village? Remember? Just so I'll be in practice."

"Oh yes, na true," Isaac said.

The other children and I exploded in laughter. "Say 'It is true,' not 'Na true,' Isaac," Chike offered spiritedly.

"Very good, Chike," I said, stooping down to let Comfort jump off my back. "Let me start again, and don't forget, speak correct English—no Igbo, and no pidgin English. Ready?"

"Yes, we are ready," the children enunciated, loudly, simultaneously.

"Why were you all running from the compound toward me?"

Patrick cleared his throat and lifted his head. "Well," he proceeded slowly, "when we woke up under the tree, we looked around, and looked around, and we did not see you."

"Then, we said to us," Isaac assisted.

"We told ourselves," Chike corrected, tapping Isaac lightly on the side of his head.

"Aou!" Isaac exclaimed cradling his head in the palm of his hand. Another burst of laughter erupted.

"Leave him alone, Chike, let him try. Go ahead, Isaac," I coaxed. "Tell me, what happened?"

"We told ourselves," Isaac proceeded haltingly, careful not to provoke another tap on his head, "to look down the road, maybe some customer came in a car."

"Good English, Isaac," I said reassuringly. "And you were all correct. A customer did come, she did have a car, and I carried her bag to her car. Come on, all of you, let's hurry and join Chukuemeka and the others under the tree, and I'll tell you all about what happened with this strange customer and about her strange request."

"Reques'?" Patrick and Patricia asked simultaneously, "Wha kin' o' reques'?"

"Wait, wait, until we're all together," I replied. "By the way, where's Ofo?"

"Chukuemeka said Ofo came back to eat, an' den went back to his hiding place," Patrick offered, "you know dee place at dee back of dat big rock, dee place where he hide when he do sontin bad?"

"'He hides,' not 'he hide,' 'he does,' not 'he do,'" corrected Patrick, who was standing behind Chike drumming several taps on Chike's head with his fingers.

Chike swung around quickly to face Patrick. "Be ciah'ful, my broda," he said, as he struggled to keep a straight face, "I'm not Isaac that you slap aroun'. Don't forget we're almost dee same age. I can beat you up!"

"Shua you can, my broada, I'm so sciah'd, see how I'm shaking like dat leaf up dat tree," Patrick replied, shaking his arms and thighs.

I tried to suppress a laugh as I observed the other siblings leaning against each other in muffled laughter. It was difficult to do when I saw Chike's audacious attitude change slowly into a sheepish smile with his body rocking skittishly from side to side as he stared into Patrick's eyes.

4

Motor Mouth

It was Sunday morning, and although the day had only begun, the air reeked with the aroma of pepper soup made with goat meat and green plantains. Mingled with the gamey aroma was the pungent smell of heated palm oil, which had been used to prepare the breakfast of sweet red beans and dry gari. All the chores at our compound, such as the sweeping of the compound and the feeding of the livestock, had already been accomplished. The middle of the compound underneath the rubber tree, which was the family reception and rest area, had also been prepared to receive Chief Udekwe, who visited the family every Sunday. Chief Udekwe was the highly respected witch doctor who had taken it upon himself, because of the popularity of my family, to heal my mother of her debilitating psychological affliction.

Our family's better colorful mats had been spread out underneath the rubber tree for the children, while a multicolored, striped, adjustable easy chair had been placed against the bottom of the tree for Chief Udekwe. On a typical Sunday, Chief Udekwe spent about two hours after his arrival with my mother; the rest of the day included dinner with the family and masterful narrations of Igbo folk tales to entertain the children.

One of Chief Udekwe's stories that never failed to render us entranced, was the story about the human intruder of a unique animal world. The animals in this forest had enough of the vicious attacks on them. As a result, they had forced their king, the lion, to hold a meeting in an attempt to find a way to put an end to the stream of mysterious events. The events were unusual because this was a forest like no other; the animals lived like one big family. It was not a threatening environment; they protected each other. The carnivorous in their midst travelled to other forests in search of preys, and returned in the evening. Thus, for the carcass of one animal after the other to be found each morning, intact, except for the missing heart and liver, was extremely disturbing to the animals. The rabbit was the first to be found in that condition; next was the monkey; then the antelope; and now the fox!

When the lion opened the meeting, the leopard was the first to speak. "For such a thing to happen to our cunning fox, of all animals, is a serious problem. No animal has been able to outsmart the fox to the extent of killing it. Therefore, I suspect that whoever is entering our peaceful forest and trying to kill us one by one in order to rip our hearts and liver out, is not an animal."

"Your suspicion makes a lot of sense," the lion replied nodding slowly. "An animal would feast on the entire body, not only the heart and liver."

"If it's not an animal that's doing this, then what is?" the tiger asked, puzzled.

"Who else but a human?" The leopard replied, with the confidence of a much older and experienced member of the animal kingdom.

"Why are you so sure?" the tiger queried.

"That's how humans do things. You see, some of them would seek to attack those of us that are useful to them in some way or another. For example, they may have a need for our fur which they use for various purposes even to cover their bodies with."

The hyena burst out into a hysterical laughter. "This is funny! Humans are a funny bunch! Covering their bodies with our fur!"

The other animals observed the hyena for a moment and turned to continue listening to the leopard.

"Or they may" the leopard declared, "Or they may want our flesh for food." Looking over at the elephant. "Or your tusk, for instance, to make things like ornaments and jewelry."

The elephant's curiosity was piqued, "How do you know so much about humans?"

"Well, I've been fortunate enough to have lived in both worlds—our world, and their world."

"How did that happen? And how were you able to return to the forest?" the elephant pressed on.

"Sometimes, humans come across our young when they get separated from us for some reason or another. When that happens, the humans take the young helpless animals into their world and raise them, and when they are old enough to fend for themselves. they are released back into the forest. I was one of those young animals," the leopard responded.

"I Know exactly what the leopard is talking about. He's absolutely right. I was also one of those captured young animals, the lion offered."

The elephant was fascinated. Turning to the leopard, he said, "That explains why you know so much about humans. Tell us more. The more we know about them, the better our strategy for trapping this one that's been after our hearts and liver."

The leopard continued, "All I can say about humans is that they're very strange creatures. Some of them proclaim interest in us, yet, they would go out of their way to kill us for what they can gain from the kill, or to display a momento of us on their walls in order to draw attention to their heroic act."

"That's funny," the hyena laughed heartily. Again, he was ignored by the other animals.

"Continue. Tell us more," the other animals urged the leopard.

"Humans are strange creatures, but they're also fascinating," the lion offered, nodding.

The leopard went on. "Then there are other humans who proclaim their interest in us, would do nothing to harm us, yet would capture us, place us in captivity, and announce to other humans that we could be viewed and admired from time to time."

Again, the hyena found that funny.

"Now, going back to this human who is after our hearts and livers, let's plan on how to capture him."

"Don't worry, he will be caught. But I have to stress one important factor. When he's finally caught, he should not be killed until he has explained to us why he only wants our hearts and liver. Is this clear to everyone? We kill him later."

"Yes, Your Highness, it's quite clear." All the animals replied in unison.

"Your Highness, you're referring to the culprit as a male. How do you know that?" the monkey inquired.

The lion turned to the leopard, "Do you want to answer that question?"

"Of course, Your Highness," the leopard replied. "The culprit has to be a male because in the world of humans, the males are more aggressive and take more chances. Most women would consider entering our forest in the night time extremely dangerous."

"How do you know what humans think?" the monkey asked, looking skeptical.

"When they express their thoughts to one another, the animals around them listen and understand everything that they say. Of course, they think that we don't understand," replied the leopard.

The hyena snickered, and then began laughing. "Good! Let them continue to believe that."

"We also have to be prepared to handle more than one human. There may have been more than one of them," the leopard cautioned. "And another factor we must consider is that we may be dealing with supernatural creatures."

"What does that mean?" asked the wolf.

"Well. that's what some humans call creatures that they believe are invisible, yet are very much part of their lives, guiding them and taking care of them. They call them spirits. They could be their deceased relatives or ancestors."

The wolf continued his line of questioning. "Do all humans believe in spirits?"

"You see, they're different types of humans."

"Different types of humans! What does that mean? You mean they are as different as we are?" The zebra finally commented, admiring his stripes.

"How can I explain it?" the leopard hesitated for a moment, and then responded, "They're basically the same. The only difference is that they look different and have different belief systems depending on what part of the world they're from."

The zebra became interested, "Belief system?"

"Yes. This is a bit complicated, but I heard them discuss the issue many times when I was in their world," the leopard replied.

"Well, give them an example of the types of things humans believe in, and let's move on to the purpose of this meeting," the lion interjected.

The leopard seemed happy to oblige. "Alright. Now, some humans believe that there're certain things in their world, such as rocks, rivers, mountains, et cetera, that have supernatural powers; and that these things have the power to protect and heal. Some call them gods, but, they also believe that there's one more powerful God, who some believe is the Creator (humans have other interpretations of how they and everything on earth were created). Others believe that all the power and protection that they need come from themselves. And yet others believe in nothing."

"Funny creatures, these humans!" The hyena went into another fit of laughter and was ignored as usual.

"That will do," the lion strotted majestically back and forth, "I can see these questions could go on forever. You'll have plenty of time to learn more about humans. But for now, I want us to come up with a plan to trap this person that has been killing us just to take out our hearts and livers."

"We could keep a vigil from this very night to trap the killer, or killers," the giraffe said, I volunteer to stand guard since I tower over everyone, including some of the trees, and can see great distances,"

"I also volunteer to be on the lookout, since I don't sleep at night," said the bat.

"I volunteer to be the one that will pounce on the trespasser since I run the fastest, should he start to run in an attempt to get away," said the cheetah.

The snake spoke pensively, "Hmmm, I'm trying to picture how the three of you are going to coordinate your activities simultaneously, when I can do it all by myself, without even losing any sleep."

The other animals were astonished at the snake's

comment, and all they could do was simply stare at him. Then, the lion spoke, "Do you have a better idea?"

"Indeed I do, Your Highness, replied the snake.

"We're listening," said the lion.

"Alright, listen to this. You know I'm always lying on the ground, sometimes stretched out, and sometimes curled up?"

"Mhh. Go on!" said the lion impatiently.

"Well, nobody steps on me and gets away with it whether I'm asleep of not. So you see, I don't even need to keep vigil. All I have to do is position myself where the intruder enters the forest, and he's bound to step on me; and when he does, I will immediately spring into action."

"But we don't want him killed right away. Before he dies, we must find out why he's in need of our hearts and livers," the lion said quickly.

"If you don't want him killed right away, he won't be. What I would do is wrap myself around him and render him immobile, that's all."

"How do you know where he'll enter our forest?" the cheetah asked.

"That's where he's been leaving the carcasses of the animals he's killed."

"If the intruder brings some kind of light with him, he's bound to see that it's a snake lying right in front of him, and he'd chop your head off before you make a move," the cheetah replied.

"That's funny!" the hyena screamed in laughter. Again he was ignored.

"I have the ability to transform myself, and blend in with what ever is in the path of my enemy. So don't worry. I won't be recognized," the snake assured the cheetah.

"What if this mysterious human encounters one of us before he gets to you, and may have no need to advance toward you?" the giraffe asked.

"Good question," the bat jumped in. "We'll be taking too much of a chance leaving the capture of this human in the middle of the night to just the snake. What if there are more humans involved?"

Once again the lion strotted majestically back and forth. "You'll have to come up with some excellent ideas, but now I will have the last say. No one should sleep tonight. We should all keep vigil, so that it would be impossible for the intruder or intruders to kill again and escape. Do you have any objections."

"No, Your Highness," all the animals answered simultaneously with much enthusiasm. "It's a great idea!"

The plan worked. By midnight, the animals had their man. As soon as the intruder entered the forest, he was immediately surrounded by all the animals. They had prepared for the capture of many men and was taken aback that one man would have the courage to venture into the forest alone at night.

As the animals questioned the man, he struck a figure of a pathetic-looking soul about to begin digging his own grave. The animals could see it was no ordinary man. On his head sat a crown of orange, blue, black, and white feathers. His chest was bare, except for five strands of coral beads. His right upper arm sported a multicolored band made of braided pieces of materials. Around his waist and down to his ankle, hung a brick colored cotton wrapper, with intricate turquoise designs of fish and shells. For shoes, he wore a pair of simple, brown, leather sandals.

To the question why he was killing animals just to get their hearts and liver, the man answered, "I'm the medicine man of my village. The people rely on me to give them advice, protect them from evil spirits, and heal them when they're ill. I communicate with the spirits, and they tell me what I need to do in order to do my job. Some evil spirits would not go away until either the heart or the liver of an animal or human is used in addition to other items as a sacrifice to appease them."

"If you can use the liver or heart of humans like yourself, why do you come after us?" the lion asked.

"According to one of our laws, we must not kill one another," the man replied.

"Well," said the lion almost sympathetically, "your biggest mistake is to come to this particular forest to kill any of us in order to collect hearts and livers. Why? Because we have a similar law in this forest that also prohibits us from killing each other."

"I'm so sorry, but I have never heard of such a forest. I always thought that all forests have wild animals which prey on each other. Besides, although there are forests or jungles somewhere where people are ordered to kill certain animals, we don't have any such rules around here."

"I'll tell you what we'll do," the lion replied, "since you did what you did to help your people, and didn't know you were breaking the law of this forest, we'll spare your life."

The man, who all the while had been standing in the midst of the animals, fell to his knees with his hands clasped in front of him, "Thank you, and God bless all of you."

The hyena went into another hysteria. "What is he talking about—God bless all of you?"

"Hyena!" the lion growled, "Stop your nonsense! You know, laughter is good, but the problem with you is that you don't know when to stop laughing. You laugh at everything and at any time, and that's an illness. While we walk the medicine man out of the forest, perhaps he can tell us as to how he could use the spirits to cure you of your illness."

Although Chief Udekwe objected to the teachings of the Roman Catholic religion, he nevertheless encouraged us to attend the village Roman Catholic church, because he knew that our parents shared his sentiments concerning the white missionaries; which were that the parents, elders and chiefs of the villages were perpetually grateful for the missionaries' efforts to educate their children. They conjectured, however, that the principal motive of the missionaries was to bring their own religion into the African continent. Nevertheless, in a gesture of appreciation, some of the villagers did attend the churches of the missionaries to worship their God, and brought their children along with them.

At home, however, children were taught the authentic African culture and religion; that the religious teachings of the missionaries were contrary to their African heritage. Children also learned through their own lives that the African tradition allowed men to be polygamous if they so desired, whereas the religion of the missionaries opposed that activity. Included in the family curricula, was filial piety. Children were taught to always demonstrate respect for authority, parents, and older citizens, in speech, behavior, and attitude. Animism and polytheism were also crucial to the African life. The worship of other gods such as the spirits of deceased ancestors and relatives, and the various gods of the heavenly bodies and the earth (the moon, sun, rivers, hills, rocks, etc.), were also on the family educational agenda. Children were taught that the spirits of their ancestors and relatives were highly involved in their daily affairs; and for that reason it was necessary to offer sacrifices to spirits and gods to mollify them.

My fascination and intrigue with Madam Ewa never left me. I thought about the mysterious stranger day and night, and the idea of making a visit to her house seemed more and more plausible as the months rolled by. Finally, I decided to seize the opportunity to pay her a visit on this particular Sunday that Chief Udekwe was visiting. I was nervous about leaving my siblings alone while I went to visit Madam Ewa, but when I asked Chief Nwokeji for permission to visit the prefabs, he thought it was a good idea, and agreed to the visit for more or less selfish reasons. He saw the visit as a promotional enterprise on behalf of the Nwokeji produce business, based on the idea that a potential friendship between the Madam and me would be one way of enticing more expatriate customers to the farm. It was well known that expatriates were big spenders and would pay whatever was asked of them without any contention whatsoever.

I respectfully listened to Chief Udekwe's line of reasoning, although I was not completely comfortable with his motives, since I was convinced that a mutual, genuine interest and liking had developed between Madam Ewa and me. I had seen Madam Ewa several times since her first visit to the farm. She had returned to buy more fruits and vegetables and had continued to extend me the invitation for a social visit.

Finally, I was ready to start the long trek from the farm to Madam Ewa's house. I strode toward the entrance of the compound and looked back to see if Chief Udekwe and the children had settled down underneath the rubber tree. They had indeed taken their rightful places on the mats in front of the Chief, but the storytelling had not begun; the preparation for my departure from the compound was still confusing to them. Each pair of eyes watched my every step; even the Chief was distracted.

When I reached the main road, I turned to wave at them one last time. Then, I swung around slowly and forged ahead.

With my back to the compound now, I imagined the way Chief Udekwe usually appeared when he spoke to the children. He was a vivacious, tall, scrawny man of about seventy-five who walked with a thick, crooked wooden cane, although there was no apparent reason for its use since his posture was as straight as that of a young man half his age. Chief Udekwe seemed to be more spry when surrounded by children. When he addressed the children, his small, narrow, sunken eyes sparkled as he scanned the children's eager faces, punctuating his phrases with mimicking gestures and sounds of the animals he talked about.

Soon, I was on the red, dusty road that led to Ahaba township, a mile or so from our compound. The hot blinding sun cast a blanket of steamy haze over the entire area. I was accustomed to the heat, though, and I had always loved the sun. I loved the way it caressed my body, penetrating into the innermost marrow of my bones. The feel of the sun, coupled with my new sense of freedom in venturing to an unknown destination to visit an extraordinary person was invigorating. I felt as though I was floating on air!

The farther I walked the more exhilarated I felt. Finally, I found the bridge Madam Ewa had mentioned and followed the narrow path at the beginning of a dilapidated wooden bridge at the edge of a small stream. I walked gingerly to the other side of the bridge. Hesitating momentarily and shading my eyes with both hands, I surveyed the area. To the left of the path, several yards down, was a colossal factory-like building under construction. Sprawled at the side of the building in small pyramids were sand, gravel, cement, and wooden planks of various sizes and dimensions, all arranged in neat rows on one side of the building. The entire complex was free of grass, trees, and shrubbery, while the surrounding area was densely overgrown with bushes and trees.

The construction site was completely fenced in. In one corner of the fence was a tall iron object that towered over everything in sight. To me, it looked like a giraffe in captivity, peering loftily over a fence. I was to learn later what the object was. From where I stood, I could see three Hausa men sitting in front of the unfinished main entrance of the building. I suspected they were of the Hausa tribe, since they wore the traditional dashiki and a turban. Besides, Uncle Jeremiah had once told me that most expatriate companies preferred using Hausa watchmen, because they considered them more trustworthy and reliable.

Several yards away from the construction site, I could see what appeared to be large cement blocks on which were built neat rows of small, bright yellow and white houses with flat round-edged roof tops. I was convinced that everything fit the descriptions and directions Madam Ewa had given me, so I continued on the narrow path leading to the yellow and white houses, which I presumed were the prefabs. Wondering if I was going to be stopped by the watchmen, I walked slowly, apprehensively, keeping my eyes on them. Suddenly, the three men shot up simultaneously like three frightened rabbits and proceeded to approach the high gate, which was surrounded by a corrugated fence. Then, their steps slowed. They probably concluded that I was only a harmless looking village girl.

"Hai, Sisi! Where you day go?" one of the men said, gesturing with his night stick as his companions peered between the bars of the gate.

"Sanunku*!" I greeted, remembering the limited Hausa Uncle Jeremiah had taught me. "Ah beg, ah de come see one white woman way don' come from Romania. Dee woman don tell me say make ah come see-am."

"Na plenty white woman day here. Waitin' be dis one name?" the watchman replied.

"Ee tell me say in-name na Madam Ewa," I replied, "and ee say her husband na Calabar man."

"Ohoh!" the watchman exclaimed. "Ewa! Ah know who dee woman be, na very very nice woman."

"Na true," one of the other men nodded in agreement.

"Go straight Sisi," the first watchman said, pointing toward some temporary looking houses with his stick. "When you don' come for prefab, make you look for number eleven." And turning to one of the other watchmen he said, "Mallam, maybe you for go wit-am?"

The second watchman then opened the gate, closed it behind him and beckoned. "Come, Sisi, make ah carry you go."

My curiosity got the best of me as I turned to follow the watchman. "Mallam," I said, pointing to the giraffe-looking building equipment which I had spotted from the bridge, "watin be dat long ting?"

The watchman looked back at the equipment and chuckled at my ignorance. "Oh-hoh! Dat na machine way day carry heavy ting up an' down. Ee go carry heavy ting, put-am here, and ee go carry heavy ting an' ee go put-am dere. You un'stand?"

I nodded, emitting a throaty sound. "Ah understan', Mallam!"

The watchman led the way towards the small yellow

*sanunku—Hausa language for "Greetings, all of you."

and white houses; and for a while, we walked in silence along the narrow pathway. Then, he asked without looking back at me, "Sisi, why you come see dis woman? You come wok for-am?"

"Work for-am?" I asked, puzzled.

"Nnnn! Ye, wok for-am," the watchman replied, tapping his stick on the ground as he walked, "like for wash dee madam cloth, sweep dee madam house, iron dee madam cloth, an' go buy sometin for dee madam for market; like so."

"Oh-hoh! Ah don see waitin you day talk," I replied. "No, Mallam, ah no day come work for dee madam. Na-in friend ee want make ah be. Na-in make ee say make ah come see-am, jus-so we be friends. You see, Mallam, dee woman like me very much, an' ah like-am too."

The watchman laughed loudly, shook his head, and turned to take a quick glance at me, "Haba,* Sisi," he said, still walking ahead, "you no know say when dee woman say ee like you, na koni† ee day play? Make ah tell you one ting, Sisi, ah know expatriate good good. Ah don' wok for dem plenty plenty time. Dis woman no wan' be you frien', na wok ee wan' make you wok for-am."

I laughed at the watchman's cynicism toward white people. I could not imagine Madam Ewa behaving that way—wanting a friendship with me so she could use me as her maid, as the watchman was suggesting. I felt as though I could trust her now. I believed her intentions were honest, and her interest in me was genuine. I had seen it in her eyes and had felt the attraction between us. So I felt obligated to come to her defense. "No no no Mallam! Dis woman not be so. Ee like me true true, an' wan make ah be-in friend, das-all. No, no, no, Mallam, dee woman no

*haba—now, really
†koni—trickery

wan' make ah wok foram. Ee jus' like me das-all."

"O.K. oh! Ah don talk finish. Make one day you no go say ah no day gee you plenty warnin'."

I replied quickly, "Make you no worry, Mallam, this woman na good good woman; ee different. Ah trust-am. Na my friend."

Wishing to change the subject, I pointed toward the yellow and white houses, and inquired, "Where dee woman house day?"

The watchman pointed to the house with the sleeping white and brown dog stretched out in front of it. "Na dat one over dere. You go, Sisi! Ah go stan' right-here because ah no like dat dog."

I approached the house and began talking to the dog to test its friendliness. The dog barked a couple of times, jumped to its feet and proceeded to approach me, cowering but wagging its tail. He then flopped on the ground at my feet, writhing on his back, and I crouched to rub its belly.

The watchman watched in amazement. "Hmmm, Sisi," he said, "dis dog nobody go near, na dog way fit bite, but ee like you. Hmmm, na one strange ting be dis."

Suddenly, the door swung open and Madam Ewa stood glaring at the watchman and me. "Yes?" she said sharply.

"Madam," the watchman said quickly, "Dis Sisi say ee come see..."

"Madam Ewa," I interrupted, "don't you remember me? It's me, Grace, from the Nwokeji farm. You invited me, remember?"

"Oh, my gootness!" Madam Ewa exclaimed, slapping her cheeks with both hands, "Ofcus, ofcus, I rememba you. Grace, you look so different. You look beautiful! Come in, come in," and to the watchman, she said, "Mallam, you can go now, tank you." Bowing slightly, the watchman turned around slowly and walked leisurely back to the construction site.

Madam Ewa hurried down the three short steps leading into her house, embraced me, and led me by the hand back up the stairs into the house. Still holding onto my hand, she kicked the door shut with the heel of her shoe and called out to her husband, "Essien, Essien, look! It's Grace, from dee farm! Rememba?"

When I entered the living room with Madam Ewa, Essien Ewa was standing with his hands crossed in front of him holding a book.

"Grace," Madam Ewa said, shifting her hand up to my shoulder, "I vant you to meet my husband, Mr. Ewa."

"I'm happy to meet you, sir," I said shyly, curtseying.

"It's my pleasure, Grace," Essien Ewa replied, motioning toward the couch. "Please sit down. My wife told me so much about you."

"Look at her Essien, she is so beautiful. Look at dee beautiful African clothes! I did not recognize her in dee African clothes."

I had tied my best lappa. It was a light blue cotton lappa, woven all over with a darker shade of silk diamond-shaped patterns. The lappa was tied over a white short-sleeved lace blouse. Circled around my head was a scarf of the same fabric as the lappa; and dangling gold earrings adorned my ears. The earrings were part of a set with matching necklace and bracelet, which Uncle Jeremiah had sent to me from Kano during a civil service conference he attended three years earlier.

"Essien," Madam Ewa began, "you rememba I tell you about the beautiful an' smat girl in dee farm? Dee one I say run dee fam only wit ha brodas an' sistas?"

Essien Ewa nodded, "Oh yes, of course I remember,"

never taking his eyes off me. His steady gaze made me feel uncomfortable. "Grace, you are welcome to our house any time," he added.

While Madam Ewa took her place beside me on the couch, Essien Ewa resumed his seat, reached for the pencil on the side table beside his chair, placed it between the pages of the book he was reading, slammed it shut, and set it on the indigenously carved, elephant-head wooden coffee table. Then, pensively, he leaned back in his chair as he continued his close scrutiny of me.

"What I give you, Grace? Coca-Cola, Orange Fanta, Sprite, vat? Or you vant some-sing like tea or coffee?" Madam Ewa asked excitedly, seeming quite anxious to please me.

"Whatever you give me, madam, is all right with me," I replied, embarrassed to be receiving that much attention.

"I have an idea, Andrea," Essien Ewa offered. "Why don't we have that dessert we couldn't eat after our meal this afternoon?"

"Das-a-good idee-ya, Essien," Andrea replied, slapping both hands on her lap as she rose from her seat; and reaching over to touch my shoulder, she added, "Grace, my husband talking about dee beautiful Swiss cake I bake myself las-night. I bake before many many time. Is very goot, you'll like-it."

I nodded, smiling overzealously, although I wasn't sure I would enjoy eating anything sweet, since I was only accustomed to the typical African diet which never included desserts. I thought about Uncle Jeremiah's stories of his travels abroad, and his comments on the excessively sweet desserts Europeans and Americans served after the afternoon and evening meals.

I observed Andrea Ewa as she glided out of the room.

I had not really noticed her beauty until now. She looked totally different out of the sun and out of her jeans. Her statuesque frame was striking in a turquoise-and-white, striped sleeveless cotton dress. Her light brown hair with lustrous curls and twirls, which were piled neatly on top of her head, gave her face a regal appearance.

I turned to look at Andrea's husband who had not yet taken his eyes off me. I thought he also had a handsome face except for the long scar which extended from the side of his nose to his chin. Since I already knew he was a Calabar man, I ruled out the possibility of the mark being tribal, because it was not customary for the Calabars to wear tribal marks. Besides, it was too deep a scar for a tribal mark. I smiled shyly at the small, brown sleepy eyes which focused unabashedly on me. In confusion, I averted my gaze, not knowing what to do or say. I reasoned that if I started up a conversation, it would seem impolite since I was younger than Essien Ewa. So I thought of a way to solve the dilemma.

"I will go to the kitchen and help Madam Ewa," I said, jumping to my feet. "Where's the kitchen, sir?"

"Where you go, Grace?" Andrea was asking, as she appeared in the doorway carrying a large tray containing a tea pot, cups and saucers, teaspoons, sugar, cream, and cake covered with red and green icing, decorated in floral designs.

"I was going to come and help you, madam," I replied, exceedingly pleased to see Andrea. For some reason, I felt more comfortable with Andrea around.

"No, no, no! You jus-sit down. I don' need help. I vill put dee tray right here," Andrea said, pulling a portable cart closer with her feet, "and den I vill sav everybody."

Later, as the three of us sat eating cake and sipping freshly brewed chamomile tea, Essien Ewa started off the conversation. "My wife told me you have completed your School Leaving Certificate exam."

I beamed. "Yes, sir. Last year, sir."

"My wife also told me that you plan to leave the village sometime in the future."

"Yes sir. I do, sir."

"Where will you go?"

"I tol' you, Essien," Andrea interrupted, "I tol' you she vill go to her uncle in Owerri."

Essien Ewa looked over at me. "I take it you will find work in Owerri then?"

"Yes sir, my uncle will help me find work."

The sudden, irascible barking of the dog outside, interrupted the conversation. Silently, the three of us listened for some time.

"My gootness! Dis dog von't shutup. I tink we have visitor. I vill go an' see." With that, Andrea hurried to the door.

Essien Ewa and I maintained silence as we listened to the voices coming from outside.

"Oh is you!" we could hear Andrea's voice. "Come in, come in, he von't bite. He just have big mouth."

Essien Ewa sat up, slid forward in his chair and cocked his head to one side as he strained to recognize the other voices coming from the doorway. He frowned and squinted his eyes; it was evident he was unable to recognize the voices of the visitors.

Finally, Andrea returned to the living room followed by a man and a woman. Essien Ewa rose from his chair, jamming his hands in his pockets, evidently waiting for the introductions. The woman, who appeared to be in her forties, was short and slender, with a blond, pixie hair-do. The bright smile on her small round face and deep blue eyes faded the instant she laid eyes on Essien Ewa and me. The man accompanying the woman, also seemingly in his forties, was stocky and much taller. The attractive deep dimples which had appeared on his smiling cheeks when he walked in, had quickly transformed into a frown. Essien Ewa looked at his wife quizzically. However, before she could begin the introductions, the woman drew closer to Andrea, stood on her toes, and whispered in Andrea's ear. Unfortunately, her voice was clear and audible.

"Who are the Nigerians? Your husband has not returned yet from London?"

Andrea turned to observe her husband's reaction. Essien Ewa's countenance was enough, in my opinion, to cause any sensible visitor to flee the house immediately and not wait to be thrown out.

Andrea looked worried. She spoke rapidly, "Essien, you remember dee couple from America I toll you I met at dee country club when you travel to London? Dis-is Maggie, and dis-is her husband Ray—Maggie and Ray Mahonny," she added, pointing to the visitors. "And dis is my husband, Essien, and my friend, Grace."

I said nothing. The message in Essien Ewa's eyes was clear. I was not to respond to the introductions or participate in whatever involved these visitors.

Maggie stood frozen and looked as though she was about to topple to the floor. Then she opened her mouth as if to say something.

"Don't say any more, Motor Mouth, just shut up," Maggie's husband said under his breath, nudging her surreptitiously. His voice was also audible.

By now, the tension had become too great for me to handle. In confusion and the expectation of danger, I shot up and stood beside Essien Ewa, almost touching him. My entire body trembled.

Essien Ewa must have noticed. He patted me on my

back and whispered in my ear, "Don't be afraid. You're safe here. There will be no trouble."

Aloud, he continued, "Sit down and relax, Grace. You're my guest, and you're perfectly welcome. This is my house." Then, turning to Andrea, he said, "All right, I've met your friends. Now, get them out of my bloody house!" He paused for a second, and then barked, "Now!"

With that, Essien Ewa picked up the book he had been reading when I arrived, flopped back into his seat, stretched out his legs and held the book up in front of his face.

"But Andrea, you should have prepared us," Again, Maggie whispered audibly. "How were we to know you married a Nigerian?"

"There you go again, Motor Mouth," Ray Mahonny reprimanded his wife, "as if you haven't done enough damage already."

"That's it!" Essien Ewa stamped both feet hard on the floor as he rose from his chair, and slammed his book into the chair opposite him. "All right, let's go! Out, out, out of my house!"

"Please let me see you out." Andrea spoke, head down in chagrin, walking quickly ahead of the unwelcome guests.

Ray Mahonny took his wife's hand and followed Andrea as she led the way toward the door. He turned to address Essien Ewa. "I'm truly sorry about this whole thing," he said. "My wife is a typical Motor Mouth; what comes out of that mouth sometimes doesn't come out right. I'm really sorry this has happened."

"Well, take your wife home and keep her there until she learns some manners."

Somehow, I wasn't afraid anymore. I began to perceive what was unfolding before my eyes as an educational experience.

"I'm really sorry," Ray repeated as he stepped outside the small prefab.

Just then, Essien Ewa rushed to the door. "On second thought, why don't both of you come back in."

The Mahonnys looked at Essien with stunned expressions on their faces. "There are some lessons to be learned here," Essien continued. "Come on, come on, come back in," he gestured with his head.

Ray Mahonny looked perplexed, confused; yet, he complied. He held his wife's hand as they re-entered the house. Inside, in the living room, Essien Ewa ordered, "All right, now. Everyone take a seat and relax. All I want is to get some information from our visitors here, and then they can go."

"What sort of information?" Maggie asked. As she sat beside her husband, her eyes clouded with tears.

"There you go again, Motor Mouth. Will you ever learn? Let me do the talking, will you please?" Then, to Essien Ewa, Ray said, "What do you want to know?"

Without answering, Essien Ewa strode toward a small varnished desk in one corner of the room, opened the top drawer, and retrieved a large, lined writing pad and a ball-point pen. "Here," he said, handing them to Ray Mahonny. "This is what I want you to do. Write down your full name, the country you come from, when you arrived here, the company you work for, and your address here in Nigeria."

"Jesus Christ! I don't believe this! Why us, Lord?" Maggie Mahonny threw her hands up in the air, and then rested her head against her husband's shoulder, sobbing softly.

"Why do you want this information?" Ray Mahonny

asked. "Why don't you let things be? I have apologized for everything. You kicked us out of your house. Isn't that enough?"

"No," Essien Ewa growled. "It's not enough. You see, somebody ought to teach some of you expatriates who travel to the so-called developing countries that you should leave your arrogance and your sense of superiority in your own country."

"You're making something out of nothing," Ray Mahonny replied.

"I don't think so. You just do what I ask, and you will be on your way in no time. If not, you can expect to spend the night here."

"Give him what he wants, Ray, and let's go. What the hell!" Maggie pleaded, still sobbing.

Ray Mahonny began writing. As he wrote, he spoke softly, directing his comments to his wife. "I knew an Italian who was thrown out of Nigeria simply because his Nigerian business partner drummed up a false accusation against him after they had had a falling out. I don't want that to happen to me. I'll give him whatever he wants. I like my work here in Nigeria. I'm happy here."

Ray handed the pad back to Essien Ewa, who looked over the information and tore the sheet from the tablet. He then folded it neatly and shoved it in his shirt pocket. Ray Mahonny stood up and bent over to comfort his teary-eyed wife. "Can we go now?" he asked Essien Ewa without looking at him.

"Yes," Essien Ewa replied, his voice heavy with contempt. "Andrea, see your friends out," he demanded.

Later, as Andrea Ewa brought a fresh pot of tea into the living room, she asked her husband, "Essien, what you going to do with dat information? I never see you act like dat before. I was fearing you vill hit dee man," and looking at me she continued, "and Grace, you so scared before, you shaking like dis," Andrea demonstrated by flapping her thighs. I covered my mouth with both hands to hide my amusement, but when Essien threw his head back in laughter, I laughed aloud also.

"So, both of you were frightened eh?" Essien finally said. Then, reaching into his pocket, he retrieved the paper with all the information he wanted from Ray Mahonny, and proceeded to shred it into tiny pieces. "That's what I intend to do with it. Both of you satisfied now? All I wanted to do was to scare them a little, to teach them some manners, that's all. And I think I succeeded."

Simultaneously, Andrea and I breathed a sigh of relief.

"Goot, I'm happy," Andrea said, "I don' vant any trable for dem or nobody."

When the Ewas drove me back to my compound, I was saddened; that whole episode was enough for me. Although a bloody fight had not occurred, I had heard and seen enough to know that the incident would affect my future relationships with white people. I wondered how it was possible for one white person to display so much warmth and affection toward me, welcoming me into her home, and really caring about me, while another was full of hatred and prejudice. I concluded, therefore, that interracial friendships and marriages were unrealistic and dangerous. Nevertheless, I liked Andrea enough to hope that she would continue to visit the farm so I could see her and talk with her. I loved her; but, one thing was certain. That was going to be my first and last visit to the prefabs.

That night at bedtime, I lay on my mat replaying the incident with the Mahonnys in my head. I wondered why

Essien and Andrew were married to each other in the first place; how they had met; why Maggie had such a negative attitude toward blacks. And what were the real motives for Essien Ewa's actions.

5
Tidings

Now that I had successfully passed the Cambridge School Leaving Certificate examination, I waited impatiently for the veritable, decisive letter from Uncle Jeremiah. Invariably, each morning for several months, I intercepted the mailman on the brick-red, dusty main road, without giving him the opportunity to enter the compound to deliver the mail. Yet, each time I met him outside the compound, his response was the same. "Still no letter for you, my child," he would say, in Igbo. "That uncle of yours should not continue to keep you in suspense like this. It's not right. He should write and say something. Either you're going, or you're not going." The mailman of course, knew the entire story. I had repeated it to him over and over again for the past two years.

    Late one morning in early August, the whole village had become one ugly mass of poto poto* due to a torrential rain which had fallen during the night, and now a light shower had taken its place. A gray, patchy blanket of clouds covered the skies, giving the morning a dusky appearance. Poto poto had made the pathways impassable for me to take my usual walk to meet the mailman outside the compound. So, I remained in the produce shed with my siblings to wait on any customers who might venture out. At least we could expect children to come by in the rain, to run errands for the adults; the youngsters of

---

*poto poto—mud caused by a heavy rainfall

the village loved to play in the puddles.

Where my siblings were concerned, the rainy days afforded them the treasured opportunity to be indoors in one place and work together as a team. As the rain pelted the thatched roof of the produce shed, we huddled together on the floor, clapping our hands as we sang popular traditional songs with great delight. By mid afternoon, when the rain showers had turned into a faint drizzle, I decided to start the preparation of the afternoon meal in the small indoor thatched-roof kitchen.

In a way, I was glad of the opportunity to finally be alone to continue my brooding over my uncle Jeremiah's silence. On this day, I prepared some okra soup, and made some gari. I carried the meal across the compound to my siblings as they sang merrily in the produce shed. I had never seen them so happy and did not want such a rare moment to end. So I relieved the younger siblings of cleaning and washing the bowls after the meal and began to gather them up to do myself.

"You our big sister. You don't pick up dee plates," Ofo said, jumping to his feet to prevent me from collecting the plates. "You sit down, we will wash the plates."

"Don't worry, Ofo," I replied, picking up the plates quickly, "I know that. I just enjoy seeing you so happy. Continue to have fun, I'll be right back." As I stepped out of the shed, I heard a man's voice reverberating across the compound.

"Anyone around?" the voice was asking, in Igbo. "It's the mailman!" Recognizing the voice, I quickly placed the plates on the ground against the wall of the shed, and waved both arms in the air, "Over here, sir," I replied, also in Igbo. The children heard the voices and crowded at the door of the shed, peering out to see who was holding a conversation with me. I hurried up to the mailman, a diminutive, rustic looking man of about sixty, wearing a loose, yellow, plastic raincoat with the hood covering most of his face.

"You must have a letter from my uncle," I said, breathless, as I began hopping up and down. Without answering, the mailman alighted cautiously from his antiquated, blue Raleigh bicycle and threw back the hood of his raincoat to uncover his face. He then brushed the beads of rain off his silver-framed eyeglasses and stamped his bare feet several times to rid them of the mud that had collected between his toes.

"Well, tell me sir, has the letter arrived?" I repeated, still hopping up and down, and twisting my body in a dance rhythm.

"Stop that jumping," the mailman laughed. "Anyone would think you have to ease yourself."

I ignored the remark and continued my dance.

"Don't look so serious," the mailman chided. "Smile! Yes, the letter from your uncle has finally arrived."

I let out a loud shriek, slapping both sides of my face simultaneously. "Where is it? Where is it? I beg you, sir, let me have it! I beg you sir!" I pleaded.

"All right, all right, here it is, my daughter," the mailman replied, as he tried to free the letter out of the back pocket of his tight khaki shorts. "I'm happy for you," he continued, handing me the letter, "and I pray there is the best of news inside."

"Thank you, sir," I replied, embracing the older man warmly, "I'll read it today, and when I see you tomorrow, or whenever you're here again, I will give you all the news."

"Very well, my child, you do that. Well, enjoy your reading, and my greetings to your family," the mailman replied as he mounted his bicycle. Slowly, laboriously, he climbed the steep incline that led to the next compound. For a few seconds after the mailman rode off, I stood motionless clutching the letter against my chest. It was as if I wanted to delay reading it if there should be some unfavorable news inside. Suddenly, my curiosity got the best of me. I dashed towards the produce shed where my siblings waited and I noticed that their heads were still visible in the doorway.

"It's the letter! It's the letter! Uncle Jeremiah's letter," I shouted, waving it in the air. The youngsters then bolted out of the shed to meet me in the middle of the compound.

"Read it to us, read it to us," they cried out.

"Of course, of course, but we have to go back into the shed and calm down," I replied, pretending to be more composed than I was. Inside the shed, the children silently proceeded to move tables and boxes around. Astonished, I asked them what they were doing.

"We are making more room to seet around on dee floor," Chike enunciated slowly, "while you read to us."

The other children chuckled at Chike's attempt not to speak pidgin English.

"Chike is showing off again!" Patricia commented.

"Leave him alone," Chukuemeka came to Chike's defense. "It is good what he is doing. We should all try as hard as he does to help our sister forget pidgin English so she will find a good job in dee big city.

I took my place on the floor. "Ready?" I asked, as I observed the anxious and curious faces of my siblings.

No one spoke. Each one sat stiffly and waited. The envelope in my lap looked almost sacred. I decided not to create jagged edges by tearing it open, so I proceeded to unglue it with great care.

"Common Grace," Chukuemeka said impatiently, "tear it open. It doesn't matter if you spoil dee envelope, what's important is dee contents of dee letta." I knew Chukuemeka was right; nevertheless, I was going to do it my way, and before Chukuemeka completed his last sentence, the envelope was already open, the flap neatly intact, and the letter flattened out ready to read.

> My dearest niece,
>
> I'm sorry for the delay in replying to your very important letter. It was a matter for careful consideration and planning, hence the delay. I wanted to write back only when I had something concrete to tell you, and here it is: Myself, my wife, and all of your cousins (all eight of them now), were delighted to hear that you passed your School Leaving Certificate exam last year, and now, you're ready to make that important transition—establishing another life for yourself away from the farm. We want you to know that we support you and agree, as you stated in your letter, that it would be for the good of your family name; and that if you succeed in your life, your brothers and sisters would be the beneficiaries of your success. We have faith in you, and believe that you will succeed in anything you do, and you will make us all proud of you. We noted also—

Here, my voice began to quiver, and I stopped reading to wipe tears from my eyes with the edge of my lappa. I looked about, to observe my audience. Their faces were solemn and reflective, and I wondered what they were thinking. Nevertheless, I continued:

> We noted also that you have great pride and confidence in your brothers and sisters, who, although they are all quite young, have been well trained to manage the farm and the compound in your absence. Yes, we too have been getting very good reports from many villagers from and around Uzoakoli, that for a farm run by very young children, it is the best place to buy worthwhile provisions. So, it is com-

forting to know that the operations of the farm would continue to run effectively even after you're away from the village.

    In your letter, you sounded a little worried about how your mother would fare without you. As you know, she does not have a physical illness. Bad spirits have taken control of her mind and there is nothing any family member can do for her. The spirits are telling her she should spend most of her time inside her hut. She is quite happy living that way, and the only person she responds to is her witch doctor Chief Udekwe. We should be thankful to all the gods that at least, the spirits want her confined in her hut, because, there are many people like her who live on the streets, abandoning their families, and getting themselves into sometimes serious trouble or accidents. So, since your mother is safe and is well taken care of, I would not worry about her.

    One of the reasons I delayed writing is because I had been waiting for word from my superior regarding a position for you at the Ministry where I work. You know, the Ministry of Agriculture. Well, I'm happy to inform you that there's now a position waiting for you.

I jumped up, letting out a deafening scream and waving the letter in the air; but I was disappointed to observe that I was now the only one, who was ecstatic at what was unfolding. My siblings remained motionless; their expressionless faces grew more solemn. Although disturbed about their lack of excitement, I decided to deal with that issue later. I continued reading:

My superior has been God-sent. He's been doing all he can to see that no one else is given the position until your arrival. You see, he's a personal friend, and is like a brother to me. So, this is a big favor he's doing me. This is a position that should not be going to someone off the street, so to speak. Positions such as this one are given to qualified, eligible people. However, when I told him about you, he wanted so much to help, and promised to arrange for a quick and intensive training period for you when you arrive. In the meantime I am supplying him with all the information that he needs to prepare your official papers. So, you see, although he has never met you, he has taken a special interest in you for my sake. What he's actually doing is ignoring some basic Civil Service regulations just to accommodate you. Believe me, it will be an opportunity of a life time; an opportunity which took even me, years to accomplish. You may as well become acquainted with my supervisor's name. His name is Ogwu, Mr. Emanuel Ogwu.

I paused once again and shook my head in disbelief. "God, together with my father, my grandfather and grandmother, and the gods of the earth, what have I done to deserve this good fortune? Do you believe it?" I searched the grim faces around me. They were still expressionless. Each pair of eyes stared blankly at me. My stomach felt as if someone was tightening a knot inside. I forced myself to read on:

You don't have to worry about accommodations when you arrive, and even when you begin to work at the Ministry. As long as you're in Owerri, you will always stay with us. I wouldn't advise you to accept your own accommodation from the Ministry until you've stayed with us for a while and experienced life away from the farm, life in a city. There's so much to learn. You're not used to living in a flat. Life in the city is entirely different from life in the village. Don't worry, we're all waiting to help you adjust. You will not be alone. You have a family here. You don't have to reply to this letter, just come when you're ready. We're anxiously waiting for you. Well, that's all for now. I will leave the rest until you get here. Oh yes, before I forget, when you come, bring us some of that good yam, plantain, and whatever else you can carry from your farm for us to sample.

Our love to all of you.

Your loving uncle,
Jeremiah Nwackuku

"All right," I inhaled deeply, slapping the palms of my hands on the page I had just read. "I have read the letter, and it's all good news. Now, tell me, why is it that all of a sudden no one is happy for me?"

No one answered or moved for some seconds; then, Chukuemeka spoke. "My sista, let me talk for our brodas and sistas here, because I tink I'm now dee man of dee house. Allow me to make a small speech in answer to your question."

"Hio, hio!" Obi chimed, breaking their silence. "Good English!"

"Hio, hio!" the other children repeated, applauding softly.

"Very good English, Chukuemeka!" Isaac said when the applause subsided.

"Tank you, Isaac," he bobbed his head twice. "Now, my sista," Chukuemeka continued, turning to me, "Of course, we are happy for you. Why should we not be? You are our flesh an' blood. We pro—pro—probably are more excited an' happier dan you..."

"Good English, good English!" Patrick interrupted.

"Hio, hio!" the other children said simultaneously.

I found my siblings hilarious. I wanted to laugh, but I stifled the impulse; I did not want to seem as though I was not taking their input seriously. After all, this was a very important issue, and although it appeared as if the children were making light of it, they were actually using play-acting to express themselves and also to practice their English language skills.

"Go ahead, Chukuemeka, continue," I coaxed.

"Yes, as I was going to say, we did not show our happiness, because, one hand, we were happy dat God is blessing you, an' on dee oda hand, we were sad dat you will leave us one day, an' dat day will be a sad day for us."

"Go on my broda, you're talking dee truth." Justine encouraged.

Chukuemeka continued, "But, we will pray to all dee gods to give us dee strength to be able to let you go, an' to guide you an' look after you no matta where you are. So, let us all hol' han's now, an' say a prayer." Tearfully, we all stood in a circle holding hands, while Chukuemeka said the prayer:

"Dee gods of dee earth, dee spirits of our relations an' ancestors, we hol' our big sista before you to protect her an' guide her in dis soon-to-come change in her life. We tank you for bringing her dis good luck, an' we also tank you for letting some of dat good luck fall on dee heads of us who will remain here on dee fam. We see how you brought dee whole family out of dee bush after dee war, an' helped us to build up dee fam. So, we are sure dat if you can do what was an impossibility..."

Obi interrupted, "Hio! Hio!"

"Shhh..." Comfort chided, nudging him in his side. "Don't annoy the gods, they are trying to listen."

"As I was saying oh ye gods and spirits, if you were able to keep our family togeda during dee war, den, it is not possible dat you will desert us as long as we live."

"Amen," the children and I intoned.

"Also, our good gods an' spirits," Chukuemeka

added, "we put our moda in your hands as long as she lives. We beg you to take care of her."

"Amen," we said simultaneously.

6

Disposition

The darkness of dawn still covered Uzoakoli like a dark brown, dewy canopy. The morning felt cool, reminding one of the cool dry Hamatan season of Northern Nigeria. It was a season that left one's skin dry, and lips cracked. Although the day had just begun, the Nwokeji compound was crowded with villagers and relations who had gathered to bid me farewell as I prepared for my journey from Uzoakoli to Owerri. I was to take the first lorry out of Uzoakoli motor park. Three months had passed since I received that very significant, long-awaited letter from Uncle Jeremiah.

From the center of the compound, gray smoke rose from the open wood fire where the morning meal was being prepared, fanning out like the branches of a tree. I was actually pleased that my personal belongings were small enough to fit in one of my lappas, since I had to worry about traveling with two heavy gari bags filled with yam and plantain intended for Uncle Jeremiah's family in Owerri. One of my lappas served as my suitcase which contained three sets of lappas; three head-ties; two sets of homemade underwear; a bunch of chewing sticks*; a small tin of talcum powder; a small jar of Vaseline petroleum jelly for my dry skin; and a large wooden, long handled Afro comb. Included in my load was a compartmental thermos bottle containing rice and stew,

*chewing stick—a specially designed stick used as a toothbrush

including a spoon. Although Owerri was only a few hours away, I had been cautioned that buying something to eat along the way at bus stops could be expensive; that the lorry could break down in the middle of nowhere, and repairs could take several hours.

At last, my entourage and I were ready for the long trek to the motor park.* There were more than enough hands to assist with the heavy bags of foodstuff. I was not concerned about how I would manipulate the heavy gari bags and my bundle on my arrival in Owerri motor park. I knew that in that region, as people traveled from village to village, and to the surrounding towns, passengers looked out for each other, sharing their food, and assisting each other with their loads.

Earlier that morning, I had entered my mother's hut and observed her as she slept. Placing a farewell kiss on her cheek, I knelt beside her built-in mud platform bed and prayed to the gods to watch over her in my absence. It was with a heavy heart and much sadness that I left my mother's hut, perhaps for the last time.

People began to file out of the compound on our way to the motor park. Surrounded by the crowd of people who had come to bid me farewell, my siblings and I had walked about a mile toward the main road, when we heard distant screams coming from the periphery of our compound. Someone in the crowd looked back and remarked, in Igbo, "A woman is trying to catch up with us."

"The woman should know where the motor park is. We will see her there," another voice replied.

At the Uzoakoli motor park, my gari bags of foodstuff were placed securely on top of the lorry where most of the heavy loads were usually kept. I began to board, holding

* motor park—bus station

firmly to my personal bundle and my rice and stew. My family and I, including the villagers who had accompanied me to the motor park, embraced, cried together, and said the necessary "good-byes" when I realized that my sister, Justine, was not in the crowd. I was not too worried however, because the lorry had another hour before beginning the journey to Owerri. So, even if Justine was not close enough to be embraced, I knew I could hold her hand through the wooden bars of the window I was seated next to. I could see clearly, which made it possible for me to see all those who had come to see me off, or touch any one of them who came close to the window.

As we continued our good-bye chatter, a shattering scream broke through the familiar buzz of the motor park crowd and the groaning engines of all the lorries preparing to roll out on their journey to various sections of Nigeria. Then, someone tried to get my attention by tapping on my window, and crying out in Igbo.

"My sister," the stranger said, "it was your sister, Justine, who had been doing all that screaming behind you on your way to the motor park. Right now, she's sitting on the roadside still screaming and she's all covered with blood." With that, my entourage deserted me, and rushed to the aid of Justine.

"Oh no!" I shouted, looking up helplessly at the ceiling of the lorry, "What has happened to my sister? I can't travel now! How do I get off this crowded bus? Somebody get me off this crowded bus! I beg you, good spirits of my ancestors, don't let me lose my mind. My sister needs me!"

I tried to stand up in order to start maneuvering my way out of the bus, and found that to be a futile attempt. The bus was already overcrowded. People and loads filled every available space. I stuck my head out of the window to get some information or help from someone I knew, but there were no familiar faces around. They had all rushed to Justine's aid. My window was two seats from the back of the lorry; and since it seemed impossible to find my way to the only entrance of the lorry, which was in the front, without climbing over the heads of some passengers, and over mountains of loads, I decided to drop my bundle out of the window and jump out after it.

Just then, Chukuemeka reappeared at my window, his face damp with tears. He said, "Grace, you can't travel today. Someting terrible has happened. You must get off dee lorry now."

I felt myself panicking, but I heard the good spirits whispering in my ear, "You're an African woman, you mustn't lose control; just go back home and face whatever it is that has happened."

"Chukuemeka," I said, tugging at my brother's arm through the window, "what happened to Justine? Get me off this lorry! How can I get off with all these people and loads all over the place? Oh, my father in the grave, I need you right now! How do I get off this lorry?"

As I continued irrationally, Chukuemeka jumped up and clung to the side of the lorry and peered inside to examine the situation. Then, he said, "Do you see dis space at the top of dee window?"

"Yes," I replied. "Oh God! What happened to Justine? I am dead. Oh, my father in the grave, I am dead."

"Pull yourself together, and listen to me," Chukuemeka said. "We don't have much time! I'm going to get you out through dis space at dee top of dee window, you undastand?"

"Help me, my father!" I said. "Where are the spirits when you need them?"

"Now, quick, flatten your bundle as much as you can,

an' pass it over to me through this space. Quick quick, do as I say, now."

I did as Chukuemeka instructed, and with much pushing and pulling, the bundle found its way outside the lorry.

Chukuemeka continued his commands, "Now, pull up your lappa all dee way over your knees, step over dee ledge of dee window. Climb up an' try to squeeze your body through dee same space. Try to get your head and your shouldas through first, an' I will pull you through."

"Now, where's everybody? Where is Justine?" I asked, as my feet landed on the ground. I was still crazed with the suspense of not knowing what had happened to my sister, and gave no thought to the demeaning and embarrassing way I had been pulled from the lorry.

"Wait, let me get your gari bags off dee top of dee lorry first. I'll explain eveyting on our way home." Chukuemeka said, as he started climbing along the side of the lorry.

I woke up late the following morning to find Chukuemeka and the rest of my siblings sitting in silence beside my mat.

"What happened to me?" I said, reaching for Chukuemeka's hand. Immediately, all the hands in the hut began to caress my whole body—my hair, my forehead, my shoulders, my arms, my hand, my legs, my feet.

"After we brought you out of dee motor park, we sat you down on dee grass nearby, and when we broke dee news about our moda to you, you fainted. So, we carried you all dee way home."

"How could she have understood enough about my departure to kill herself over it? Maybe the bad spirits killed her," I replied.

Chukuemeka began to stroke my hair. "My sister, dere are a lot of tings we humans can never understan. Our moda wasn't of dis world, but obviously she knew more than we tought she knew."

"How did she kill herself?" I asked, sitting up. Justine rose, and ran out of the hut whimpering. The other children ran after her.

"She stuck a knife in her stomach and bled to death."

"How awful! Tell me, honestly, my brother, do you think our mother would have the courage to do such a thing to herself?"

"But she did stab herself, my sister. She was still holding the knife in her hand when she was found dead. Everybody has been wondering dee same ting, but Chief Udekwe cleared up dee mystery for us. He said that dee evil spirit forced her to do it. So, actually, she didn't know what she was doing."

"How did Justine get blood all over her?"

"Justine found her. She was dee last person to leave dee compound yestaday as we were all going to dee motor park. She said she heard some noise coming from our mother's hut an' she went to investigate. Anyway, our mother had already stabbed herself an' was dying. A lot of blood was flowing. So blood got on Justine when she trew herself on our moda's body."

"Where is our mother now?" I asked.

"She is all ready for burial for dis evening. We put her in dee spare hut. We have been waiting for you to wake up so we could start dee burial ceremonies."

That evening, as my siblings and I were walking away from my mother's resting place at the innermost section of the farm, Comfort asked, "Sisi, you still going to Owerri?"

"Yes, but not for a long while. Mourning period usually lasts for one year. After that, I will go."

"What is mourning period?" Isaac asked.

"Well, it's a time when the women in the family dress in black in honor of a family member who has died. They remain home all the time and do not participate in any merriment if it does not concern the person who has died. When our father died, we were all children, and did not go through the mourning period like grown-ups do. I am a woman now, so I'll be wearing black for a year, and remain quietly on the farm."

"What going to happen with all de yam and plantain you were going to bring to Uncle Jeremiah's family?" Patricia asked.

"I went back to dee motor park dis morning and explained to dee lorry driver what happened," Chukuemeka offered. "I told him dat since my sister had already paid for her passage from Uzoakoli to Owerri an' did not travel, I would like to go in her place tomorrow morning to bring the foodstuff to our uncle an' his family, an' also give dem dee bad news about our moda."

7

Transition

The end of the mourning period for my mother brought back normalcy once again to our compound, and my trip to Owerri was re-scheduled. Finally, the travel date arrived.

On entering the Uzoakoli motor park, I was astonished to see how much more congested and busy it was than the first time I had tried to travel, and I wondered how my entourage and I were going to make our way through the throng to reach the Owerri lorry. It was decided that only Chukuemeka should accompany me into the park, while the rest of my entourage would wait along the roadside leading to Owerri, where they would get a better glimpse of me as the lorry rolled by.

The Uzoakoli–Owerri lorry was also mobbed. Again, passengers sat or stood in any available space. Even the steps leading into the lorry were not immediately visible since they were used by some passengers as sitting or standing platforms.

"I may have to wait for the next lorry," I said to Chukuemeka, taking a deep, futile breath.

"Don't worry; you should be used to dis sort of situation by now, my sister. People don't get discouraged by the lack of space, they jus' squeeze in somehow, an' you're going to do the same." Chukuemeka replied firmly. "All you need is for your foot to jus step insigh' dee lorry an' you will be fine. Anoda ting, after dee lorry makes a few stops, dees passengers sitting an' standing on dee steps are dee ones who will be getting off first. Den, people from dee insigh' will take dere place. Maybe if dis happens a few times, you will find a seat."

Chukuemeka put my mind at peace. I wasn't worried anymore, I was ready to go through any hurdle.

Soon, Chukuemeka and I found ourselves in the midst of the small crowd shoving its way through the front side door of the Owerri bus. As we moved closer to the steps of the bus, Chukuemeka pulled me closer to him by my shoulders and whispered in my ears, "Listen to me, my sister, I have a plan of action. Open up your bundle and put dee flask insigh' so you'll have one load, and put the whole ting on your head."

Without questioning, I did as Chukuemeka instructed, holding firmly to the compartmented food flask inside my bundle to prevent the soup I was carrying from spilling onto my clothing. "What now?" I said.

"I'll prac-ti-ca-lly lift you up, bundle an' all, an' put you right inside dee lorry."

"What about all these people standing in the way?"

"When dey see me trying to get you on dee lorry, dey will join in and help me carry you along. You'll see."

Chukuemeka was right. It seemed everyone was eager to get me on the lorry. In no time at all, I was already inside where passengers sat cramped in the regular seats, on the floor, on window ledges, on bundles and loads strewn about the floor. Some women had children sitting on their laps, while others had babies tied to their backs.

Finally, I found a space that was big enough for my bundle. I placed it down gently, took out the food flask, tied the bundle back up, and used it as a seat for the rest of the trip.

As the lorry crawled out of the Uzoakoli motor park on the way to Owerri, I was already beginning to feel the loss of my family and village. From where I sat, it was impossible to see anyone who had been waiting along the roadside to catch a glimpse of me. Although I knew they would understand if they could not spot me on the lorry, I nevertheless, felt extremely sad, alone, and lost and I would have liked to wave to them. I tried to console myself by rationalizing about my dislike for "good-byes"; that it was just as well that I was not able to see my people for the last time.

Since I was unable to enjoy the scenery along the way, I clutched my flask and closed my eyes, saying a prayer to the gods and my deceased parents for the safe-keeping of my family and for my own safe journey. The prayer eased my sadness and loneliness somewhat, and soon I began to wonder how my life would be changed as a resident of Owerri. Could I fit into the city life? I pondered over the contents of Uncle Jeremiah's letter regarding the differences in maintaining a village hut and a city flat; and the difference between working in a government office, and working on a farm. I thought about my nieces and nephews in Owerri who were my age-mates, and wondered whether I would find marked differences between us. Would the differences make me uncomfortable? Would they be conspicuous to others?

As I brooded on these imponderables, I also became aware of the various stops being made by the lorry, for refueling, or to pick up and drop off passengers. At each stop, the conductor announced either the reason for it, or our arrival at a particular destination.

At last, the conductor called out "Owerri" as the lorry approached the bustling Owerri motor-park. My heart and stomach fluttered with excitement. Still sitting on my bundle, I was amazed at how quickly the lorry emptied out even before it screeched to a halt. Passengers were jumping out of windows and doors like toads finally set free from an extended entrapment. Clutching my food flask, I stood up for the first time and peered out the window, watching people scurry in all directions. I observed names like Onitsha, Umuahia, Maiduguri, Bauchi, Sokoto, Ilorin, Akure, etc., on the signs in front of the other parked lorries scheduled to travel within the eastern and southern areas of Nigeria, including the north.

I picked up my bundle and proceeded toward the driver who was still behind the wheel observing me in his rearview mirror. The conductor was, of course, nowhere in sight. He also had vanished quickly with the passengers.

I had not expected to be met at the Owerri motor-park. I had decided that a surprise visit would be more expeditious than waiting more than a week to allow the letter that would inform Uncle Jeremiah of my arrival, to reach him. Besides, he had stressed in his letter to me that I should "just come"; that I did not have to prepare his family for my arrival as long as I knew his address. Chukuemeka had also advised me to take a taxi from the motor-park to Uncle Jeremiah's house.

Just before I reached the driver's seat, I placed my bundle and my food flask on one of the seats in order to recheck the address on Uncle Jeremiah's letter, which I had stuck down the front of my blouse. Although I had memorized the address, I was afraid I might be too nervous and excited to speak coherently to the cab driver. I read the return address aloud, "Number 12 Okpara Street, Owerri."

"Are you lost or what? Where are you supposed to be heading?" the driver finally spoke, in Igbo. Startled, I looked up, but when I saw his amiable face, I sighed with relief. Although I understood what was said, I was able to detect some variations in the driver's dialect.

"No, sir," I replied in my own dialect, "I don't think so, sir. I'm supposed to take a taxi to where I'm going. I have the address here with me."

"Is this your first visit to Owerri?"

"Yes sir," I replied. "And a taxi, sir, how do I get one?"

"Where are you coming from?"

"From Uzoakoli, sir."

"Hmmm!" the driver uttered shaking his head from side to side. "You remind me of my own daughters. I have eight of them, between three wives. You're very young and extremely beautiful so you must be very careful. Come, wait outside while I lock up my lorry and I'll walk you over to the taxi stand. I'll personally see that you get one. This lorry is not due back to Uzoakoli for another hour."

"Thank you very much sir, and may the gods bless you and bring you much luck." I replied quickly, picking up my bundle and flask. As I waited beside the lorry, I wondered how I could ever repay the driver for his kindness. Then, an idea came to me as he led me out of the motor park carrying my bundle and the flask. I would give him my rice and stew. I was certain he would like a home-cooked meal. After all, he had not eaten since we left Uzoakoli, and I would soon be fed by my uncle's family.

"You know sir, I was so excited about making this trip," I said, before I climbed into the taxi, "I lost my appetite completely! I thought I would be hungry at some point, so I carried this flask filled with some rice and stew, but I never even thought about food. Since I'm going to be fed on my arrival at my uncle's house, and I'm sure you haven't eaten since we left Uzoakoli, I want you to please have the rice and stew. And I want you to know that I cooked it myself."

"You mean it?"

"Yes sir, I do. Please take it. You've been so nice to me, and I don't know how else to express my gratitude."

"What a considerate girl you are! The gods have not only made you beautiful, they also made your heart beautiful. How can I refuse such generosity from someone like you? Some men would kill to have an opportunity to eat food cooked with those beautiful hands!" As the taxi started its journey to Okpara Street, the driver of the taxi eased off slowly, obviously to allow me to complete my conversation with the lorry driver.

"By the way," the lorry driver continued, speaking loudly and quickly now and holding up the flask as the taxi picked up speed, "your flask? How do I return your flask to you?"

"Don't worry sir, you can keep that too. Let it be my gift to you. You cannot imagine how much I appreciate your help. You made my arrival in Owerri less scary. Goodbye sir, and I hope I run into you again sometime, and thank you again sir!" I added quickly as the taxi sped away.

I looked back to get a last glimpse of the lorry driver as he stood by the roadside clutching the flask against his chest. He was a short, slim, and energetic looking man. Back on the lorry before he had told me about his daughters, I presumed that he was about twenty-eight. He had not divulged how many children he had altogether. Therefore, since it was possible that he could have had a few sons in addition to his eight daughters, he could have been in his early fifties.

* * *

The transition to life in Owerri had not been easy for me. Already in Owerri for three months, my existence still seemed dream-like. It was as though I might awaken any moment and find myself in the familiar surroundings of my village compound, with my brothers and sisters. Here, in Owerri, I woke up every morning, not on my mat but in a bed assembled with a mattress, clean white bedsheets, and pillows covered with clean white pillowcases. The bedsheets felt luxurious; however, I felt more comfortable covering myself up with my lappa as I slept at night. The transitional shock I was feeling was more severe because I found myself spending most of my time indoors. I missed the ample compound in the village, where one space was our lounging area, another was our frolicking area; and there was an area that served as our kitchen. I missed the trees (including the fruit trees), the bushes, the melodious singing of the songbirds early in the morning, and the wake-up call of the crowing cocks. I missed the smells, the farm, the fresh fruits and vegetables, the grinding stone to grind peppers, tomatoes, onions, and other cooking ingredients. Using electrical gadgets here in Owerri to grind cooking ingredients, and pounding yam foo-foo indoors, were still strange and awkward for me. I also missed going into the farm in the village to collect ingredients with which to cook, as opposed to going to the open market to buy what was needed. Yet, I marveled at the various items offered by the open markets. Besides food items, they carried hardware and household items, such as plates and silverware; some furniture; clothing for men, women, and children; or whatever one might want. What gave me much pleasure was my shopping spree for dresses appropriate for office wear in preparation for my employment at the Ministry, where my uncle worked. Eva, one of my cousins who was my agemate, assisted me with the purchases. She explained that the younger office girls wore fashionable dresses, shoes, and accessories to work; that the older women wore mostly lappas, and wore dresses only occasionally.

Working at the Ministry constituted yet another transitional shock. However, to my surprise, I was able to adjust much quicker than I thought possible. My determination to succeed, made the transition manageable. In addition, interacting with a different category of people made my business hours interesting and exciting. It was always a pleasure to go to my job. My superiors marveled at my sagacity. Soon, I gained the respect of the entire Ministry, earning the reputation of being sedulous, intelligent, and someone whom anyone would want to work with.

My immediate superior, Mr. Ogwu, and Uncle Jeremiah's lifelong friend, taught me all there was to know, and very quickly. Soon after my training, Mr. Ogwu expressed much satisfaction with my performance, and fought hard to get me promoted to a much higher level in the Ministry. It was a tough fight, because promotions normally were given based on seniority, in addition to receiving outstanding evaluations. However, Mr. Ogwu used his influence to circumvent the usual procedures and regulations to have me appointed head of one of the prestigious departments in the Ministry. No objections to such an unprecedented move rose from either other administrators or employees. The acceptance to the move was unanimous; subsequently, the consensus was that my presence in the department had enabled it to be the most organized and most efficiently run. Even I was astounded by my own abilities and success.

It was one of those routine mornings in my office. There were files to look through, letters to sign, and telephone calls to make. I was interrupted by a knock on the door which was already wide open. I looked up to find Mr.

Ogwu entering my office. His visit was not a surprise to me, since we met routinely, once a week for about fifteen minutes to rehash the discussions of the weekly administrative session. I immediately dropped the pen I was holding and rose to my feet to demonstrate my respect for him as my superior.

Mr. Ogwu was a short, portly, balding man of about sixty. On entering my office, I noticed that he shut the door behind him, which I presumed meant that we were about to have a brief business meeting. Before uttering a word, he brought out a large light blue handkerchief from the side pockets of his trousers and proceeded to wipe his damp, shiny face, forehead, and head. Then, thrusting the handkerchief back into his pocket, he extended his hand to greet me. I wondered why the handshake, since a handshake had never been a type of greeting for us, either in or out of the office. Although he was my superior, I also respected him as I would my own father, not as an equal, or a stranger. Hence, verbal greetings without the handshake I thought would have been more appropriate for our relationship. Nevertheless, I stretched out my hand eagerly, surmising that the handshake was probably to congratulate me for a job well done on some specific assignment; but, when I went to withdraw my hand, Mr. Ogwu would not release it.

"No, no," he said, still holding onto my hand, "come away from behind that desk and stand beside me."

Although surprised and confused, I did as he requested, and wondered why his whole attitude and behavior was different—unprofessional.

"You're so fresh and beautiful. Did you know that you're going to be my wife?" Mr. Ogwu continued, brushing his hand across my breasts.

My mouth flew open, and my throat felt constricted. I

was unable to speak. I simply gaped at him, feeling as if I was being molested by my own father.

"Yes, you! I'm going to marry you! Why are you so surprised?" he said with a chuckle. He then added, "Close your mouth, my wife. I don't understand why you're so shocked. What did you expect? Did you expect that I would do all I've done for you for nothing? How could you be so naive? Have you ever heard of anyone who rose so quickly to a high rank in such a short time, and of all places, in the civil service?"

My voice returned. "Your wife! Did for me! I don't believe this." I managed to release my hand from his grip, swung around, and placed both hands on my head. I felt my legs giving way under me. So, I groped my way back to my desk, sank heavily into my chair, placed my elbows on the desk and buried my head in my hands.

Then, I felt Mr. Ogwu's hand on my shoulder. "Why are you behaving as if this is the worst thing that could happen to you? Most women would be honored that a man like myself would want to do so much for them, and that I would even want to marry them."

I raised my head wearily. "But, Mr. Ogwu, you're like my own father, and besides, you already have four wives. And speaking about what you have done for me; yes, you did give me the opportunity, for my uncle's sake, but I have worked very hard to prove myself and you know it."

"That you have. There's no denying that. But in your situation, where would hard work get you so quickly without someone pulling some strings? For your information, it takes sometimes a lifetime to get where you are now! As one of my wives, you would have the best of both worlds. You will maintain your top position here, travel, and do whatever else your heart desires. No other wife of mine would be in that position."

"If I say 'no' to all this?" I replied audaciously.

"You're an intelligent woman, extremely bright, you're popular, well-liked and respected. You will not say 'no.' Think about it, and don't be foolish. I'll see you tomorrow."

With that, Mr. Ogwu left my office. However, he returned a few minutes later to find me in the same position, and still in a state of shock. "Shame on you!" he said, "I was just thinking about what you said. You call yourself an African woman, and you're horrified when an African man wants you to be one of his wives. What kind of an African woman are you?"

"Mr. Ogwu," I pleaded, "please don't ruin our relationship. I respect you as my superior, and love you as my own father. I cannot perceive you as anything else. Please try to understand. I admit I'm an African woman who wants a little bit more than usual, and I don't know where that's coming from. For example, marriage—what you're proposing to me now is something I can't imagine myself doing, not at this time in my life, and not even to a man who is single. I am more interested in having a career and traveling to different places. Please try to understand. I don't want us to fight. I just can't help the way I feel. I'm even surprised at myself for seeming so different."

"I don't understand where all this is coming from." Mr. Ogwu replied. "You've never travelled out of Nigeria. You came here straight from the village, yet, you're talking and acting like a foreigner. Anyway, bear in mind what I've said, and I advise you to start thinking like an African woman, or you'll continue to miss out on significant opportunities. An African woman lives for her husband and children, not a career. You say you see me as a father figure? Look, my dear, I don't want to be your father, I want to be your husband."

That episode in my office marked the beginning of Mr. Ogwu's constant lecherous advances. His once professional demeanor had now been transformed into aggressive, revolting wet kisses on my cheek and neck, each time he came into my office. After the nauseating kisses, his clumsy, heavy damp hands would rest on my shoulders, and then brush down surreptitiously over my breasts.

I felt helpless, and considered ways to stop Mr. Ogwu's harrowing advances without creating a scene, and without making the harassment public knowledge. I had even promised him that no one, particularly my uncle, would ever know about what was going on, if he would only stop his unwanted attentions. The last thing I wanted to do was to be the object of a dispute between my uncle and Mr. Ogwu, two men whose friendship was as significant as the relationship between two blood brothers.

It had already been three years since my arrival in Owerri and since joining the Ministry. Aside from the problem with my superior, Mr. Ogwu, my job brought me much gratification and contentment, and so did my private life in Owerri. I was now renting a two bedroom government bungalow, which I had acquired only six months after I began working at the Ministry. Of course I had acquired it through Mr. Ogwu's influence. Otherwise, my life was perfect. Things were going so well, I gave no thought to making any changes in my life, but now, my benefactor, Mr. Ogwu himself, was about to shatter that perfection. His lascivious behavior was getting out of control and turning my life into an insufferable nightmare. Yet I was afraid to discuss the situation with anyone, and unable to put a stop to it on my own. As a result, I fell into the depths of a despondency so acute that every aspect of my life was beginning to be affected. My job performance began to decline, but Mr. Ogwu's daily advances continued, along with his constant reminders of how he had made me what I was; and how even the acquisition of my bungalow had been due to his influence.

Soon, my concentration began to deteriorate. At home, I became a recluse who ate little and slept most of the time. The novelty of going to work each day finally vanished, along with my zest for life.

The knock on the door was loud enough to awaken a dead man, I reflected, as I dragged myself out of bed to see who was there. I was confused as to what time of the day it was until I opened the door to find my uncle standing there in his light blue cotton suit, white shirt, and navy blue tie. The bright hot sun which was too much for my eyes helped to organize my senses.

"Come in, Uncle. Please sit down. My goodness, what time is it?" I said, rubbing my eyes with the back of one hand and holding my loosely tied lappa with the other.

"What is wrong? This is not like you," Uncle Jeremiah said after observing me for a few seconds. "You have not been to work for three days, we have not seen you at my house for the past month, and frankly, you've been behaving quite strangely. What is the matter? Remember me? I'm your uncle. If you cannot talk to me, who can you talk to? I know you're an independent woman now, and a successful one at that, but I still consider you my child, and I'm still responsible for you."

I said nothing. I loved, adored, and respected this man who had taken my father's place in my life. I knew I could not keep the secret from him any longer.

"Look, my daughter," he said, rising from his seat,

"I'll go and put some petrol in my car. When I get back, I want you to be ready to take a drive with me to my farm, away from everything, so we can talk."

By now it was dusk, and Uncle Jeremiah's light gray 1982 Toyota headed east on the usually congested Aba road, which was almost devoid of traffic. The drive was so invigorating that I forgot its main purpose for the first few miles. Then I became distracted as I found myself immersed in the sheer splendor of the view. I felt a special bond with nature and the universe. The setting sun splattered the sky with all the colors of the rainbow and more, covering the landscape with resplendent colors.

At the periphery of the Owerri boundary was the highest point of the hilly Aba road. Then at the lowest point, where the road was only partly tarred, it stretched for miles, snaking its way through luscious, fertile green hills and valleys and occasionally through small, sleepy villages. I was awed by the sight. I had not paid much attention to the beauty of my surroundings, even back at my village. I venerated the moon, since it was one of our many gods and I had appreciated it particularly as a child, because its incandescence made it possible to continue playing games in the compound when it grew dark. Also, the brightness of the moon saved the villagers the cost of leaving lighted kerosene lamps in the compound at night, since the nights were usually bright enough even to read by.

"You haven't said a word since we left Owerri," Uncle Jeremiah finally said as he observed me from the corner of his eye.

"Uncle, I'm enjoying the ride and the spectacular view," I replied, "I guess the beauty of the scenery has left me speechless."

"Some sections of Nigeria are absolutely enchanting, yet some of us don't appreciate the beauty."

"You're right, Uncle, I was that way until I came to Owerri. I have only just begun to appreciate the beauty of the villages and the fantastic roads and fields which separate them. By the way, Uncle, when I accompanied you and your family to your farm some time ago, I found it as impressive as our village farm back in Uzoakoli. When do you city people find the time to tend to your farms?"

"As you know, there's nothing to do now, especially with the fruit trees. All the trees are full grown now at this point, and all we have to do is harvest them when it's time. But the small shrubs, the vegetables and the like, we take care of during planting season. Families who live in the cities travel back and forth to their farms on weekends to do what has to be done, or if they have the extra money, they hire farm hands who live nearby to do some of the work. Take my farm for instance; years ago, when we started the farm, my family and I spent every weekend doing that very hard work. One of my colleagues at the Ministry manages to keep a well cultivated produce farm on the other side of Owerri, off the road leading to Aba. It has corn, sweet potatoes, tomatoes, and all sorts of vegetables. Yes, as I said, many people who work in the cities bring along all their family members on Saturday and Sunday to do whatever is necessary."

By the time we arrived at Uncle Jeremiah's farm, I felt comfortable enough to reveal the truth about Mr. Ogwu. We sat underneath one of the grapefruit trees, and I spilled the whole devastating nightmare to my uncle. I expected the revelation to come as a shock to him; however, after listening intently, he took my hand and sighed, "My daughter, you're a beautiful woman. It's natural for any man to want you. What's wrong with at?"

"But uncle, Mr. Ogwu is like my father, and besides, he already has all those wives."

"How do you know that?"

"Uncle, you know how it is at work. People talk, and they know everybody's business."

"True. But so what if Mr. Ogwu has other wives? Either you agree to marry him or you don't. You know that's our tradition. A man can have more than one wife if he wants to."

"Uncle, I understand the tradition. But why do men take it for granted that the woman they want also wants them?"

"What do you mean?"

"Well, what if the woman is not attracted to the man?"

"I still don't know what you mean."

"I mean, the woman may not feel anything for the man or may not like him in that way, and therefore does not want to marry him. I'm talking about love, Uncle; what about that?"

My uncle laughed. "Love? What are you talking about? The woman doesn't have to have love or feel anything for the man, as you put it. All she needs to know is that the man is a good man from a respectable family, and a good provider. That feeling and the love you talk about, that will come in time."

"Uncle, I must have come from another planet then, because I'm not going to marry a man I don't love. And another thing, even if I do like him, or love him, once he's already married, whether he has one wife or a hundred, I wouldn't want him."

Uncle Jeremiah let out a robust laugh. "My daughter, you really must be from another planet then; you're definitely not talking like an African woman." But when he stopped laughing, he added quickly, "But look, what's important here is what you want and what you don't want. If you don't want what my friend, Mr. Ogwu is proposing, then, the case is closed. I want you to be happy, my child."

"Oh thank you, good spirits of our ancestors!" I cried out looking up to the sky with my hands clasped.

"The problem now is what to do about your situation, since you've told me how miserable your life has been since all this started," Uncle Jeremiah responded.

"And I can't take it any longer; I'm about to lose my mind!"

Uncle Jeremiah and I fell silent for some time. Then, he said, "I have an idea, and we'll talk about it on our way back to Owerri. First, let's pick some grapefruit and oranges to take back."

The headlights on Uncle Jeremiah's gray Toyota shone brightly on the dark road, and the night lights on the outskirts of Owerri township glowed dimly, like distant stars. I took deep breaths as the refreshing breeze seemed to be cleansing my body from the pain and depression which had consumed me since the start of the trouble with Mr. Ogwu. Even before knowing the idea which my uncle promised to discuss with me, I felt confident that a solution would soon surface.

"Now, about that idea I mentioned," my uncle finally said. "Although I don't agree with your line of reasoning, I respect your wishes and your own personal philosophy. You say you don't want Mr. Ogwu to know that you have told me what happened; and he will not know. So, the idea is this: you have served the Ministry now for three years. At this point in your career, it wouldn't be unusual for you to request a transfer to another Ministry, anywhere else in

Nigeria. We will all miss you if you leave Owerri, but this is the only solution to your problem with Mr. Ogwu. By the way, whatever happened to your old dream of going to Lagos someday anyway?"

"Oh, yes, Uncle," I replied. "That had been my main goal, but I had become so happy and contented here, I never gave it another thought. You're absolutely right, Uncle; transferring to Lagos is the perfect solution. It's not only a legitimate excuse to get away from Mr. Ogu, but it would satisfy my life-long dream." Then, I sat up, straightened my shoulders, held my head up high, and turned to my uncle. "Where do I start?"

"There are some standard procedures to follow. Don't worry, I will obtain the form and assist you in filling it out. You and I will sit down and select an appropriate Ministry. Then, you will take a fortnight leave of absence and travel to Lagos to deliver the transfer packet personally. It's faster that way; otherwise, the whole thing takes forever."

"Where would I stay in Lagos for the fortnight?"

"I thought about that too. I have many friends and colleagues in Lagos who would be glad to help out. But for our purpose, one specific couple comes to mind. The man was my roommate in a university we both attended in the United States, and we became very good friends. He married a black American woman after his graduation and brought her to Nigeria."

"Who are they? Do they have any children?"

"Bola and Helen Balogun, and no, that's one of the reasons I think their place would be ideal for you. They have this very big house with plenty of room and there are no children. At least he has no children with the American woman."

"Uncle, don't tell me he also has other wives..."

"Just one more. He was already married to his Nigerian wife in the village, with three children, before he left Nigeria."

"Does his American wife know about his other family in the village?"

"Nope."

"What about the wife in the village? Does she know about the American wife?"

"She should know by now. I imagine he must have told her; he goes to the village only on weekends."

"Yes, yes—it's the culture, so she knows. Right?"

"Right," Uncle Jeremiah replied, "but, it's not always that the Nigerian wife knows about her husband's other wives. It all depends on the circumstances. Sometimes, the husband keeps this information from the wife he lives with, regardless of who she is. If she finds out, it won't be from him. It generally doesn't make any difference anyway; our women understand the culture."

"How do you think Mr. Balogun's American wife would take the news that her husband is already married? This business of having more than one wife is not something she is accustomed to."

"I don't know. We'll see when the time comes. Then again, he may decide not to tell her; it all depends on the woman's attitude and personality, and how well her husband knows her. You know, how he thinks she would react."

"Isn't it possible that she could find out from other sources, sooner or later?"

"That's a chance some men take. It could get very complicated when a foreign woman is involved, since she does not understand our culture; or if she does, she may not accept it. But that's not your problem. Both Bola and Helen are extremely nice people. Helen doesn't work and

I'm sure she'd be happy to have you around for company. She has just arrived from the U.S., hasn't made many friends, and she's left all alone in that big house when Bola goes to work everyday."

8

The Interview

Helen Balogun had prepared me well for this outing. I was to continue walking from bus stop to bus stop until I reached Kofo Abayomi and Musa Yar Adua Streets, hoping to find a taxi that would go to Race Course. She had warned me that taxis were scarce in that section of Ikoyi, so I stood with a small crowd of people; some seemed to be waiting for the bus, and others were, like me, waiting for a taxi.

Finally, a taxi appeared, swerving roughly into the curb, causing a few people to jump out of its path. Then, several people, including me, rushed over to the taxi. "Race Course, Broad Street, Ebutte Metta," the driver called out, "Ah get room for one more passenger."

Hissing sounds emanated from the crowd as people turned away in disappointment to await the arrival of another taxi.

"Race Course," I yelled.

"Get in, get in, quick quick," the driver commanded.

A young man sat next to the driver in the front. He wore a white safari suit, and seemed to be brushing off some imaginary dirt from his short sleeves and collar. In the back seat, sitting behind the driver, was a woman who looked about thirty-five, dressed in a light green silk lace buba* and lappa, with gele[†] of the same material tied

---
*buba—the blouse that is commonly worn by Yoruba women with lappa
[†]gele—the stiff head-tie worn by Yoruba women

skillfully high up on her head. Seated on the other end, was a young man in Khaki shorts and a white, short-sleeved cotton shirt. He sported a bandaged knee.

I opened the door where the woman in lace sat. "Excuse me," I said. "Please move over." Madam Lace creased her forehead, pursed her lips as her eyes travelled from my brown low-heeled shoes to my hair, which Helen Balogun had taken great pains to style. "Pass over," she finally said, "and make you watch my foot."

I climbed into the taxi and tried to ease into the small space between Madam Lace and the man with the bandaged knee, when the taxi pulled off with a sudden jerk, depositing me on Madam Lace's lap.

"AAAH...!!!" she shrieked. "My bloody toe! God punish you, you bloody fool! What's dee matter with you!" With that, she pushed me over sideways, causing me to land on my shoulder—on Bandaged Knee's bad knee.

"I'm dead...OHHHH!!! It's my spoil knee dat she fall on top," he exclaimed, holding his knee and writhing from side to side.

"I'm sorry, but the taxi took off before I sat down."

The driver immediately screeched to a stop, exited the taxi and slammed the door shut with so much force, that I felt my ears clog up. Then, jerking open the door of the side where Madam Lace sat, he peered into the taxi, and addressed each of us individually:

"Waitin be all dis? You!" he said, pointing at Madam Lace. "So, na my fault way your lace an' your foot don doti? You!" pointing at me, "So, na my fault way you jump in dee taxi like some crazy fool an' fall all over dis woman an' dis man. And you!" Pointing at Bandaged Knee, "So, na my fault when somebody don jump on top of your spoil knee, eh, eh, eh?" Then, addressing the three of us together, "Oya, oya, dee tree of you! Comot for my taxi, now now. Oya, comot comot."

"For what?" Madam Lace demanded. "You put me out of your taxi because I say sometin when dis foolish woman fall all over my lace an' my foot?"

"Look here!" Bandaged Knee said, hopping out of the taxi and pointing his forefinger in the driver's face, "If you drive like man way get some sense, an' not like some bloody idiot, de woman no go fall on top of us."

"Who you day call idiot?" the taxi driver shot back, slapping the man's finger away from his face. A boxing match quickly ensued between the two men.

Madam Lace and the passenger who was sitting in the front seat rushed to break up the fight. Soon, the two belligerents were surrounded by a small crowd, who had gathered to hear both sides of the argument as soon as the fight came to an end.

"What you doing in dee taxi when dee driver is over dere fighting?" a school-uniform–clad girl said, peering through the window of the taxi.

I got out of the taxi quickly and stood beside her. "Listen," I said. "How far is Race Course from here? Can I walk it? I haven't had any luck with taxis today."

"It's a little far to walk, but it's not too bad. You see dee main road over dere, by dee police barracks? Get on dat road, an' make a right turn. Walk straight all dee way to dee end. Den, make a left turn, an' go straight, an' keep on going an' you will run into Race Course."

I must have made a wrong turn somewhere, because I ended up in a section that appeared to be the commercial and financial district of Lagos, where hundreds of people could be seen scurrying about the narrow, dusty streets. The level of noise was at a deafening pitch. Loud conversations and tooting of horns added to the incredible cacophony, amid the clatter of danfos,* buses, taxis, and other automobiles. Walking briskly amid clouds of dust, I discovered very quickly that a pedestrian required a unique skill to navigate the streets of downtown Lagos, and lack of attention while walking could result in serious altercations. For instance, at one point on the sidewalk, a man, perhaps distracted, bumped into me. Then, in a chain reaction, I, in turn, bumped into a shopkeeper who was ringing a bell in front of his small store to attract customers. The bell-ringer quickly shoved the bell in his pocket and pulled me toward him by the sleeve of my dress.

"You crazy? Look where you day go, you bloody fool!" the man screamed at me as he shoved me into the path of a danfo which barely missed me. The bus conductor, who was standing on the steps of the danfo, leaned over, struck me on the side of my head, and gave me another shove that sent me back on the sidewalk into a final collision course with yet another pedestrian. Fortunately, unscathed from being tossed around like a soccer ball, I quickly crossed over to a busy and crowded intersection by Broad and Bamgbose Streets, where a sign read, "Tinubu Square." It was there that I asked directions to the Ministry of Establishment.

Going through Tinubu Square was yet another adventure. Scores of street vendors crowded the area trying various gimmicks to attract customers. Some stood at makeshift stalls, beckoning to prospective customers, holding up samples of their wares. Others rang small silver bells, calling out the items on display and promising reduced prices. And then, there were others who followed passers-by, pulling them by the arm and virtually pleading with them to buy something.

*danfo—a small private transport van

At the center of Tinubu Square, amateur street photographers clicked their instant cameras feverishly at strollers who wished to have their picture taken. Some of the photographers were so desperate, they even prevented the unwilling participants from passing through.

After traversing Tinubo Square, I came to an area where one could buy cooked or snack foods by the roadside. Light gray smoke from fireplaces and grills could be seen rising in the hot, hazy sun amidst the nearby trees and houses. The smell of roasted corn, mingled with the smell of dodo* and acara† permeated the whole area. The smells and sounds were all new to me, but I was suddenly homesick for my village and thought about Uncle Jeremiah's statements about Lagos. Somehow, I took comfort in those words, "Lagos is the type of city that grows on you," Uncle Jeremiah had said. "Despite its madness, it is magical, full of excitement and wonder, and after you stay a while and then have to leave, you feel as if you should stay longer, and you begin to look forward to coming back again." I thought about my ordeal with the taxi, the way I was bounced around like a ball, being struck on my head by the danfo conductor, and wondered whether this was the sort of madness that Uncle Jeremiah meant. Yet, despite those unpleasant experiences, by the time I reached the Ministry of Establishment, where I had an appointment, I had already fallen in love with Lagos.

Finally, I was sitting face to face with Mallam Saidu, the Permanent Secretary of the Ministry of Establishment. I seated myself in front of him and placed the folder I was carrying on his desk. I observed him as he went through my papers—the transfer application, my letters of recommendation and the like. It was easy to tell that Mallam

*dodo—fried yam
†acara—fried crushed beans

Saidu was of the Hausa tribe. He had the classic Fulani face—smooth, ebony black velvet skin, with large, oval-shaped, piercing eyes, and teeth as white as cotton.

Without looking up, Mallam Saidu studied the papers before him. Occasionally, he adjusted the wide, draping sleeves of his agbada* which appeared to be a nuisance to him at times. Finally, he looked up at me and smiled, revealing red cola-nut† between his teeth.

"Grace Nwokeji," he said, blinking his eyes rapidly, "I see here that you're a popular and well liked and respected officer in Owerri. Hmm...And a superb administrator too! It's all here in your reference letters and evaluations. Quite impressive, quite impressive!" he added nodding his head and flipping the pages.

I was not sure whether "Thank you" would have been appropriate, so I did not respond.

"Why do you want the transfer to the Ministry of External Affairs?"

"Sir, I see the External Affairs Ministry as an office where I would have the opportunity to serve both Nigerians and foreigners; a place where I would develop a general knowledge of the world around me and beyond, so I could render appropriate services to the people I encounter."

Mallam Saidu seemed to have gone into a trance. With his elbows on the desk, and his chin resting on the palms of his hands, he stared at me without blinking. It appeared he had not realized that I had finished speaking. A few more seconds went by. Suddenly, as if responding to a snap of the finger, he said, "Did you attend university here in Nigeria?"

*agbada—a loose outer gown worn by a Yoruba man
†cola-nut—the seed of the cola tree, used in carbonated drinks and other products

"No sir, I never attended any university. I only completed my secondary schooling and sat for my School Leaving Certificate exam."

"But you speak such good English, I thought you might have gone to the Ministry in Owerri straight from college."

"No, sir."

"Is this your first time coming to Lagos?"

"Yes, sir."

"Are you originally from Owerri?"

"No sir. I was born in Uzoakoli. I left my village to take the Ministry position in Owerri."

"Interesting!" Mallam Saidu remarked, leaning back in his chair and observing me for a few moments before continuing with his questions. From time to time, Mallam Saidu would return to his trance-like state, making me extremely uneasy. His unblinking eyes seemed to penetrate mine. When that occurred, I would look down at my lap and brush off imaginary pieces of groundnut.* Then, I decided that turning the pages of my own papers in front of me would look more natural.

"You know, Miss Nwokeji, your Permanent Secretary in Owerri, Mr. Henry Aguocha, is a personal friend, and he says you're such a good worker that no matter where you go, or what you do, he's convinced that you'd be successful. That's enough for me. I would be a fool not to approve your transfer. Congratulations! Your request for a transfer is approved." Mr. Saidu concluded, rising from his seat, hand outstretched.

"Thank you sir," I replied, rising as I received his hand.

"Now, sit down, sit down, let me explain what is going to happen: I will summon my messenger. When he

*groundnut—peanut

comes, he is going to bring you and your file to Mr. Udofia. Mr. Udofia will go through your file, and then give you the necessary papers to take to your new Ministry, awright?"

"Yes, sir. Thank you very much sir."

"When are you moving from Owerri permanently?"

"I'm on a fortnight leave now, sir. I should be moving to Lagos in another three weeks or so."

"Let Mr. Udofia know if you will need government housing, so that he will put in the request for you through your new Ministry."

"Thank you, sir, but, I won't worry about accommodation just yet. Where I'm staying now is quite comfortable."

"Where is that?"

"I'm staying with a married couple, friends of my family. They have already asked me to stay with them as long as I want. It's a big house with plenty of room and they have no children."

"That's perfect, then. Where is it?"

"In Victoria Island, sir."

"You should be fine then, at least for a while. Victoria Island is nice. You're all set then. Good luck!" Mallam Saidu added.

"Thank you very much sir," I replied, extending my hand, which he cradled with both hands. His grip was strong—and long. "Don't forget, I'm here if you ever need anything. And take care of yourself when you finally move to Lagos. You are a beautiful woman. The men will be after you like flies, so, watch your step!"

My hand was still held captive. I was extremely uncomfortable, and Mallam Saidu's comments about my looks made matters worse. Memories of my encounter with Mr. Ogwu back at the Ministry in Owerri flooded back. I felt myself trembling. To force Mallam Saidu to release my hand, I twisted my body to the side and looked down on the floor about me, as if I had dropped something. The strategy worked and my hand was once again free.

"Goodbye sir, and thanks again," I said, as I hastened toward the door.

"Wait!" he called out. "Wait for my messenger. He will be here shortly to carry your file and take you to Mr. Udofia's office." I had stopped to listen, but did not turn around and, with my back still toward him, I replied, "Thank you so much, sir. I will wait outside. I really appreciate your help. Goodbye, sir."

"Bye now, Miss Nwokeji, and don't forget—I am here for you whenever you need me."

He probably had no ulterior motives in saying that, but I did not respond. Nevertheless, the words left a bad taste in my mouth. I was haunted by Mr. Ogwu's hands.

9
Friend Everlasting

"I don't believe this; it's like a river outside. Water everywhere. Just look at that! Children are the only ones enjoying this. Look at them! They're actually swimming in that dirty water."

"Grace, when did you start talking to yourself? And who's swimming out there in that flooded street?" Helen said, as she joined me at the French window in the living room. "Are you still upset you can't report to work because of the floods?" Putting a comforting arm around my shoulder, she continued. "I told you not to worry. Not many people will be at work today."

"Look at me," Bola Balogun joined us. "I can't go anywhere today either. All Lagos is flooded, even up to Apapa where I work. Just relax and enjoy the day off. Tomorrow should be fine."

I turned and stared at him. "How could everything be back to normal by tomorrow, when the whole island is one big river today after such heavy rain?"

"It is amazing what happens. It is about 9 o'clock in the morning, right?" Bola said, looking at his watch. "By 5 o'clock this evening, most of this water will all be gone."

"Where will it all go?" I replied, astonished.

"The sun drinks it up; that's how hot it gets. So, tomorrow, you can report to your new Ministry and everything will be fine."

"What if my supervisor tries his best to get to work, knowing that I'm supposed to start today?"

"Believe me, he would not be trying to get to work. Supervisors know what to expect on a day like this. How would he get to work anyway? You have no idea where he would be coming from."

"But he may be coming from a few streets from the Ministry."

"You don't know that."

"No, I don't, so I don't want to take any chances," I replied.

"Hmmm!!! What does that mean?"

"It means that since we don't live too far off from the Ministry, I'll walk it."

"You will *what*!" both Bola and Helen chimed simultaneously.

"I will walk to the Ministry. I can hold my shoes in my hand, together with my handbag and all my papers." I replied. I was adamant and could not be stopped.

Helen laughed, "Look, Grace, I'm new in Nigeria, but I learned quickly how things are done here. Even if the streets were not flooded and you don't report today, it won't be a big deal. They'll know that you're transferring from another state, so, if you're one or two days late they won't get excited. They would understand that anything could prevent you from reporting on time."

"I still don't want to take that chance."

"You know, I tell you what," Bola said, as he climbed the stairs to the second floor. "If walking in all this water to report to work is going to give you peace of mind, go ahead, and go with my blessing."

Helen laughed again. "Grace, you mean it? You're really going to walk to the Ministry in all this water?"

"Mmm...hmm! Since it's not raining anymore I don't think I'll have much of a problem," I replied.

Helen shook her head and started up the stairs as

well. "Good luck, my sister."

I stood outside the gate of the house and surveyed our entire street before I began my arduous journey. With my reporting papers tucked safely inside my black vinyl handbag, I pulled the long strap over my head and underarm so as to leave my hands free for holding up the skirt of my dress and carrying my shoes. I was now ready to begin my walk.

As I waded in the murky rain water through those few streets that were passable, I thought about Bola and Helen Balogun and how lucky I was to have two people who were not even members of my family to be so concerned about me; and then, to go so far as to insist that I should live with them as long as I wanted to. I also pondered about their relationship as a couple.

From my first encounter with them, I wondered why the two ever got married, since I saw no compatibility between them. Helen was a loquacious, gregarious woman of about twenty-eight, huge and broad-shouldered, with an effervescent and ebullient personality. Bola, on the other hand, was a quiet, diminutive, and unpretentious man of perhaps about fifty-five, who, when he was home, sat off by himself, his silver-rimmed spectacles resting on the tip of his nose, devouring a book, a magazine, a newspaper, or any reading he could get his hands on. Aside from breakfast and supper times, it was a rare occasion that the couple would chat together. Nevertheless, it was evident that they loved each other. When they spoke of each other to friends, "I love my husband," or "I love my wife," never failed to be expressed by either one of them. To each other they spoke respectfully, and never disagreed about anything.

Meanwhile, I was covering much ground as I continued my adventure. I tried to remain on major roads, so when I reached Alexander and Gerald Avenues, I knew I was not far from my destination. Soon, I was gazing at the impressive buildings of the Secretariat and the black, wide iron gates which opened onto the grounds. I stood on the flooded street for some time, hoping that someone would come along so I could ask whether the Ministry was open or not. Nothing of the sort happened. Twice, men crossed over from one building to another, but my attempt to attract their attention was futile; neither man looked toward the gates.

I decided to take my chances and follow the directions that were given to me by Mr. Udofia back at the Ministry of Establishment. I was to enter the Secretariat building, find the main lobby, and ask anyone around to direct me to the correct floor.

Water from the flooded streets gushed onto the grounds of the Secretariat, but I was unaware that there was a large, open sewer alongside the walls of that section so I proceeded through the gates. Suddenly, I felt my right foot slide down the side of the concrete slab that served as a bridge over the open sewer which was now completely covered with rainwater. I immediately sank to the bottom of the colossal gutter. Spitting out debris that had managed to lodge on my tongue when some of the water entered my mouth, I struggled to remain on my feet, groping at the edge of the gutter for something to hold on to.

I stood inside the gutter with the mixture of sewage and rainwater up to my neck, and noticed that my shoes were not on my feet. I thought that was fortunate for me, because I could now use my bare feet to feel for some ridge or crack on the walls of the gutter which would make it possible for me to climb out to safety. I held on to the edge of the gutter with one hand; with the other hand, I wrapped the strap of my handbag twice around my neck to shorten it and to prevent it from obstructing my impending maneuvers. Then, my right foot began a search for cracks and ridges. However, the cracks I found were neither large nor deep enough to create make-believe steps; that was when I realized that I might have to remain where I was for hours, or drown from fatigue and shock, if I was not rescued. I began to pray to my parents' spirits. Just then, I heard a woman's voice behind me.

"Who is this? What are you doing in the gutter?" she was laughing hysterically. I detected a Yoruba accent. I could not turn around to look at the woman's face for fear that I would lose my grip at the edge of the gutter.

The woman, still laughing, came around to face me, and gave me her hand. "What happened? Did you fall in there just like that? Where were you going?"

"I'm so glad to see you," I said, spitting out sand and debris. "I'm so embarrassed!"

"Excuse me for laughing," the woman replied, pulling my hand as hard as she could, "but it's a funny scene—you inside the gutter, and the filthy smelly water up to your neck."

"I bet even funnier now," I said, as I finally climbed out of the gutter. "Look at me: smelly, soaked to the bones, no shoes...I guess it is funny, but most of all embarrassing."

"Where were you going?" the woman repeated.

"This is my first day at the Ministry of External Affairs. I'm on a transfer from Owerri." Then, I suddenly remembered my reporting papers. "Goodness!" I said stamping my muddy feet. "I'm sure the water must have ruined my reporting papers in my handbag."

"Why did you bother to report for work on a day like this? No one goes to work or anywhere when the streets are flooded like this."

I took a good look at the woman for the first time. She looked to be about thirty years old and she was dressed for the floods in what I found out later to be a vinyl jump suit. It covered her whole body up to her neck, and she also wore knee-high plastic boots, looking exactly like the image of the "classy Lagos girl" that had been described to me back in Owerri. Lagos girls, I was told, sported permed, professionally coiffured hair; flattering make-up which included bright red lipstick; expensive fashionable outfits, and lots of gold jewelry. This woman fit that description.

I decided to answer her last question. "I didn't think the floods would stop supervisors from carrying out their duties. I thought my supervisor at the Ministry of External Affairs would expect the same from someone reporting for the first time."

The woman's face was serious now, "You poor thing," she said. "You must be cold and extremely uncomfortable in those wet clothes."

"I am," I replied, shaking murky water off my arms and legs like a wet puppy. Then, the woman unzipped her small, navy blue handbag (which matched the color of her jumpsuit), retrieved a large floral handkerchief and handed it to me. "Wipe yourself off."

"Thank you so much," I said, and began wiping my face, neck, and arms.

"By the way, I'm also a civil servant and I work at the Secretariat. I came this morning, not to work, but to pick up my keys. I had left them in my office yesterday! But they can wait while I take care of you. Here, hold on to my arm and let's walk together, it's not far from here. You're coming home with me. You need to take off those clothes and scrub the germs off your whole body as soon as possible, and then drink something hot, like some Ovaltine."

I could not thank her, as I was too choked with emotion. I would have expected such treatment from anyone back at the village, but not in Lagos. I had been told by my cousins in Owerri that the "fancy Lagos girls" were arrogant and would not associate with people whom they considered were of a lower class than they were. Yet, this woman who represented money, class, style, and elegance, was bringing to her home a seemingly lower class stranger who reeked of the foul drainage system.

"Where do you live?" the woman asked.

"Victoria Island," I replied, still in awe of her.

"Victoria Island!" the woman exclaimed. "I thought perhaps you walked all the way from Mushin."

My assumption was correct then, I thought to myself. She had concluded from the very beginning that I was of a lower class, yet she reached out to me. "No, I'm living temporarily with some family friends who have a house in Victoria Island."

"Good. So you actually live in the next community from me. My house is here in Ikoyi. So you just walked from Victoria Island then; that's not too bad."

"Yes." I replied, "Actually, walking long distances has never been a problem for me. We're used to that in my village. It's walking in all this smelly water! And now I feel awkward walking so close to you and brushing against your nice clothes."

"Don't let that bother you. This is my flood-and-rain outfit. I have many of them. My maid tells me that everything washes right off. By the way, my name is Bisi."

"And my name is Grace," I offered quickly, "Bisi, I don't know how to thank you."

"But helping you out seems natural to me. Frankly, I don't know what woman would find another woman in the same situation and *not* help her, no matter who that woman is. I'm sure you would have done the same for me."

Her response made me ashamed of my prior evaluation of her—that she had already categorized me as someone much below her status and with whom she would never socialize.

"You're right about that," I replied. "And when a woman is shown this kind of kindness by another woman, that kindness sooner or later becomes a bond between both women—a bond that remains forever."

"Grace, what I'm going to say may sound ridiculous, but, for some reason or other, the bond was sealed when I saw you in that gutter. It's something that is difficult to explain." Bisi chuckled, looking somewhat coy. "It was more than coming to the aid of someone in distress. It was as if I already knew you, and when I was laughing, it was like teasing a close friend who had gotten herself in some hilarious situation. I tell you, the whole experience was strange. And then, bringing you home with me now is something that I felt I must do. It's a strange thing!"

I smiled, because I knew the answer. But I decided to keep it to myself, although I realized that, as an African woman, Bisi had to be knowledgeable about the culture. I knew that the spirits of my deceased parents wasted no time in coming to my aid when I called to them for help. They had sent Bisi to me immediately and caused her to go through the emotions and actions she was describing.

I offered another explanation. "Actually, you were simply going by your instincts. I believe that women are blessed with very strong instincts, the same ones that tell you someone you don't even know is perfectly all right and can be trusted."

We waded silently along the streets for some time. It was a comfortable and peaceful walk despite the circumstances. Still a village girl at heart, I marveled at the idea that I was developing an instant rapport with a glamorous, sophisticated, worldly stranger such as Bisi. When she had said that she felt as if she already knew me when she saw me in the flooded gutter, I wanted to tell her that the feeling was mutual, but I refrained from verbalizing my emotions, because I thought it would not have sounded genuine.

"You know Grace," Bisi finally broke the silence, "I feel as if I've known you all my life. I feel comfortable with you."

"How strange!" I replied, changing my mind about making this known to Bisi. "I was thinking the same thing."

"Hmm...mh! The hands of fate sometimes cause things to happen in mysterious ways. It has taken your funny and disastrous experience this morning to bring us together," Bisi said.

"Yes, to make us friends everlasting," I replied resolutely.

"Everlasting friends indeed!" Bisi replied pulling me closer to her.

10

The Professor

It started out as a normal day at my office at the Ministry of External Affairs; however, before long, it became one of the busiest. Dozens of telephone calls flooded in. Numerous walk-in visitors were attended to between scheduled appointments. It had become so hectic that it became necessary to instruct Moses, my secretary, to screen future calls and to take messages.

Then, my secretary rang my buzzer, signalling an urgent call.

"Yes," I responded.

"It's a Mr. Paulucci, Madam. He says he must talk with you; that it is urgent."

"Fine. Put him on, Moses," I replied, picking up the receiver.

"Yes, Mr. Paulucci, and how are you?"

As I spoke with Mr. Paulucci, I looked up to find Bisi opening the door to my office gently and tiptoeing to the comfortable, black velvet chair by the wall beside my desk. I waved my fingers at her and continued my conversation with Mr. Paulucci. "I'll see you in the morning then, Mr. Paulucci. Goodbye! And don't forget, you must see me first before you go to the Immigration Office. O.K.? Bye!"

I dropped the receiver and instructed Moses not to put through any more calls until after lunch.

"What was all that about?" Bisi asked, as she approached my desk.

I looked at my watch. "My goodness! Lunch time! If you hadn't come to get me, I would have continued on until closing. No wonder I am hungry."

"You didn't answer my question," Bisi chided.

"It's a long story," I replied. "We'll talk at lunch."

"I also have something very important to tell you," Bisi responded, "Let's get away from all this. Let's go to Ikoyi Hotel for lunch."

"Why do you do this to me," I replied, faking anger. "You know I don't like all that fancy food. I'm still used to my foo-foo or gari with some nice vegetable or agbono soup."

Bisi conceded. "All right, all right, let's go to dinner at Falomo then, at the canteen."

"Good," I said, dragging out my handbag from under my desk.

Later, as we sat devouring some rice and chicken stew with sweet red beans and dodo, Bisi reminded me about my phone call with Mr. Paulucci.

"What was all that about the Immigration Office?" Bisi insisted with a steady gaze.

"It's a big mess," I began. "Mr. Paulucci, as you may have guessed, is an expatriate from Italy. He went into partnership with a Nigerian and they formed an automobile sales company. Well, to make a long story short things have gone sour between the two men."

"So, what happened?" Bisi opened her eyes wider.

"Well, Mr. Paulucci said that his Nigerian partner has accused him of stealing the company funds, but he also says that if anyone is stealing, it's the Nigerian partner. And each one says he has evidence to prove it."

"Woh!! Serious stuff. What's going to happen now?"

"Mr. Paulucci said that his Nigerian partner has reported the matter to the Immigration Office in an attempt to get him out of Nigeria. And as if that wasn't enough, the Nigerian partner showed up at his flat at the company estate with four strapping Hausa men and instructed them to physically throw him and his wife and child and all their belongings out into the street."

"Were they thrown out?"

"Hm...hm, physically!"

"What an awful thing to do," Bisi replied, her tone compassionate, "and they have a child, too. That's plain wickedness. You mean Mr. Paulucci and his family are now out in the street?"

"Yep."

"Where are they now? Did he tell you?"

"No, but he probably moved in with a friend, or checked into a hotel. You see, he doesn't have to worry about furniture. All these company houses and flats are furnished."

"How's your office going to solve this problem?"

"My office will try to prevent this sort of arbitrary action by the Nigerian partner until we have proof that the expatriate has indeed broken the law."

"Good." Bisi sounded relieved. "But that means the police might have to be involved."

"Of course."

"Well, I trust you to handle this the way it should. By the way, what's the Nigerian partner's name?"

"Mr. Oyerokun," I replied.

"Oh no, not him!" Bisi exclaimed.

"Do you know him?"

"Yes, he's a well known business man, very successful and rich, and he's notorious for mistreating those who work for him, not just the expatriates. He has a terrible reputation! He pays his employees only when he feels like it, and sometimes much less than they're supposed to get. It's also said that as soon as he feels he has no more use for an employee, he throws the person out without cause. Oh yes, Mr. Oyerokun—he's well known in Lagos."

"I'm glad you're telling me this," I replied. "It will help us in our investigation. People like that give Nigeria a bad name and discourage foreigners from doing business with us."

"You're right," Bisi replied, biting into a piece of dodo.

After enjoying our meal in silence for some time, I said to Bisi, "Your turn."

Bisi raised her eyebrows, "My turn for what?"

"You said you had something to tell me," I replied.

"Oh yes, yes, yes, of course!" Bisi said, "Talking so much about good old Mr. Oyerokun, I almost forgot what I wanted to tell you."

"You know, it's almost time to get back to the Ministry," I said, looking at my watch.

"I tell you what we do," Bisi replied. "When we get off work, wait for me by my car in the parking lot. We can drive to the Federal Palace Hotel and sit in the gardens at the back. There's a breathtaking view from the lounge. We could sit there. It's sort of like a gazebo, you know. We could order drinks and sit there and chat."

"Sounds good to me," I replied as we headed back to the Ministry.

Later, we sat amidst the magnificent profusion of multicolored tropical flowers facing the Lagos Lagoon. Bisi thought she needed a drink and a cigarette, but after a futile search in her handbag, she said, "I must have left my cigarettes at the office. Wait here on this bench while I go inside the hotel and buy a pack. I'll also get us something to drink."

"And remember, no alcohol for me," I called out, as

she headed toward the entrance.

"I know, I know!" Bisi replied, without turning around.

I looked all about me, savoring the beauty of the early evening, especially the flamboyant arrangement of flowers stretching all the way out to the jetty. The evening sun was playing dazzling tricks with the blue lagoon, where pleasure boats could be seen moving about. On the other side of the jetty, more pleasure boats appeared to be anchored, swaying from side to side while prospective customers could be seen negotiating the cost of cruising the waters with the boat-owners.

"Beautiful sight, isn't it?" said a man's voice from behind me. Before I looked to see who was invading my private pleasure, I responded, "Yes, it is. I could sit and watch this view forever." Then, I turned. Two expatriates were standing behind me.

"What a face!" the one who spoke earlier said.

"What a gorgeous creature!" the second man added. Both men were now standing in front of me.

"Are you here alone?" the first expatriate asked.

"No, I'm here with my girlfriend," I replied, and both men looked at each other and smiled. "She went to buy some cigarettes and get us some drinks," I added.

Both men began searching frantically in their trousers and shirt pockets and came up with cigarettes and lighters. The first expatriate had found his pack and shook it in my face to eject a cigarette; the second man quickly struck his lighter and was poised ready to light it for me.

"No thank you," I said, waving both hands. "I don't smoke. The cigarettes my girlfriend went inside for are for her, not for me. She's only bringing me a soft drink."

"Well then, can we join both of you and enjoy the view together?" the first expatriate asked, lighting up the cigarette in his hand.

"I'm so sorry, but the reason my girlfriend and I came here is to discuss a private matter," I replied quickly.

"Can I contact you for an evening together...dinner, dancing, whatever you wish?"

"Hello there!" Bisi's voice rang out, as she approached holding a drink in each hand. "And who are these handsome men?" she beamed as she handed me my drink in a water glass and keeping hers in a tall champagne class.

"This is your friend? We were—" the first expatriate said, stepping aside.

"We were just saying hello to your girlfriend and wondering if we might join both of you," the second expatriate interrupted him.

"Why not?" Bisi replied flirtatiously. "Go get yourselves some drinks and join us. We could sit over there in the gazebo."

I rose to my feet, glass in hand and glared at Bisi, "The discussion! The discussion! Remember?"

"Hey! Don't get all excited, my sister, we can always talk at my house some other time. What's wrong with sitting in a public garden, in broad daylight enjoying the view with two handsome gentlemen?" Bisi countered, shrugging her shoulders and sipping her drink.

"It's just that I thought that the matter at hand was urgent," I said, raising my eyebrows and bobbing my head.

"My sister, relax, we see each other every day, we have plenty of time to talk. Let's be social!" Bisi added, digging into my ribs with her elbow. Then, she addressed the expatriates, "You know, my girlfriend here is a big* woman; you can't imagine how big. But she's also a bush

---

*big—in the Nigerian society, "big" is used to describe someone with a high status.

woman, and I've been trying my best to get the village out of her for the longest time. I'm sorry, but she doesn't think she should deal with expatriates on a personal level."

"Bisi, stop it!" I said, feeling betrayed, hurt, and embarrassed. "You've said enough to these strangers." Then, turning to the two men, I said, "It's really been a pleasure meeting you gentlemen, but my girlfriend and I are here to discuss an urgent matter."

"What about you?" the second expatriate addressed Bisi. "Is it possible to see you again? Can I telephone you?"

"That would have been lovely, but I'm afraid I have a boyfriend," Bisi replied. "I'm sorr...y!"

After both men left, I turned to Bisi angrily. "My sister! I'm truly disappointed in you. You embarrassed me in front of those men. There are certain things that should remain only between women or between friends."

"What I told them is not a big secret. I'm sure they thought it to be a matter of cultural differences, but you saw it as a betrayal of trust. What I was actually doing was giving the expatriates a lesson about the African culture in an indirect way, and I think they understood. It wasn't a personal attack on you. I'm sorry, my sister, if you took it that way," Bisi concluded, squeezing my arm.

I smiled. "I forgive you. Bisi, you're a true teacher and a counselor all right, but your teaching techniques are sometimes strange. I guess that's the reason I disagree with most of your philosophies; perhaps it's the way they're presented."

"Perhaps. Speaking about philosophies and one's culture, it's funny that the issue has come up, because that's exactly what I wanted to talk to you about."

"You mean the reason we came here?"

"Precisely why we came here, yes," Bisi replied. "You

see, what I told those two expatriates is just what worries me about you. Maybe that's why it came out the way it did. You have come a long way in your life, my sister, and you're still very young. To get where you are, and as a woman in an African country, in this day and age, is remarkable. You always handle your job with extraordinary skill, and—"

"Coming from you, my sister, it's a nice compliment. Thank you. Go ahead." I interrupted.

"I mean it. I'm even envious of you and your accomplishments and your position, but I'm not envious in a vicious way, because I love you like my blood sister, and I want the best for you."

"I know, my sister, and I love you too," I replied hooking my arm around hers. Then I took a sip of my Sprite. "So, what's wrong? What's the problem?"

"Well, you see, right now, you're sitting on top of the world. You have everything, but there's something missing."

"Oh no, not you too! Don't tell me I need a husband!" Once again, I was reminded of Mr. Ogwu.

"No, no, no, no! It's not that."

"Thank you, all you good spirits!" I replied, rubbing my hands together and looking up to the sky.

"You see, the problem is that with all your experience and education, you should be thinking in terms of social interaction. You should be able to transcend cultural philosophies. That's the meaning of education. You're fabulous when dealing with all types of people, including expatriates. However, on a personal level, you behave as if someone with white skin has the plague. Specifically, you don't give expatriates an opportunity to be friends with you."

I quickly replied, "I'm sorry, I can't help that; it's cultural influence. You, of all people, should understand that. You know that, as Nigerian women, we're taught directly, and sometimes indirectly, to marry men from our village. If that's the case, where would an intimate relationship with an expatriate lead to?"

Bisi replied, "I know exactly what you're saying, but my point is this: Is it really the right thing to do? I understand that many cultures dictate to their citizens how they should interact on a personal basis with people who are different from them, but does that make it morally right?"

I was becoming a little agitated. "You're lecturing me again? Why don't you become a politician and lecture the whole country?" I gestured with both hands still holding my glass of Sprite.

"Oh, I can't change the whole country, but I can try to change someone that I love."

"Why do you insist that I need changing? You yourself admitted I handle all types of people superbly."

"That's what I brought you here to talk about. I believe that friends get along mostly because they have much in common, particularly their ideologies."

"Not necessarily," I replied. "Take you and I, for example. Our common ground is that we're Nigerians, we enjoy each other's company, and we love each other. Other than that, we're very different."

"Awright then; if you can love me as your blood sister and are able to maintain a friendship with me in spite of our differences, why isn't it possible with someone who has white skin?"

"I've answered that question. The culture teaches us that it's inappropriate."

"That's when the problem arises; when we follow our culture blindly, without question, and allow the rules to apply in each and every situation."

"But, if we don't do that, how would the culture remain intact?" I replied.

"A culture is not necessarily disrupted simply because of some intermingling."

"I strongly disagree," I said.

"You then obviously believe in a strictly divisive world, where each culture, group, or community would refuse to acknowledge outsiders in their midst."

"Not that strictly," I said. "We could work together, trade with each other, and so forth, but that's it. No intimate stuff."

"My sister," Bisi replied. "You're contradicting yourself. Let me explain. First of all, why did you even bother to get an English education and then leave your village?"

"To be able to communicate and interact with all types of people. To travel to different places in Nigeria, maybe the world; you know." I shrugged my shoulders.

"Does it mean then, that you will return to your village someday?"

"Definitely! When I retire. I would do whatever I wish to do—work, travel, and then return to my village in my old age."

"If in the course of your work and travels, suppose you happen to meet a man that you become emotionally involved with, and the man is not from your village...or is not even a Nigerian...and you fall in love with each other, and he asks you to marry him. What would you do?"

I shook my head. "First of all, I would never let myself get that involved with such a man. So, there's the answer to your question. I can't answer it any other way."

"But how could you stop your emotions?"

"Easy!" I replied, "There is such a thing as self-control, you know. By the way, why is this issue so important to you?"

"You are my best friend, and you're part of my life now. We're supposed to be honest and truthful with each other, right?"

"Right," I replied, curious as to where this was heading.

"We have known each other now for the past two years, yet I live another life that you know nothing about. I have kept this part of my life from you simply because of your strong cultural beliefs, and because I don't want to lose you as a friend."

My heart sank, as I prayed and hoped that my best friend, whom I loved dearly, was not engaged in some kind of illegal life style. "Common now Bisi, hurry up and tell me what this is all about. You're scaring me."

Bisi was silent for a moment as though she was thinking of the best way to begin. "We've known each other for the past two years, right?"

"Right, right, common, what is it?"

"Well, I've been dating a man for the past five years, and that's the part of my life you don't know about."

I was relieved. Bisi was not in some kind of trouble. The whole thing was all about a man. "Is that all? What's wrong with that? Have you been hiding him from me because he's some big politician or something?" I snickered.

"No...oh, he's not some big politician. He's an expatriate."

I jumped to my feet. "He's *what*?"

"He's an expatriate," Bisi repeated. "Please, my sister, sit down and hear me out."

I remained standing facing Bisi and bent over toward her to stress my point. "Are you telling me he's an ex-patriate?"

"Yes, and we've been in love for five years."

I was angry. "No wonder you've been giving me all that fancy talk, all that lecturing about people being morally wrong to shun mixed relationships with people who are not of their culture. Oh...oh, now I know exactly why I'm getting this lecture, professor! To cover up the fact that you sold out on your culture?"

"Grace, calm down and think about what you're saying. You believe I sold out on my culture because I fell in love with a human being. That's what I was trying to explain to you. When it comes to matters of the heart, it's not easy to control." Bisi stopped suddenly at this point. "Grace, your mouth is open, and you're looking at me as if I've just killed someone. This reaction is the very reason I've kept this information from you. You're my best friend, and I don't want to lose you the same way I lost my family and my old friends. You are the only one I have now."

"You're not joking then?" I asked stiffly.

"Haven't you ever wondered why I hardly ever talk to you about anything personal?"

"Yes, I did wonder about that and thought it was very strange that you never mentioned your family, and I never see you with other girl friends," I replied.

"You see, before I met you, I had already been ostracized by everybody in my life because of my personal involvement with an expatriate. That's the reason all of my friends are expatriates. I decided that if my family and friends abandon me because of such nonsense, then, I don't want any part of them either."

"How can you live without any family ties?" I asked, more concerned now than angry.

"I've managed to do it. Of course, my boyfriend's love, affection, and support has helped a lot. Since cultural and societal concerns seem to be more important to my family and friends than my happiness, I decided to make another life for myself. Doesn't it make sense to surround myself with people who care about my happiness and show me love, consideration, and respect? I truly hope *you* will remain one of those people. You remember? Friends everlasting?" Bisi added, as she searched my eyes.

I did not answer. I also searched Bisi's eyes. There was much to consider. Much to learn. However, regarding my friendship with Bisi, there couldn't be any compromise. The bond had been sealed, as Bisi put it, the day she rescued me from the murky gutter. I extended my hand to her. She received it, rose from the bench, and we embraced and wept softly on each other's shoulders.

"I'll get us more drinks," Bisi said, as we pulled ourselves away from each other and sat back down heavily on the bench.

"No more for me," I said.

"I must have another drink. This is a celebration! There will be no more secrets between us. I also want to smoke a cigarette inside; I know how you're bothered by cigarette smoke."

I appreciated being alone at this time, because, I was still thoroughly confused and needed a few minutes by myself to think about what had just happened. I loved Bisi with all my heart, but was not quite convinced that her relationship with the expatriate had to happen. I could not understand why she had allowed herself to fall in love with the "wrong" person. *All she had to do was to simply walk away,* I thought, *when the relationship started getting too intimate.* Nevertheless, although the revelation infuriated me, and I didn't know if I could associate with Bisi's expatriate boyfriend, I had no intention of abandoning her. I heard footsteps and turned to find Bisi walking gingerly holding a glass in each hand, her handbag hanging down her shoulder, and I hurried to relieve her of one of the glasses.

"I told you I didn't want any more to drink," I said.

"I heard you. It's all for me. One is a chaser."

"A chaser? What's that?"

Bisi placed the glass in her hand on the bench, removed her handbag from her shoulder, and sat down beside the glass. "Well, what you're holding in your hand is the chaser; it is nothing but soda water. And what I have here is the whisky. You see, I don't like the whisky diluted. So I take a sip of the whisky, and then take a sip of the soda water, take a sip of the whisky, and then take a sip of the soda water. That's how it goes, you see?"

"Mh...hm, quite clear," I replied, but thinking how silly the idea was. I wanted to change the subject. "Tell me about this boyfriend of yours. The five years you've known him; is that how long he's been in Nigeria? What's his name?"

"His name is Peter, and he's been in Nigeria on and off for the past eight years."

"Oooh! That long! He must like Nigeria."

"That's what he says," Bisi replied. "He also says he likes Nigerian women a lot, too."

"Where's he originally from?"

"Germany."

"Hmm, if both of you feel so strongly about each other, why haven't you gotten married, not that I would approve?"

Bisi bent her body forward, burying her face in her hands. She did not answer.

"Why? What's wrong?" I was concerned.

Then, raising her head, she sat back on the bench and stretched her arms and legs out in front of her, still saying nothing. Finally, she answered my question without looking at me. "He is a married man, my sister. We all know that in our African heritage, it is normal for a man to have several wives, but it's not so in the European culture. It's against the law! A man has to divorce one wife before he can marry another woman."

"Why doesn't he divorce his wife then, and marry you?"

"It's a long story."

"I'm interested," I replied, shifting from side to side and straightening my back.

"According to Peter, his marriage broke down some time ago, which is the reason he has been working out of Germany for many, many years now; and he has not been on good terms with his wife for the past eight years."

"What does that mean?"

"It means that Peter and his wife have not lived together as husband and wife for a very long time."

"So, why don't they divorce each other?" I repeated impatiently.

"Well, this is his story: Peter and his wife have a grown daughter who married a prominent English doctor in a small village outside London. Both their daughter and the doctor knew even before they got married that he was unable to have children. However, two years into the marriage Peter's daughter became pregnant, by another man. And this became a big scandal in that little village. The doctor had no mercy, and threw Peter's daughter out of the house immediately, and eventually divorced her.

"Peter's daughter went back to Germany to live with her parents, and then she rejected the baby after it was born. She wanted to go back to being single and free. So, Peter and his wife adopted the baby and part of the court settlement was that the child must be raised in a stable home; which means that if they divorce each other, the child would not have a stable home."

"So their child is actually their grandchild."

"Exactly," Bisi replied. "And today, the child thinks that her grandparents are her real parents."

"What a story!"

"Mm-hm. And everybody's left it that way," Bisi replied.

"How old is the girl now?"

"Nine years old."

"Has she ever seen her biological mother?"

"Yes, but she thinks her biological mother is her aunt, because that's how she introduced herself to the child the first time she visited Sonya. That's her name. You should see her, my sister! She's gorgeous!"

"You've seen her then?"

"Many times. She travels to Nigeria often to visit her father. Besides, I also see her in Germany when I travel to Europe with Peter," Bisi replied.

"I was beginning to wonder how she gets that stability when both parents live in different countries. By the way, how do you feel when Peter's wife brings Sonya to Nigeria to visit Peter?"

"Well, Peter's wife hates Nigeria. So, after that first trip with Sonya, she vowed not to return. So, Sonya has learned to travel in the care of the airlines. She has been traveling alone since she was a little baby."

"People arrange for even babies to travel alone?" I asked.

"Of course! It's quite safe. There is nothing to it," Bisi replied, "and children love it. Sonya receives special attention from the airline crew, and she's completely in their care until she's picked up at her destination. Peter says that when she arrives either here or back in Germany, she talks about her experience for days."

Bisi suddenly glanced at her watch and jumped to her feet, "We must get going! Peter is picking me up in another hour and a half; which reminds me; I had told Peter I was going to discuss this issue with you tonight, and he wants to know when you can join us for dinner. He says he is dying to meet you."

I broke out in a nervous laugh and stood up beside Bisi. "My sister," I said, "each time we're together, I learn so much from you. And sometimes, it's after some fierce battles. But, my love for you will always be, no matter what. Of course! I will have dinner with you and Peter. I admit it will definitely be extremely awkward for me, but I will be there as your best friend and support you all the way. Who knows? I might get accustomed to the idea someday."

"Thank God!" Bisi replied, embracing me. Then, holding me at arm's length, she asked, "Now, what about this weekend?"

"Not so fast, my sister." I quickly added, "You're forgetting one thing."

"What, what?" Bisi asked moving her shoulders up and down.

"You yourself tell me that I still dress like a bush woman and that you hate all the clothes and shoes I brought from Owerri. Remember? You say they are all horrible. You call them 'market dresses.' I know that you and Peter will take me to a fancy restaurant. If *you* laugh at my dresses, what would people in those fancy restaurants do? Laugh me out of Lagos!"

Bisi stumbled about in uncontrollable laughter.

"You see what I mean? Even the vision of my clothing makes you laugh," I said, laughing as well.

"But your dresses are horrible," Bisi confessed, still

laughing. "I don't have to visualize anything. I can see it right here in front of me," she continued, as she stepped back to examine my entire outfit. "I swear, you are extremely lucky that God gave you that gorgeous face. I'm probably the only one who notices your 'market dresses'. I think people are so busy looking at your face, your clothes don't seem to matter to them. Anyway, from now on, we'll begin buying decent clothes and shoes for you, and tossing out all the 'market' ones. This is Monday; we have a whole week to shop for this weekend. As a matter of fact, the first dress we pick out will be on me."

"Oh my!" I exclaimed. "This is exciting! Let's begin the shopping tomorrow afternoon, if you're buying."

"One catch," Bisi added quickly. "If the shopping spree becomes too expensive, you'd have to borrow one of my dresses."

"No way!" I protested. "Me, wearing a gari bag?"

"I was just teasing. I really intend to pay for the first dress no matter how expensive. By the way, why are you calling my dresses 'gari bags'? I buy all my dresses in Europe. They're all very classy."

"I know. That's not what I mean. Your clothes are gorgeous! I'm just trying to say that your dresses would be too large for me."

"What are you talking about? I'm not that much larger than you."

"Don't you remember the drainage water? Whose clothes did I wear home that day?"

"Oh no, please, don't remind me of that incident," Bisi replied, trying desperately to suppress a laugh. "I've laughed at you enough for today."

"No, go right ahead and laugh. Don't you think I know why you want to pay for my new dress? It's because you want to make up for all your insults. Yes, go ahead, don't hold back, laugh, because you are going to pay for the dress, shoes, handbag, jewelry, and anything else that I buy in preparation for the dinner this week."

And in between much laughter Bisi and I reminisced about that fateful day.

11
Stepping Out

I pivoted in front of the full length mirror behind the bedroom door. I liked what I saw. Although I realized that it couldn't really be me, it was virtually a magnificent replica of me. I was quite baffled at the idea that clothes and makeup could create such a striking transition.

Sprawled on the bed and leaning back on her elbows, Helen Balogun watched with the countenance of a village artist admiring one of his completed, intricately designed handicrafts. "You look absolutely stunning, Grace!" she said. "The makeup does wonders for you. Don't get me wrong," she added quickly. "Not that you're not naturally beautiful, but now you look like a movie star."

I understood what she meant. I stopped twirling, brought my face closer to the mirror and examined the faint green shadow over my eyelids; the black eyeliner under my eyes and under my eyelashes; the subtle plum blush on my cheeks; and the matching lipstick.

"The makeup is not too much?" I asked.

"No way!" Helen replied. "If I say so myself I did an excellent job. It's all there, but you can hardly see it. I made it all look natural. You feel it's too much because you never wore makeup before, so it seems too obvious to you. You know what I mean?"

"Mm...hm. And my hair, you did a good job there too. Wa...ooh!"

"I'm glad you're happy with it. I didn't straighten it too much. All I did was touch it up slightly with the hot comb and make a lot of tiny little curls with the hot curler and fluff it up to look like a nice curly Afro."

"I like it!" I beamed.

"Awright, that's enough of the primping. Let's go downstairs and wait there for Bisi and her boyfriend."

"Oh no! Where's my handbag? I think I hear a car," I said, suddenly nervous. Helen pulled herself up quickly, rushed to the window facing the street, pulled the curtains to the side, and peered out, "You're right, they're here! I see Bisi. Wait a minute! It's an expatriate driving the car. Don't tell me that's Bisi's boyfriend. You didn't tell me he's an expatriate!"

"Let me see," I said, scurrying to the window as though I did not know that Bisi's boyfriend was an expatriate. "I know, I know," I replied sheepishly, "I didn't know how to tell you. Not that I was worried about you. You Americans are used to seeing that type of relationship, but it's Bola I'm worried about. He's not going to be too happy about it. I don't like the idea myself. Bisi knows that, but she's my best friend and I love her. What can I do?"

"Do what you're doing. Continue to love her and be her friend," Helen replied.

I thought Helen deserved an embrace for saying that. "Thank you for your support, Helen," I said, squeezing her tightly.

"Let me warn you; brace yourself for some trouble when Bola sees Bisi arriving with her expatriate boyfriend. It will be even worse when he realizes that you knew all along and never bothered to mention it to him. He doesn't like that type of surprise. Well—let's get going downstairs and see what happens. All we can do is hope for the best."

"But Helen, do you think he'll be that angry?"

"The man is my husband, isn't he? I know him well.

He did date white women in America before he and I knew each other, but his attitude changed after we got married. Since then, he has expressed his disapproval of interracial relationships."

"Do you think that's quite fair?" I asked, feeling sad for the white women Bola had dated.

"What do you mean?"

"I mean his double standard. The white women were good enough for him to date, but not good enough to marry? Why waste their time? Don't get me wrong, Helen. I like you very much and I'm glad Bola married you; but do you think what Bola was doing was fair to those women?"

Helen placed her forefinger over her lips. "Shhhhh! He will hear us. Let's get going."

"He's already outside. I saw him walking toward the car," I offered.

"Come, let's see what happens," Helen said through her teeth, as we stepped outside.

"Why do you think Bola didn't wait for Bisi to bring her expatriate boyfriend into the house?" I said, also through my teeth.

"Grace, I think you and I know that answer. Shhh, they'll hear us."

Peter quickly got out of his car and hurried to the passenger's side to open the door for Bisi. He then extended his hand to Bola, who swung around instead, and proceeded to walk back toward the house. "I'll speak to you when you get back home tonight, young lady," he said, looking back at me.

Bisi emitted a long hiss as she got back in the car. "How rude! What arrogance!" Then, turning to me, "I hate it when he talks to you as if you're a child. When is he going to realize that you're more than grown up now and that you're even a big woman now in Lagos!"

I shook my head. "My sister, you know our culture. Some of us never become adults in the eyes of our elders."

"As for that Bola, he's a stupid goat!" Bisi continued. "He could've at least been polite. Why didn't he shake Peter's hand and behave like a human being?"

"Forget it," Peter said as he reached in the car and squeezed Bisi's shoulder. "Don't let this sort of thing upset you. Your girlfriend also understands him. Let's go and have a nice time."

Helen approached Peter and extended her hand. "My name is Helen. Nice to meet you."

"It's my pleasure, madam, and I'm Peter." Peter replied, receiving her hand warmly.

Peter then turned to me. "You must be Grace," he said.

"Yes," I replied. "It's good to meet you."

"It's my pleasure indeed," he replied as he opened the back door of his 1984 maroon Mercedes-Benz to let me in. No one spoke during the ride to Eko Hotel. It was as if we were trying to cleanse our memory of the incident with Bola in order to focus on the impending events of the evening.

As we walked away from the car in the parking lot, Peter positioned himself between Bisi and I, hooking his arms around ours. Involuntarily, I stiffened, pressing my arm tightly against my side.

"Relax!" Peter chuckled, "Bisi knows I don't hurt women. A woman who is in my company will be cared for, protected, and will always have a good time. Besides, both you look so gorgeous, I want the world to know you're with me!"

Somehow, although I felt self-conscious and nervous

walking with my body touching Peter's, I was calmed by his voice, his forthright words, and his humor.

"I understand Grace, that this is your first night out here in Lagos?" Peter asked me.

"Right," I replied. "Never been to a night club or a fancy restaurant for dinner, if that's what you mean."

"Well then, we have to make this a night you will always remember."

"Thank you," I replied, feeling more and more comfortable.

At the entrance to the dining room, Peter seemed to revel in the attention we aroused from everyone inside. Even after we had been asked by the waiter to follow him, Peter still held Bisi and I tightly, his eyes scanning the room as though he was searching for a lost friend.

"Dis way sah," a white-jacketed, puffy-faced waiter beckoned for the third time. Finally, we were seated, amidst a sea of curious and admiring eyes.

"A table for four sah like you want. You wana stat with drinks? Or you wana order dinner right away, sah?" the waiter asked bowing slightly. Peter bent forward looking from me to Bisi, and back again, "What do you say, relax with some drinks first?"

"I'll go along with whatever you do," I said.

"Order the regular for me, please, dear," Bisi replied.

"Fine," Peter said, "and after we order the drinks, I'll make a quick phone call."

"Hey, Mister!" Bisi teased. "Who are you calling?"

"Our friend, Jacques, to see whether he can join us. I phoned him earlier, but he wasn't home."

"Jacques Pialeau!" Bisi said, contorting her face as if she had just tasted some vinegar.

"What's wrong with Jacques? He's a good man." I knew immediately that Peter was trying to be a matchmaker, and worse yet, he was matching me up with an expatriate! I sounded out the name in my head—'Jacques Pialeau!' and I was sure only an expatriate would have such a name.

"Smile." Peter reached over and touched my arm. "You shouldn't be looking so serious. Let me order a nice wine for you."

"No, please no!" I said quickly. "I don't drink."

"But, it's only a light wine," Peter insisted. "This is a special night... Commo-n!"

"Peter, order her a fruit drink for now, maybe later for the wine," Bisi said, her eyes and voice pleading.

Peter agreed. "Well then, I'll order the drinks, we'll toast, and then I'll go and make that phone call."

When Peter left the table, Bisi asked "What's wrong with you? Your mood has suddenly changed. You weren't like this when we first walked in."

"I know Peter means well, but you yourself told me that he knows how I feel about having a personal relationship with an expatriate. And you can't tell me that person he is calling to join us is not an expatriate!"

"Grace, my sister, relax. It doesn't matter who joins us. Nobody is trying to make you do anything. We're all just going to have dinner together and have a good time, that's all. You came out to meet Peter, right? After dinner, we'll take you home. It's as simple as that. Now, what's to be afraid of?"

Although Bisi did not say so, her eyes were telling me that I was creating a problem where one did not exist. I was embarrassed. I looked away and did not answer her question. Then I took a sip of my fruit drink. "This is very good; I like it," I said, in an attempt to change the subject. "What are you drinking?"

"Dry martini," Bisi replied.

"What's it made of?"

"Gin. You want a taste?" Bisi reached over, offering me her glass.

I replied, shaking my head, "No, please no! I'm sure I'd burn up inside. By the way, what did Peter order for himself?"

"Same thing. Oh Grace, it's so nice to be so compatible with a man you love. And he shows me in countless ways how much he loves me. I'm so happy with him! Except for that snag in our relationship, and that's driving me crazy."

"But, Bisi, are you going to continue this way forever? You know he can't marry you until his daughter is of age. Don't you see how hopeless this is?"

"That's how you see it. To me, it's not. As long as Peter wants me, I'll continue to love him and be with him. My sister, I cannot leave him now. I never knew the meaning of love until I met Peter. I never even knew happiness and contentment until I met him. How can that be hopeless? About his wife: who is he having a relationship with? Me, not his wife. Their marriage is over. She would get a divorce, according to Peter, if it weren't for that grandchild who is now their daughter."

I listened to Bisi with great interest, yet I still believed her relationship with Peter was senseless. I looked up to find Peter returning to the table. "Peter is coming," I announced.

"We'll continue this conversation some other time," Bisi said, and when Peter took his seat, she added, "Well, what about Jacques?"

"Yes, I finally reached him and he's on his way," he replied. When I looked across the table at Peter, I found myself paying attention to his looks for the first time. His eyes were the bluest blue I had ever seen, and I was amazed that the paint brush of the God of the expatriates had so skillfully painted such a beautiful color in a man's eyes. And when Peter laughed, which was usually a quiet chuckle, his eyes also laughed. He was not what I would perceive as being handsome, but he had a certain buoyancy, elegance, and charm about him that made him exceedingly appealing. Peter was also a joke teller, and it was his warm personality and his jokes that finally made me feel comfortable and less self-conscious in the company of an expatriate. What he was wearing also attracted my attention—a light cotton, beige safari suit with a brown and beige polka dot silk scarf around his neck, which was tucked neatly inside the jacket of his suit.

As we chatted, sipped our drinks and laughed at Peter's jokes, I surreptitiously observed the ambiance and decor of the dining room. I knew I should not make it obvious that I was impressed with the opulence of my surroundings, or Bisi would give me one of her "You're a typical bush woman" looks. Nevertheless, I unabashedly admired the exquisite chandeliers, the red velvet draperies with delicate white lace between the panels, and valances to match the draperies. On the center of each table, was a globe-like wine colored glass jar which held a burning candle with a flame that danced provocatively in the dimly-lit room. Peter leaned forward on folded arms. "There's Jacques now!"

I did not turn to look. I kept my eyes on Bisi who was sitting directly opposite me.

When Jacques reached our table, Peter rose and shook his hand vigorously with both of his hands. "I'm glad you could make it, my friend!" Then he shoved his left hand in his pocket and gestured with his right hand, "You know Bisi, and this is Bisi's dear friend, Grace. Grace, Jacques. Jacques' a very good friend of mine."

I started to rise as I extended my hand, but Bisi's sudden cough drew my attention to the message in her eyes. I was to remain seated while I shook Jacques' hand.

"Pardon, mademoiselle, mais vous êtes la plus belle femme noire j'ai jamais rencontre," Jacques said, bringing my hand to his lips.

"Hey, you!" Peter chided him, faking contempt. "Speak English. Jeez! Who told you she could understand French? A show off; that's what you are! Jeez!"

I could not understand why I made no attempt to shrink from Jacques' touch as would have been my normal reaction to an expatriate. I felt a warm and honest hand and instinctively understood the language coming from the enchanting eyes that were now looking down into mine. If he had been trying to impress me with those French words, however, he did not succeed. What did it was the seductive way he looked at me, enfeebling my usually unflappable emotions. I was immediately bewitched by this proscribed stranger. I felt embarrassed, because, I was unable to prevent betraying my own convictions. Holding my hand with one hand now, Jacques sat down in the vacant seat beside me.

"Jacques, that's enough with the hand-holding," Bisi laughed.

"The lady doesn't object," replied Jacques.

"Yes she does." Bisi was still laughing. "She's only being polite. I know her."

Jacques picked up my glass which was half full of fruit juice and held it to the dim bowl of light. "What are you drinking?"

"She doesn't drink," Peter quickly said, "so I got her some fruit juice."

"No, no, no," Jacques replied as he beckoned to a waiter.

"Sah?" the waiter said, approaching the table.

"Bring us a bottle of Montrachet and two dry martinis, and then we'll order."

"Yesah," the waiter replied bowing from his shoulders, "I bring now, now sah."

"Where have you been hiding this gorgeous creature?" Jacques looked at Bisi, and then at Peter.

Peter shrugged his shoulders, "Don't blame me. I'd never laid eyes on her until this evening."

"Stop it now, Jacques." Bisi looked serious. "Enough of your playacting. Haven't you been busy with Gentry's wife? Isn't that why you have that scar over your eye? You were lucky Gentry himself was also busy with Hansen's wife, otherwise he would've killed you that day."

Suddenly, Bisi's revelation gave me the strength to withdraw my hand from Jacques' grip. I looked at Jacques furtively and was dismayed at what I saw. His face had turned the color of the tomatoes we grew at our farm back in the village. I wondered what was happening to him. I looked again, this time quite openly and with much concern. His face had turned a deeper red like the ripest, larger, hot peppers on the farm. He was speechless, motionless, as he glared at Bisi.

"Why are you kicking my foot, Peter?" Bisi asked ingenuously, searching the floor.

Peter ignored the question. He looked about him and waved to the nearest waiter although there was no need to, since instructions had already been given to another waiter.

Jacques finally spoke. "Bisi, that was cruel. My God!! What a thing to say in front of this gorgeous creature, this princess!"

"Oh yeah? Well, this gorgeous creature, this princess, happens to be my sister, and as long as I'm alive, I'm not going to sit back and watch her step into a boiling volcano," Bisi replied haughtily, snapping her head back.

"Sah?" the waiter Peter summoned approached the table.

"We're waiting for our drinks and we're ready to order. Oh, never mind," Peter added quickly. "I thought you were our waiter. We've already ordered drinks."

Just then, the waiter with the drinks appeared, and Peter seemed to be pleased that some activity was taking place which would temporarily interrupt the bickering between Jacques and Bisi. "Put the bottle inside an ice well to keep the wine cold. The martini is for me and this madam, and the wine is for this madam and that master."

"Yessah, right away sah," the waiter replied and got busy.

No one uttered a word as the waiter poured the drinks. I stole another glance at Jacques to see what was happening with his red pepper face and was surprised to find that his color had reverted to normal. I felt relieved and still wondered what could have happened to him.

"You ready to order now sah?" the waiter said, holding out his pad and biro.*

"Yes," Peter said quickly.

"No, wait," Jacques said, looking slightly angry. "Look," he addressed the waiter, "give us another fifteen minutes." The waiter glanced at his watch. "I come back fifteen minutes, sah."

Then, Jacques began. "This is supposed to be a special evening for Grace and a fun evening for the rest of us. I don't want to pretend everything is all right because I was hurt by what you said, Bisi, and I want to clear the air so we can put it behind us and concentrate on having a good time."

*biro—a writing pen

"Fine!" Bisi replied closing the menu she held in her hand and placing it beside her placemat. "Clear the air." She then clasped her hands, rested them on her lap and glared at Jacques. Peter sat back with arms folded and waited. With downcast eyes and hands in my lap, I also prepared to listen.

Jacques began. "Bisi, this incident that you brought up happened a year ago. Right after that I went back to France for a while and came back just a few weeks ago."

"True!" Peter said, sitting up, and moving his chair closer to the table, "Bisi, I forgot to tell you that."

"Come to think of it, I guess you did," Bisi replied.

"Anyway, I want you to listen." Jacques looked at me and squeezed my hand. I tried not to reveal any discomfort. He continued, "I'm a single man. I've never been married. I have done a lot of travelling, and yes, I've met a lot of women. If I'd found the woman I wanted, do you think I'd still be travelling and working in all these different countries?" he added, squeezing my hand once again. This time, my heart fluttered, and I hoped that no one noticed.

"There was nothing between Gentry's wife and myself," Jacques continued earnestly. "She practically threw herself at me that night. I'm not going to go into the details; but we got caught. We had both been drinking, that's why I didn't have the strength to defend myself from her husband who made a punching bag out of me. Even if that woman were single, I wouldn't want her. She's not the type of woman I'm looking for. I'm not attracted to the worldly type. This is the type of woman I want." Jacques raised my hand to stress his point. "—sweet, unspoiled." And when I turned to him, he gave me that same look that rendered me vulnerable under his spell.

Bisi's cough broke our trance. "Awright, the air has

been cleared." Then, she turned to Peter. "Don't you agree, Peter?"

"Definitely," Peter replied, bobbing his head.

"Where's the waiter? Let's order; I'm starved!" Bisi said.

Soon, our table was crammed with the various dishes we had ordered. Since I was not familiar with the European dishes on the menu, I had allowed Jacques to select a dish he thought I would like.

My eyes moved from dish to dish in admiration of the skills I thought it took to make each serving so appealing to the eye. As an appetizer for Jacques and me, we were served escargots in cream with pernod. For the main course, it was chateaubriand bouquetier, topped with bearnaise sauce and served with fresh mixed vegetables. The appetizer for Peter and Grace was shrimp salad. The main course for Peter was roasted, boneless duckling with kumquats, sliced and prepared with amaretto sauce, and served with brown rice. Bisi's main course was sirloin steak with marrow, also served with bearnaise sauce.

"Grace, you think you'll need some hot pepper for your food?" Bisi asked.

"Why don't I try it without hot pepper and see what happens?"

"Are you sure about that? It's not a problem you know, they have everything here. You want hot pepper, you will get hot pepper," Jacques said.

"I'm sure, I'm sure. I want to try it that way," I insisted.

For dessert, Jacques and I had caramel custard, while Peter and Bisi enjoyed some chocolate mousse.

"You did fine," Jacques, whose eyes had observed my every move as I ate, said. "By the way, have you ever had cappuccino?"

Bisi and I looked at each other. Then, placing down

the glass she had brought to her lips, Bisi clutched her chest in amusement. "How d'you expect a bush woman to know anything about cappuccino?"

"Perfect. She'll find out tonight," Jacques replied. "If you don't mind, when we leave here we'll all stop at my house for some delicious cappuccino."

Bisi was still chuckling and Peter said, kissing his finger, "Jacques makes some great cappuccino. You'll love it, Grace."

I smiled and nodded my head. Suddenly, I felt a queasy sensation in my abdomen and it spread quickly up to my chest and throat. I pushed my chair back quickly and addressed Bisi. "You were right, I should have used some pepper in my food. I need to get to the ladies' room fast."

"Oh no!" Bisi said, as she opened her handbag, whipped out a large, white cotton handkerchief and handed it across the table to me. "Here, you'll need this, let's go!"

I began retching from the time I rose from the table until Bisi and I reached the ladies' room.

"I told you to put some hot pepper in that food," Bisi said as I bent over a sink swishing water in my mouth.

"Eating that European food without pepper doesn't affect you?" I asked, dabbing my lips with Bisi's handkerchief.

"At first it did, that's why I was worried about you. Then I got used to it, and now, I can't handle food that has too much hot pepper in it."

"Oh, Bisi, I'm so ashamed. How can I face Peter and Jacques out there. I spoiled everybody's dinner."

"Don't worry about it. Here, let me help you with your lipstick."

"I wish we were going to your house instead," I said.

"Why?"

"So I could use a chewing stick."

"I'm sure Jacques has a toothbrush you could use when we get to his house. By the way, are you still using chewing sticks?" Bisi replied.

"I use both. I found out about toothbrushes and toothpaste when I stayed with Uncle Jeremiah and his family. His wife and children used chewing sticks all the time, but he alone used a toothbrush."

"Getting back to Jacques; my sister, I've never seen you look at a man the way you were looking at Jacques. He's an expatriate, remember? Was it the lecture I gave you the other day that did it?"

"No way!" I exclaimed,. "Your talk made no difference in the way I perceived things. It is something extraordinary that I'm feeling toward this man. It's difficult to explain. When he touches me or looks at me, it's like a magnetic force that is almost electrical passing from his body into mine. The more I become engulfed by that feeling, the more helpless I become. My sister, it's so scary that, silently, I even asked my mother's spirit to intervene."

Bisi laughed, slapping my shoulder. "You bush woman, you don't have to pray about such things. These are natural emotions; you just ride with them."

I frowned, trying to understand. "But he's an expatriate!"

"What difference does it make? He's a red-blooded man." Bisi snapped.

I sat beside Jacques in his 1984 red Ferrari as we led the way down Ahmadu Bello Road onto Ozumba Mbadiwe Avenue, to avoid Falomo Bridge. Jacques and I rode in silence. I was grateful for that. After my embarrassing ordeal back at the restaurant I was not in any mood for a conversation. Peter and Bisi followed closely behind. We finally reached the tail end of Five Cowrie Creek, off Ademola Street on Olokun Close. Jacques' headlights shone on the yellow and white house at the end of the close. As we drew closer to the house, the headlights also singled out Jacques' danchiki clad night watchman, whose neatly wrapped turban fell loosely around his mouth. Flapping against his full-legged trousers, gleamed a sword which rested against its casing. Bending forward and squinting his eyes, he observed us. On recognizing his master's car, he quickly kicked off his sandals and rushed to open the painted iron gates.

The cars ground over tiny brown pebbles into the spacious yard through a large garden blooming with bright, colorful tropical flowers. At the section of the house facing the stream, elegant, white outdoor furniture stood in sharp contrast with the glowing colors of the flowers. Off in one corner of the yard was a kennel which housed a couple of monkeys, five rabbits, assorted birds, and a snake. On the opposite section, hovered a paw-paw tree about fifteen feet away from a guava tree; and at the back of the house which faced the creek, was a slanting coconut tree bowing gracefully to the dark waters below.

Inside the house, Jacques immediately became occupied with the preparations for his famous cappuccino, while Peter became the tour guide for Bisi and me. It was a massive two-story house with rooms so spacious that each one could easily be converted into two large individual rooms. To my surprise, I felt comfortable going from room to room. The nagging twinges about the company I was keeping had vanished, at least, temporarily. The African room was particularly unique, housing dozens of Nigerian art works, including some antiques from other parts of Africa. Not even in the village where most of these artifacts were made, had I seen such unusual pieces. For example, a ceramic lamp with intricately carved forms of chained slaves forming the base of the lamp, which supported the stem which depicted a whip-toting slave master.

After the tour of the house, Peter brought us to the living room where Jacques awaited us with the promised cappuccino. I could not understand why it was served in tiny cups, and wondered how many of those cups it would take to satisfy anyone. I inquired what it was made of but was deliberately ignored. However, when I took the first sip, I realized I was drinking coffee for the first time. It did not smell like tea, cocoa, or Ovaltine, so I assumed it was coffee.

I became distracted by the colossal television set occupying one half of the wall. In Owerri, at Uncle Jeremiah's house, was the first time I laid eyes on a television set; then, there was the set at Bola and Helen Baloguns' house. However, the television set I was staring at now had to be the largest in the world, I thought.

"You're quiet," Jacques said, leaning over me from behind my chair.

"Not really. I had a good time going through your house. I'm just resting from a busy night."

"Did Peter show you my African room?" he said, as he came around to sit beside me, his cappuccino in hand.

"Why would you have such a thing in your house?"

"What, the room? I think it's exquisite."

"Not the room, that lamp!" I replied sharply.

"Oh, that! Interesting," Jacques replied placing his cup on the coffee table before us. "But everybody else likes that lamp. Tell me, why d'you object to it?"

"I see it as a celebration of slavery. You shouldn't celebrate slavery; you should condemn it." I replied.

Jacques took my hand and buried it in his. "I never thought of it that way, but I can see your point. Well, you can be sure that lamp is going out the door tomorrow."

"You're throwing the lamp out?" I sat up and looked at him wide-eyed.

"Of course! Whatever you don't like, has to go."

"Just like that? But I don't live here, we hardly know each other, and you're going to throw the lamp out for my sake?"

"Grace, it's true we've just met. All right, let's start now to get to know each other, because I would like very much for you to be that special person in my life."

I knew what he meant, because, obviously, our attraction to each other was indubitable from the moment we met. I should have said, "A special person in your life? What nonsense! You're an expatriate, and I'm an African woman." However, when I gazed into his pleading gray eyes and saw, again, that special look that stirred my entire being into a quivering, shameless pulp, I became speechless. I did not want to think about the ramifications of such a relationship: a relationship that would appear as a blatant defiance of my own cultural norms; possible ostracism by my family and my village; Bola Balogun's wrath; the constant derision that was bound to follow; and many more problems than I would ever be ready to endure. I was also unwilling to delve into the reason I was allowing a perilous union to enter my life rather than elect for a less complicated situation with an African man. There was no doubt now that I liked this man; but why? After all, he was an expatriate! I also wondered why I hadn't, up until meeting Jacques, felt this way for any of my countrymen. I realized that there could never be an answer to that question. It was a feeling that just happens;

but why a feeling emerges for one person and not for another, will continue to be a mystery. Was I going to allow myself to "ride with the feeling," as Bisi put it, or let Jacques know immediately that I wanted to be the special person in his life?

My decision was clear. I would disregard my overwhelming attraction to Jacques, and decline to see him after this night. That would be the end of it. There was too much at stake.

"What are you thinking?" Jacques asked, shaking my trapped hand, as though he was awakening me from a sound slumber.

"Nothing."

But I could not believe that was all that I allowed myself to say, after having arrived at what seemed like the most rational decision of my life.

"Well, let me tell you what I was thinking."

"What?" In spite of myself, I had to continue this conversation.

"I was thinking: Tomorrow is Sunday. It would be nice to have a quiet dinner right here, just the two of us. Remember? You said that we hardly knew each other. So how about dinner for two, just to get to know each other. And guess what? I will give my cook the evening off and do the cooking myself; just for you. You won't have to lift a finger. You relax, and then you eat. How does that sound? When should I pick you up?"

I avoided those dangerous eyes, and looked over where Peter and Bisi sat engrossed in an intimate conversation. As I did that, Jacques cradled my chin gently in his hand and turned my head to him, forcing me to look into his eyes.

"I asked you a question. When should I pick you up?" he repeated.

"Around two," I replied, unequivocally. There was no doubt in my mind now that I did want to be a special person in the life of this expatriate, regardless of the ramifications.

12

The Dove

The sea at Bar Beach glistened under a baby-blue, cloudless sky. It was twelve midday, and the temperature had already soared over 40° Celsius, but the sea breeze had reduced the humidity to a pleasant level.

"I wanted to pick you up earlier so we could work up an appetite walking along the beach," Jacques said as he parked by the shore.

I silently observed him as he hurried to open the door on my side and assisted me out of the car.

The fresh scent of the sea breeze filled my nostrils as we began our walk on the gritty brown sand along the beach. Although I was not a stranger to Lagos at this point, this was my first visit to any of its beaches. I shaded my eyes with both hands and looked about me at the iridescence of the sea, and realized we were at the section that is known as the Bight of Benin, on the Atlantic coast. Jacques was silent, gazing at me with a smile on his lips, as though he was enjoying my fascination with the beauty of the environment. I gazed at the distant, well-defined horizon, the short green trees and the shrubbery in the nearby marshland. Swimming and wading in the bluish-gray water were mostly expatriates in colorful bathing suits, while others sun-bathed beside make-shift cabanas with large multi-colored striped canopies.

"Let's walk toward the water's edge where there's a market. You'll like that." Jacques finally spoke.

"They sell things here on the beach?"

"Of course!" Jacques replied. "They sell everything but food."

Even before we reached the beach market we were surrounded by aggressive peddlers, and the air was filled with pleas to buy their wares.

"Master, madam, buy mask. I give you good good price."

"Master, madam, buy bag. Na £10.00. What you give me? I give you good good price."

"Master, madam, buy cloth. I make myself. Ee cheap." And so it went.

The market consisted of dozens of makeshift stalls, in which were displays of various African artifacts and clothing—jewelry, items carved in wood, ebony and bronze; baskets; and jewelry boxes. Other items available were embroidered gowns and dashikis; leather goods, such as handbags, briefcases, wallets, sandals, and slippers, made of crocodile, lizard, and snake skins.

"Do you want to look around?" Jacques asked.

"No," I quickly replied. "We're out to walk along the beach, not to shop. Let's move on."

"By the way, this market is here every Sunday. Just let me know when you want to come back."

We finally reached a peaceful and desolate section of the beach and sat on a large blue beach towel Jacques had brought along.

"This towel is as big as a mat. Ten people could sit on it," I said, admiring the design of sailboats, with a hint of the sky, water and birds, on the towel.

Simultaneously, Jacques and I looked at each other. Then, he spoke: "So, you haven't been in Lagos long."

"Yes and no," I replied. "Some people might call two years long, and some people might say that's not so long."

"Peter told me you're a civil servant and that you're a big woman in your Ministry. How did you do all that when you're still so young?"

I smiled and shrugged my shoulders.

"Your parents are in Owerri?"

"My parents are dead, but we all came from Uzoakoli village. I just happened to go to work in Owerri. My uncle is there."

"I'm sorry about your parents."

"That's all right. I believe some good came out of what happened."

"Have you gone back to your village since you've been in Lagos?" Jacques asked, leaning back on his elbows, knees raised.

"Of course! I go back to the village at least once a month. I'm still a part of my family and I try to help out with the work on our farm."

"You see, it's this kind of attitude—commitment and responsibility to family—that attracts me to Nigerians."

I heard him, I understood him, but I was mesmerized by his eyes, and by the way the French-accented words rolled out of his mouth. I felt I could listen to him forever.

"Enough about me," I said. "Tell me about yourself."

He looked surprised, "You really want to know?"

"Very much so," I said, sitting cross legged facing him.

"Well, I come from Martiques. It's a small town in the southern part of France."

"You have brothers and sisters?"

"I don't have any family really."

"Nobody at all?"

"I was an orphan and an only child, and so I was raised by distant relatives." At this point, Jacques stopped, cocked his head to one side and observed me quizzically. "I can't remember when I ever talked about my life to anybody, and nobody ever asked. I'm not complaining. I guess that was good, because I don't really like to remember some things in my life."

"Well, I'm asking now. I'm interested. I want to know."

"I've never told anyone about my childhood, not even my father." Observing the confused expression on my face, Jacques added, "You see, the man I call my father is not even related to me. We sort of adopted each other. Anyway, the relatives who raised me were very, very poor. That would have been fine, if they hadn't been so cruel to me. I almost thought they blamed me for their situation."

Jacques paused and shook his head slowly, seemingly overcome with emotion. "I don't usually talk about these things and why I'm telling you this, I don't know."

"Because I asked you. Remember? I want to know. You can trust me," I said, placing my hand on his arm.

Jacques searched my eyes for some time, and then turned his gaze toward the ocean. "It's not a pleasant memory."

"Tell me anyway," I urged.

"There were three other children in the family. I was constantly beaten by somebody. They beat me for the slightest reason, sometimes for no reason whatsoever."

"How awful! They should have been ashamed of themselves," I said, frowning.

Jacques continued. "School was a nightmare. I got teased about my shabby clothes all the time. I had no friends. Nobody wanted to be friends with a boy wearing rags. As a teenager, the girls didn't want me either because I never had any money to buy them gifts or take them to the cinema. My life was miserable. So, as soon as I graduated from secondary school, I left town without telling anybody."

"How old were you then?"

"Seventeen. But, fortunately, I looked much older."

"Where did you go?"

"I thought I could hitch a ride to Paris. It took me two weeks of living on the streets, in different places, before I eventually reached Paris."

"Why did it take so long?"

"I got very few rides so I had to walk a lot. Then, sometimes, in order to eat, I would have to hang around somewhere looking for an opportunity to either steal some food from a store, or ask for work in the kitchen of a restaurant."

I shook my head slowly. "Oh, Jacques."

"Let's walk back to the car," Jacques said, springing to his feet and reaching out for my hand to help me up.

I picked up the towel, shook it, folded it twice, and threw it over my arm.

"Give me that," Jacques said reaching for the towel. "Let me carry it."

"Go ahead," I said, "continue the story. What happened when you got to Paris?"

"In Paris, I continued to live on the streets, and you won't want to hear what I had to do sometimes in order to survive."

"Yes, I would. Tell me," I said looking up at him, my curiosity piqued.

And those captivating eyes again searched mine, and then he said, "These are things I'm sure you've never even heard of. How then could you understand? These are things that people keep to themselves. Why am I telling you all this?"

"It's amazing! I know what you mean. I feel the same way too! Being in your company makes me feel as if you had grown up in my village with me and I had known you all my life. You see what I mean?

"Yes," Jacques replied. "Let me have your hand. Touching you will give me courage to tell you what happened in Paris."

Suddenly I felt apprehensive. I almost wished that he would not divulge any more secrets, but he was eager to talk now and couldn't be stopped.

"I had to survive. I had no job, no money, nowhere to sleep. So I began to sleep around with widows and older, married women, for money, clothing, and someplace to stay. I became a gigolo basically and—"

"*Gigo* what?" I asked.

Jacques replied, "Gigolo. That's a man who lives off women. The man doesn't work and depends on women to supply all his needs. And you know, the funny thing about that was, I was actually proud of the way I was able to get whatever I wanted from those women."

Jacques paused, perhaps to give me time to decipher this information. I was glad that he stopped. I had to stifle the urge to express disgust at such a lifestyle. However, I realized we appeared to be following an unwritten rule to become supportive friends. Consequently, it took all the strength I could muster to blurt out instead, "You were young, and didn't realize what you were getting yourself into, I'm sure. But how did you finally get yourself away from all that?"

Jacques squeezed my hand and kissed me on the cheek before he answered. "That's where my father comes in. From the moment I met him, my life changed. When I met Monsieur Suquet (that's his name), I was living with a widow, but I had saved a lot of money and was looking in the newspapers for a flat. Finally, I came across

Monsieur Suquet's advertisement. He owned a big house and was looking for someone to rent a room. When I went to answer the advertisement, he and I hit it off right away. I moved in the same day, and that's how our relationship started."

"I like this story. Just like that—two complete strangers become father and son."

"Yes, he was a lonely widower and had no children, and wanted us to live like a family. After we became very close, I told him the truth about my lifestyle, and that was the end of it."

"What happened after you told him all that?"

"You see, when he adopted me, he told me that no son of his would be a gigolo. And because he was an engineer, he wanted me to follow in his footsteps and become an engineer as well."

"What a man, your father! What happened next?"

"He offered to send me to England to learn English and engineering."

"No wonder you speak English so well, although you still do have a French accent. I had been wondering about that since last night." Then, I added, "This man has done for you what very few men would do for someone they're not even related to."

"Well, all those who know me think he is my real father. You're the only one who knows the truth."

"And it will remain a secret with me. How often do you see him?"

"As I said before, I've not been working in France for many years now. But, no matter what part of the world I am in, I still find time to visit him in Paris several times a year."

"How did you find the job here in Nigeria?"

"I had been working in Saudi Arabia for two years

when I heard about the position in Nigeria and I decided to look into it. I thought it would be a nice change to work in Nigeria."

"How long have you been here?"

"Three years."

"Three years! Time for another change?"

"I've been thinking about that. After about three years in a country, I begin to get restless and want to move on."

"So, you might be leaving Nigeria soon then?"

"Yes, unless something beyond my control forces me to stay on."

I did not respond; I couldn't think about Jacques leaving Nigeria. He squeezed my hand.

I looked up to find three young Nigerian boys hovering over Jacques' car. "What are those boys doing around your car?" I asked.

"They're all right. They wipe off cars, they just want some money."

"But your car was spotless when we left your home this morning!"

"That's all right. I give them twenty-five kobo here, and twenty-five kobo there, and they go away. By the way, when I was here in Nigeria before, just after the civil war, the currency was pounds and shillings."

"Yes, I remember. I was a young girl in the village then."

"Massa! Massa," the boys yelled simultaneously, "we clean your motor. You owe us two naira."

"No, no, no, no," Jacques replied, fishing for some coins in his pocket. "I owe you only one naira; fifty kobo for you and fifty kobo for your friend. My car was clean before, you made it all dirty now. Go away!"

It was pleasant stepping inside Jacques' air-conditioned house out of the intense heat of the sun. I stepped into the kitchen to see what Jacques was doing. He looked up from his chore at hand—dicing onions. "What are you doing here? I thought I told you to remain in the living room and relax."

"Are you sure you don't want me to do anything?"

"I'm sure. Go sit down, put your feet up and watch television; or look through some magazines; go, do something, anything. Take a nap."

I left the kitchen feeling extremely uncomfortable. I had been taught that it was the woman's place to do the cooking, take care of the house and the children, and wait on the man. In order to really relax and not be concerned that there was a man in the kitchen cooking for me, I rationalized that Jacques' behavior was due to his culture and his upbringing. After all, he was not an African, and his behavior was probably normal where he came from. Nevertheless, it was still incomprehensible to me.

I sat in the lounge chair that faced the television set, threw my head back, pushed myself all the way back in the chair, and was a little startled when my legs were raised automatically, putting me in a totally reclining position. It was a soothing feeling, yet strange. I closed my eyes, but not in sleep. I appeared to be dreaming; dreaming about what was actually taking place—my willingness to be out on a date with an expatriate and feeling very comfortable in his presence and even quite at home in his house. In my dreamlike state, it was apparent to me that I must be losing my senses; however, what was more frightening was that I was not terribly disturbed about it. Instead, I was consciously allowing myself to tumble into a perilous abyss of insanity.

Then, I heard Jacques talking to himself. "She's asleep, that's good." I kept my eyes closed and pretended

I was indeed asleep. This time however, I decided to examine the reality of the situation, since it was virtually impossible to deny the mutual attraction Jacques and I had for each other. I wondered, *How can I explain such absurdity to Bola, to my Owerri relatives, to my family and neighbors back in my village, and to my colleagues when the news of my relationship with Jacques begins to spread throughout the Ministry?* Again, I decided that I must open my eyes and do one of two things—succumb to my uncontrollable feelings toward Jacques, or rise quickly before Jacques reappeared, flee the house, disappear into the afternoon sun, and out of Jacques' life forever.

"You must wake up now," Jacques said stroking my forehead. I opened my eyes to find him on his knees beside my chair. I was relieved; he had foiled my plan.

"I don't mean to startle you, but dinner is ready," and continuing to stroke my forehead, he added, "You're absolutely gorgeous, even when you're sleeping. You're definitely my princess."

Then, without warning, Jacques turned my head gently to the side, brought his face closer to mine, parted my lips with his tongue and began kissing me for what seemed like an eternity. Although it was my first kiss, I was not surprised that my response came naturally. And when he took me by the hand and led me into the dining room and kissed me again, I knew I had to prepare for an impending battle with my world.

At the dinner table, I was suddenly overwhelmed by the emotions and thoughts that consumed me. So I ate in silence, grateful that Jacques also was silent, although I felt his eyes on me continuously. Finally, I was forced to say something when I tasted hot pepper in every dish I ate.

"Jacques, thank you very much; I taste hot pepper. That's very thoughtful of you."

Jacques nodded and smiled. "I like hot pepper too. My cook makes me Nigerian dishes as well."

"You have a cook and you were prepared to cook all this yourself, today!"

"As I told you, Sunday is his day off. Besides, I wanted this dinner to be special. This is a dish he doesn't prepare very well and I wanted it done properly for you."

I could not speak; I had just put a combination of sauteed mushrooms and creamed spinach in my mouth. I looked at Jacques tenderly, hoping he would read my thankfulness in my eyes.

For dessert, Jacques served fruit salad and rice pudding. At the end of the meal, I said, resolutely, "I'm washing the plates, so it's your turn to sit and relax."

"What plates?" replied Jacques, chuckling triumphantly. "I'll put everything in the dishwasher."

I frowned. "What do you mean, dishwasher?"

"You see that machine over there?" Jacques pointed toward a machine that looked like a cooking range without the burners. "That's the dishwasher. All you have to do is stack up all your dishes inside, push a button, and it will wash them just as clean as you would."

"Impossible!" I replied, "A machine can't do a better job than the human hand."

Jacques turned to look at me. "You go back inside and relax while I stack the dishwasher. I'll turn the telly on for you. There should be some kind of a variety show on," Jacques said, leading the way to the livingroom.

Alone once again in the livingroom, I sat in the corner of the couch that faced the television set and tried not to think about what Jacques was doing. I did not want to entertain guilt feelings while trying to enjoy myself! A commercial for Pablum baby food flashed on the screen. A beautiful, bouncing, robust baby sat on his mother's lap, joyous and frisky, enjoying each mouthful of Pablum. After the commercial, a dynamic Miriam Makeba appeared on the screen belting a song in French before an audience in French-speaking Sekou-Toure, Guinea. One after another, she crooned most of her famous numbers in her usual electrifying fashion. Although I did not understand the words, her stage presence and the pulsating beat of the accompaniment kept me spellbound. After Miriam Makeba's show, a special documentary on South Africa came on, and I learned for the first time, about the plight of the black South Africans. It made an enormous impact on me. I was suddenly filled with rage and resentment toward a country that would allow such demoralizing treatment of a group of its citizens. I did not realize that I had risen from the couch and was standing in front of the television set with fists clenched.

"What's wrong with the telly?" Jacques asked on entering the room, "You look as if you're about to punch in the screen."

I relaxed my fists and walked over to where I had been sitting. "There was nothing wrong with the television. This is a documentary about black South Africans. I just got very upset and didn't realize I was reacting that way."

"It's been a terrible situation for the blacks there," Jacques replied as he sat beside me. "Someday things are going to be reversed and I hope we live long enough to see it."

"I hope so," I said, although I could not envision any way out of that dilemma for the blacks.

"I shouldn't have turned on the telly; now your day is all ruined. And that's just the opposite of what I wanted to have happen. I wanted to make this a special day for us to get to know each other."

"I'm sorry," I replied, wishing also that I hadn't watched the documentary. A deep frown on Jacques face had replaced the smiling eyes that I found so alluring.

"You're right," I said. "I shouldn't let something like that ruin this day; you took so much pains to make everything so beautiful for me. Jacques, I'm really sorry."

Jacques did not reply. Instead, he placed my head on his chest and proceeded to massage the back of my neck and shoulders gently. "You're so tense. Just relax," he finally said.

The movements of his magical fingers were beginning to have a calming effect on me. I wanted it to continue. I shifted and lowered my body gently, placing my head on his lap. But, I had seen that familiar gleam in his eyes which always caused the fullness in my chest to plummet downward, centering in the lower part of my abdomen. And when Jacques finally stood up, reached out for my hand, and led me out of the livingroom and up a flight of stairs, I knew I would go anywhere with him.

13

Outcast

It was the late afternoon rush hour in Lagos and the traffic on all the major streets flowed at a snail's pace. Awolowo Road in Ikoyi was no exception. As usual, Bisi was driving me home after work; she decided to cut through Obalende to Keffe and St. Gregory streets on to Awolowo Road.

"This is no ordinary 'go slow,'" Bisi observed. "We haven't moved in twenty minutes; this is ridiculous!"

"Something else besides 'go slow' must be happening," I offered.

Bisi had already turned the car engine off. "This is so annoying!" she said, banging the palms of her hands against the steering wheel. Then, she pushed the car door open with her elbows. "Ah beg oh, what's going on here?" she continued, as she stood on her toes and craned her neck. "Grace, I think I see what's going on. A visiting V.I.P. is passing by. Don't you know, they invariably pick a time like this to whiz a V.I.P. by, knowing too well it would interfere with the already terrible, terrible, Lagos 'go slow'!"

"I know, it's awful, and in this heat too! Goodness, it's hot!" I responded, fanning myself with my hand. "I might as well get out of the car too. At least I can stretch my legs, and besides, I may catch a glimpse of this V.I.P., whoever he is."

"Well, we'll find out when the motorcade reaches us," Bisi replied. "Look, look! I can see the V.I.P. car now; they're almost here!"

Soon, gleaming black government cars adorned by small green and white flags and escorted by military men on motorcycles, came zooming by. Following closely behind, were other shimmering black government unmarked cars. Suddenly, it was all over; the motorcade vanished.

"Did you see who it was?" Bisi asked.

"No," I replied. "The cars went by so fast I didn't recognize anybody."

Finally, the "go slow" began to inch forward; we jumped back in the car and Bisi quickly started the motor. It took us one whole hour to reach Victoria Island which was the very next community. Turning into Ojora Close, Bisi pointed with her lips. "Grace, isn't that your house, where all those people are gathered around?"

I raised my head and shaded my eyes, "My mother in the grave! It is right in front of my house. Hurry, hurry, Bisi, something bad must have happened. My mother and father in the grave! I wonder what is going on?"

"Look! There's Bola! What's he doing home this time of the day? Look! It looks as if he's throwing things out of the house," Bisi said, leaning forward and squinting.

"Hurry, Bisi, hurry. I wonder what's happening? You think maybe he had a fight with Helen and is throwing her out?"

"He would not do that. What could she have done? Besides, she's from America. Where would she go? She doesn't have anybody here to run to," Bisi replied.

Quickly, Bisi parked the car along the street away from the small crowd that had gathered in front of the house. Thrusting our way through the crowd we entered the yard with its two drooping paw-paw trees by one side of the house. I focused my attention on the things strewn all over the yard, and in horror, began to recognize my own belongings. Just then, my light green vinyl suitcase came crashing at my feet. I jumped out of the way just in time to prevent my feet from being severed from my legs.

"Grace," Bisi turned to me, her eyes blazing with rage, "these are your belongings! For what reason? How dare this bastard!"

"Who are you calling a bastard?" Bola yelled, looking out his livingroom window, "You're the bastard. It's your example Grace is following. Are you satisfied now that you have turned her into a loose woman? I have no room in my house for loose women."

With a slight jump, Bisi swung around quickly and stormed toward Bola, pointing her finger at him. "Hoo-ooh, you bastard! Are you saying I've turned my sister here into a prostitute?"

"You said it!" Bola replied.

"How dare you!" Bisi said firmly. "Do you want to talk about prostitution? Let's talk about prostitution. I bet you have no idea that I know all about you, do you? Let me tell all these people here who the prostitute really is." Bisi pointed at Bola, "It's you Bola Balogun!" Then, advancing toward the gates, Bisi addressed the mesmerized crowd, "You want hear true true story about this man?"

"Ye-ah, ye-ah, madam, talk true true story about dee man. We wan' hear." One voice after the other responded eagerly:

"Yes, madam, tell us dee true true story."

"Dee man call you and your sister asawo,* so, explain yousef, madam."

"Talk madam, yes, talk."

"We wan' hear your side. Ee look say dee man day lie. You an' dis your sista no look like asawo atall. You look like big big woman way get good good job and plenty

*asawo—a prostitute

money. So, talk your side; we day listen."

Bisi began, "First of all, as you can tell, me and my sister here are big big women in one Ministry here in Lagos. We get our money from the Ministry. We don' beg any man for money. We get our own house, everything. Now, you tell me, how we can be asawos? We look like asawos?"

The crowd became restless and the sounds of "No, you can't be prostitutes; you don't look like prostitutes" veberated in the air.

"Mm-mn, God forbid! you an' your sista no be asawo."

"Noo-oo, noo-oo, noo-oo, you no be asawo. Dee man day lie."

"Yes, dee man lie."

Bola disappeared into his house. I felt proud of the way Bisi was handling the crowd. She continued her defense quickly. "So, because my boyfriend is expatriate, this foolish man think he has right to call me asawo? And because one expatriate care for my sister she is asawo? That make sense?"

"Noo-oo, madam," the crowd replied.

"Now, let me tell you about this foolish man over there," Bisi turned and pointed at Bola's house, "who is calling me and my sister asawo. This is what you must know about this man. The reason he's talking all this, is because guilty conscience is killing him. You see, I know people who know the man when he live in England and in America. You want hear what the man day do when he go to school in England and America?"

"Yes, madam, tell us madam, we wan' hear, madam," voices in the crowd yelled out.

Another voice rose from the crowd, "How dee man live, madam? Tell us, madam."

Bisi continued, "First of all, let me ask you one thing: Do you know that men can be asawos too?"

Some of the spectators stared blankly at Bisi, some gave a "no" answer by turning their heads from side to side, while responses such as the following could be heard from the crowd: "Eh—heh? man? asawo?" "Wha-t? Is dat so?" "What kind world be dis?"

Bisi continued, "Yes, na true, true. Some men are asawos too, and this man over there, this Bola Balogun, was asawo himself with women in England and America. And you see, the same man is calling me and my sister asawo just because my boyfriend is expatriate!"

A man in the crowd gestured impatiently. "Madam, go on, go on, tell us more about dee man."

Bisi knew she had the crowd in the palm of her hand. She went on quickly, "You see, this same man who call me and my sister asawo, live off white women all the time he day for England and America when he day for school, before he marry this black American woman. I mean, the white women give him place to put his head, give him food, put clothes on his back, pay his money for school, give him car to drive; the women do everything. Now, tell me, what you call a man like that?" Bisi added, as her eyes scanned the crowd.

Voices in the crowd responded by chanting, "Asawo! Asawo! Asawo! Asawo!" and "Dee madam talk true; dee man be asawo."

Bisi tried to cut in. "Listen, listen, listen, I haven't finished yet!" Finally, the crowd calmed down and Bisi went on. "And what you think he did as soon as the foolish man get degree, you know, finish all his studies?"

"What he do, madam?" a young man chuckled, nudging the man standing beside him with his elbow.

Bisi replied, "As soon as he finish his studies, he

never say 'Thank you' and 'Goodbye' to those white women who helped him. He disappear, just like that, marry this black American woman and come back with her to Nigeria. Now, you judge for yourself. Who na the hypocrite? Who na the liar? He throw my sister out because I get one expatriate boyfriend, and then he call me and my sister asawo."

Instead of responding to Bisi's questions, one man said to another, "My broda, come, make we go. Like dee madam say, dee man na hypocrite and lie man. Come, make we go."

Another spectator said to the man standing beside him, "My broda, dis man na disgrace for African man. We work for take care of our woman and children, not for woman for work an' give us money! Come, make we go."

The second man replied, "Where dee man go? Ah want look him face!"

"T-u-a!" The first man spat on the ground. "Ah no want look him face. Him face ugly! Come, make we go."

Then the crowd began to disperse. The spectators each looked to see if they could get a glimpse of Bola Balogun. They would wave their hands in disgust or shake their heads in disbelief, and then walk away.

After most of the people in the crowd had disappeared, two women came through the gates and approached me. The younger woman dropped to her knees and began to pick up my scattered clothing. The older woman approached Bisi who had now turned away from the crowd and was surveying the remnants of my belongings. "My child," the older woman said, "me an' my daughta here go help your sista finish pick up her tings and carry dem to your car for you. We come to help you because dis man wrong when he say you an' your sister be asawo. But I know you not asawo, an' everybody who come hear dee trouble know you not asawo. But you see, my child, many young young Nigerian gals stan' aroun' all dis big big hotel an' asawo demselves with expatriate. So, dis young young asawo gals who do dis with expatriate give good good Nigerian woman like you bad name. So you see why people an' foolish man like dis one over dere go call you an' your sista asawo? You see what I mean?"

"I see ma," Bisi replied. "What you just talk make plenty plenty sense ma."

"Anoda ting, my child; you see, we African, we tink say African an' expatriate not natural togeda, because we fear say we go lost our culture. You undastan' me? Das why all dis trouble."

"I understand you, ma. I know all this, ma. I know why our people do ting like dis. But ma, if na true true friendship, and true true love between African woman and expatriate, why people no understand and leave them alone?"

"My child, our culture strong strong too much, an' our mind go dat way. You see? Even for me, when you talk how you feel, I undastan' you, but all dee time, I tink our culture be dee right way for African people. You see?"

"Yes, ma," Bisi replied, looking dejected.

"My child, you have big big trouble, but, if your mind strong strong for your expatriate, an' you happy, den, explain someting to your family, explain someting to all your friend. You see, when you no explain someting, an' you don't beg dem to undastan' you, an' beg dem to try an' get plenty plenty patient, das when you get big big trouble."

"You're so right, Ma. Na dat exactly happened to me. I never try to understand how my family and friends feel about me and my expatriate boyfriend, when they tell me what I do isn't natural. I just pushed what I do down insigh' their throat, because I think only of my happiness. No wonder they say, 'You do that, stay away from us; we never want to look your face again.'"

"Eh—heh! You see? You see what I mean?"

"Yes, ma," Bisi replied, bending down to embrace the older woman who stood about four and a half feet tall. "Thank you, ma. You don' teach me big big lesson today."

The woman looked up at Bisi. "You love dis man true true?"

"Yes, ma, I love the man true true."

"You want dis man bad bad?"

"Yes, ma, I want this man bad bad."

"Den, my child," the woman replied, "go back to your family an' all your friend an' explain dee true true love you get for dis man, an' kneel down an' beg dem to try an' undastan'. My child, you need your family. You mus' never live your life with no love from your family."

Bisi gave the woman another embrace. "Thank you ma, I go take your advice. I see now my mistake. Before, I never want to 'gree say my family mean a lot to me, and I never want to 'gree say I miss them plenty plenty. I thank God for your wisdom, ma."

"Good!" the woman replied with a triumphant smile. "Now, come, make we carry all your sista's tings to your car. Where your car?"

"Over there, ma," Bisi gestured.

That night at Bisi's house was a particularly difficult one for me. The situation was stressful and sleep eluded me. Staying up most of the night, however, afforded me the opportunity to reevaluate my feelings toward Jacques, and to reconsider a potential relationship with him. Again, I deluded myself into thinking that this time, I would be more resolute in my efforts to go over the pros and cons of such a relationship. Then I asked myself whether Jacques was worth the trouble—the sacrifices, the aggravation, and the other adversities that were bound to follow if the relationship continued. I was astounded by my own response. In spite of what had taken place at Bola's house, I did not hesitate in deciding that I wanted Jacques if he wanted me, and that I was prepared to go through whatever it would take for me to be in his life.

My room was dark, but the illuminated numbers on my nightstand clock made it possible for me to see the telephone receiver. The time was 3:08 A.M. I felt uneasy ringing Jacques at such an untimely hour. However, I reasoned that after all, an emergency had occurred, and since he was directly or indirectly involved, he should welcome hearing from me. Besides, he had promised to ring me at the Baloguns' that evening and must have been shocked to learn that I did not live there anymore. Therefore, hearing from me would relieve his anxiety. I dialed Jacques' number now without any compunction. I waited. The telephone rang five times, and then, a sixth time. After the eighth ring, I surmised that he had probably gone out with friends and had not returned. I was about to hang up the receiver when a woman's voice answered.

"Hello!"

The voice was lusty, alert. The woman had obviously not been asleep. I thought quickly. "Oh my heavens, I have the wrong number!" I said. "I'm awfully sorry to have awakened you."

"Wait, wait, wait," the woman said, "are you calling for Jacques?"

"Yes," I replied. "Is this his number then?"

"Yes. One moment," the woman replied.

As I waited for Jacques to come to the phone, my

heart began to sink into the darkest abyss. *Why was a woman in Jacques' house at 3:15 in the morning?* I had convinced myself that Jacques had no one else in his life, and that he wanted me to be "that special person." I had fallen for my own fable, allowing myself to be captivated by him to the point that I myself really wanted him now. I had to be strong, since the relationship was just starting. So, I decided to remain on the phone and give Jacques the opportunity to explain what was going on.

Finally, Jacques' sleepy voice came on. "Hello! Who is it?"

I hesitated.

"Hello!" Jacques repeated.

"Jacques, it's me, Grace," I replied.

"For goodness sake! Grace? Am I glad you called! Where have you been? I rang you at Mr. Balogun's house and he was extremely rude to me and wouldn't tell me where you were. What's going on?"

"It's a long story, but you have a guest with you." I gave him an opening to initiate an explanation. "I don't want to disturb anything."

"No, no, no, I don't have a guest. I'll tell you all about it when I see you. Where are you ringing from?"

"I'm at Bisi's house. I'm staying with her now. As I said, it's a long story; I'll explain when we see each other."

"Grace, there's so much going on and it's all so important. Can you take off from work today? I intend to do the same. I'll come and pick you up now. You can ring the Ministry from my house later on this morning."

"Bu-bu-but," I stammered, "you're going to pick me up now and there's a woman there?"

"I told you, I'll explain when I see you. Trust me. Can you be ready to leave in thirty minutes? I'm already dressed. I fell asleep in a chair in the den upstairs. I'll see you in thirty minutes." Jacques hung up quickly. I couldn't even ask for some additional time to dress and throw a few things together. I had no choice now but to do what I could in thirty minutes.

As Jacques and I rode in the warm, dark, and quiet morning, the thought of the woman in his house haunted me. I could not wait for the explanation. "Is that woman going to be gone by the time we get to your house?" I mumbled.

"Maybe, but don't worry about it. This is the woman Bisi was talking about the first night we met. You remember?"

"Mm-hm, I remember," I replied, feeling jealous.

"She should be gone by the time we arrive. I told her to leave because I was going to pick up my girlfriend." Jacques paused and shook his head. "Grace, I thought she had disappeared from my life and had gone back to England with her husband, because I hadn't seen her in two years. All of a sudden, she appeared at my door last night and would not leave, even after I made it clear that our one-night affair was a terrible mistake on my part. I reminded her that we had been drinking an awful lot and I must have been out of my mind. Her husband was a friend of mine and had been in Kaduna on business that night. She and I ran into each other at a club and she clung to me all night, telling me how much she had always wanted me, and insisted on going home with me. So I took her home; it all seemed natural to me until I woke up the next morning and realized what a stupid thing I had done. Naturally, someone told her husband she slept at my house that night! And worse yet, I got in trouble with a good friend, and wasn't even attracted to the woman, and I'm still not attracted to her."

I was satisfied with Jacques' explanation. I sighed, feeling relieved, but I wondered what would happen if the woman was still at Jacques' house on our arrival.

Jacques looked over at me and seemed to have read my mind. "Listen! As I said, I told her that I expected her to be gone by the time we arrived, but she might be hanging around just to see who you are. You see, she's been drinking since last night. She refused to leave when I asked her to; instead, she made herself comfortable and began helping herself to the liquor in the cabinet; that was when I went upstairs to sleep in the den."

Jacques' suspicion that the woman might still be there was on target. As we turned into Jacques' driveway, we saw the woman standing in front of the main entrance to the house, holding a glass of what seemed to be liquor. When we came into her view, she raised the glass as if to toast our arrival.

I looked at Jacques. "What do we do now?"

"No problem," he replied casually. "I will keep her outside, and while I do that, just say nothing. Slip right into the house and make yourself comfortable."

I nodded and relaxed.

Jacques parked, hurried to assist me out of the car, and held my hand as we walked toward the door where the woman stood. Jacques let go of my hand at the door, placed himself in front of the woman and proceeded to address her. I took that as my cue to slip into the house quickly. However, before Jacques could utter a single word, I felt the shatter of glass on the side of my forehead. She had thrown her drink at me! I panicked when I felt my own warm blood trickling down my face and arms.

Jacques immediately grasped the woman by both wrists, pinning her against the side of the door. "Martha, what did you do that for?"

"I hate blackies!" she replied. "So you prefer this slut of a blackie to me, heh? This *thing*? This prostitute?"

"Listen to me, Martha," Jacques said, tightening his grip around her wrists and shaking her vigorously. "This young lady is far from what you think she is. Actually, she is more of a woman than you are! Furthermore, she is the woman I want to marry if she'll have me. Do you hear me?" Jacques added as he became more and more infuriated. "I have no patience with people like you who automatically think she's a prostitute because she's with me!" Jacques then released Martha's wrists, pushing her away from him. "What's the use, you're drunk anyway! Now, my steward will get you a taxi, get in the taxi with you, and personally see that you get to your room at your hotel. And by the way, before you go, I believe you owe my girlfriend an apology for calling her all those nasty names."

"Ne-ver! Nev-er!" Martha slurred, wobbling on her feet. "B-oth o-f you a-rre crazy!"

Gesturing angrily, Jacques commanded, "You stand there and don't you move! I'll go get the steward." Then, turning to me and cradling me in his arms, he examined my wound. "I'm so sorry. Thank God, it doesn't seem serious, although there's a lot of bleeding. I'll get you to the clinic right away. The nearest one is at the marina, not too far from here."

Later, all cleaned and patched up at a private clinic at the marina, Jacques and I returned to his house to a plantain and egg breakfast prepared by Sunday, his cook.

"What an ordeal for you in the past twenty-four hours!" Jacques said, as he brought his cup of coffee to his lips.

"I know, and I hope that's it with surprises—I don't

think I can take any more for a while," I said, shaking my head.

"Yes, you can; you can take one more." Jacques replied.

"Oh, no, not another surprise! What is it now?" I said, as I tried to chew some plantain.

"That's one of the reasons I love you. You're beautiful, bright, delicate, yet you are very strong. I'm sure you can handle one more surprise."

"Oh no!" I said, dropping my fork. "I mean it Jacques, I can't take any more."

"What if it's a pleasant surprise?"

"It all depends," I replied.

"Well, that was what I wanted to tell you when I tried to reach you last night at the Baloguns'. I wanted to tell you that I have to travel to France. It's an emergency."

"That's supposed to be a pleasant surprise for me?"

"It may just be. Wait, I haven't finished yet," Jacques continued with a mischievous gleam in his eyes.

I glared at him. "I'm listening."

"Well, my father rang me last night."

"He's not ill, is he?"

"No, nothing like that."

"What then?"

"Some sort of family affair. He thinks it's time to turn over his business to me at this point in his life. He just wants us to talk about it and to bring a few things to my attention."

"Then what? Does that mean he will then retire?"

Jacques chuckled, "Not my father. If he could, he would work forever. As he puts it, he just wants his important papers to be in order while he's still alive." Jacques paused and searched my eyes, which were now so transfixed on his, I was afraid to blink for fear that I would miss some of the enchantment. I had more than once found myself lost in the magic of his charm when he spoke.

He seemed distracted. "A penny for your thoughts, madam."

I nodded, still mesmerized.

"You'ren't paying attention. When I say, 'A penny for your thoughts', you're supposed to tell me what you're thinking."

I looked at him seriously, and said softly, "Believe me Jacques, I'm always with you, a hundred percent."

"I'm happy about that because I have something very important to ask you."

The hint of mystery caused me to be extremely impatient with Jacques. "Jacques, you're playing with me and it's not fair. Common, what is it? Ask me, ask me."

"No, not now. Later, after I make us a drink and we're relaxing in the livingroom."

Later, in the dimly lit room, I found solace in Jacques' warm, protective arms, and he finally cleared up the mystery.

"I want you to come to France with me. I can't wait to introduce you to my father."

"What? You mean it? Me? Your father? What about my job at the Ministry?"

"That's part of what I want to talk to you about," Jacques replied. Then, extricating himself from me, he dropped to his knees, cradled my hands in his and continued, "Don't say anything. Just listen to me. Grace, my love, think about it. Why would I want to introduce you to my father, someone who lives all the way across the ocean? Because you're what I had been looking for all my life and I can't wait to show you off. Grace, I fell in love with you the moment I laid eyes on you; I'm sure you sensed it. I love you, Grace." Jacques released his hand from mine. "Oh, never mind that we've just met. I loved you instantly and I decided right then that I'd marry you if you want me. And admit it Grace, we came together like magnets! I could sense that you also fell in love with me; I could see it in your eyes. And that's what's giving me the courage to propose to you today.

"Grace, let's be honest with each other. We know what's happening to us, so why should we wait so many months, so many years, that sort of thing, in order to find out whether we really love each other, or whether we are suited for each other? As far as I'm concerned, it's foolish to go through all that formality when we already know how we feel and what we want. Besides, I never want to see you hurt or unhappy for any reason whatsoever. You don't deserve to be called all those nasty names! Now, you asked about your job. That's the reason I want an African woman. I want a real wife; one that I will work very hard for, in order to support her and our children; one who will be home waiting for me with a hot meal, when I arrive from work; one who will put me and our children first, not a job, because I will be making enough money to support my family."

Suddenly, Jacques interjected, chortling, "You look funny; you haven't closed your mouth since I started talking."

I closed my mouth, pressed my lips together tightly, and swallowed hard. It was an arduous task trying to condense and decipher so much and so quickly. My lips and throat had become parched. I was pleased Jacques had asked me not to speak. I pointed at my drink feebly. Quickly, Jacques reached out to get it with one hand, as he continued to hold on to both my hands with his other hand. Then, he also reached for his drink and took a quick sip.

"Do you love me, Grace? Do you want what I want?" Jacques asked me finally.

I did not answer. I threw my head back and thought of all my dreams when I was in the village, even as a little girl. I thought about what I had gone through to get where I was now. I thought about my enviable position at the Ministry. I thought about how proud my family was of me because of my dogged ambition and success. I thought I was ready to answer Jacques' questions...if I could only avert those dangerous eyes that had been peering into my soul, I was sure to give Jacques the most reasonable answer. So, I gently pulled my hands away from his, sat up on the couch, clasped my hands in front of me and looked straight ahead at the blank wall. "Do I love you? Do I want what you want? Wel—"

"Look at me when you answer," Jacques interrupted, shifting sideways on the couch and turning my face toward him. And when I looked into his eyes, the words that I spoke were implausible even to me. "Jacques, is this what love is then? What we're feeling and what we want above everything else? If that's what it is, then I love you, Jacques; I love you, I love you, and I want everything you want. Yes, Jacques, I love you and I want, more than anything, to be your wife."

14

Wild Cat

The sun was still at the center of the pale blue and white sky, although it was around 6:30 in the evening. A light gray film hovered over the hot, steamy sand along the sidewalk on Araromi Street in Maroko. Food vendors sat on low wooden stools beside smoking black grills as they tended to the cooking at hand. The air reeked of a combination of hot palm oil, dundu, acara, fried plantain, and roasted corn. Across the street from the food vendors were small tables with neatly stacked household items such as tinned milk, toilet soap, matches, candles, chewing sticks, and bottles of assorted homemade liquor.

"Let's stop and get some corn," I urged.

Bisi frowned and looked at me. "Don't you remember where we're going? We're all dressed up going to that nice new restaurant I told you about, and you want to stop and get some corn! That's one of the things I like about you, though; at heart you're still a bush woman," she added, shaking her head.

"You sound like Jacques," I chuckled. "What's the difference when I eat corn?" I shrugged my shoulders.

"I bet you won't mind some moi-moi* on top of that, eh?" Bisi chided.

"Mmmm, I'd love some!" I taunted, smacking my lips.

Bisi responded by first giving me her "You're-out-of-

---

*moi-moi—a bean cake

your-mind" look. Then, she accelerated the car, zoomed onto the next street and out of Maroko.

I was anxious to open the conversation. "Bisi, you haven't asked me about this 'big news' I have for you."

"I didn't ask because you yourself said you won't tell me until we sit and relax in the restaurant over dinner. Remember?"

"That's right, that's right, let's wait," I replied, although still impatient.

The dimly lit restaurant was devoid of customers except for a lone expatriate sitting on a stool at one end of the bar chatting with the smiley-face bartender. We took our seats at the opposite end of the bar. We had agreed to have a few drinks at the bar before we ate; we had also agreed that we would not rush whatever we decided to do, since we had planned to use the whole evening to gabble, gossip, have some drinks, and dine. I jumped on the bar stool quickly, and without giving Bisi the time to order our drinks, I got to the point.

"Bisi, Bisi, listen! Jacques has asked me to marry him," I said quickly.

Bisi's mouth flew open and her eyes seemed to double in size.

"Is that how you receive the news?" I asked, feeling a little disappointed. "Aren't you happy for me? No hugs, no nothing?"

Managing a weak smile, Bisi finally composed herself. She sat up straight and looked over at the bartender who was still engaged in a conversation with the expatriate. "Bartender!" she called out; and turning to me, she said haughtily, "So, Jacques asked you to marry him, eh? So soon? What kind of nonsense is that? You only met him just the other day. And what was your answer?"

"I said 'yes,' of course."

"Bartender!" Bisi called out louder. Then, turning to me, "What does 'yes, of course' mean? Does that mean it's natural to marry someone you don't even know, someone you met only three days ago? And the person you said 'yes, of course' to is an expatriate! Of all people;' one of the people you've been so much against. What's come over you?"

"Aren't you happy that at least my attitude towards expatriates has changed?"

"In a way, yes; but I don't care what nationality a man is, you just don't jump up and marry him three days after you meet him without having some knowledge of his background."

"My sister, I know Jacques and I have just met, and this may sound crazy, but I already know a lot about his background."

"Oh yeah? How?"

"We've had long talks together, and he's even planning to let me see everything with my own eyes."

"Mm-hm, how?"

"I'm traveling to France with him to meet his father."

Bisi waved both hands, "Wait just a minute, you people are moving far too fast for me. I need a drink! Where's that bartender?" Then, Bisi tried for the third time to get the bartender's attention. "Bartender!" She made an attempt to walk up to where the bartender was, but I pulled her skirt, forcing her to remain on her seat. "My sister, listen to me. Jacques and I found out from talking that we both fell in love with each other instantly when we met. We talked about it and agreed that it's silly going through all kinds of hypocritical formalities when we already know how we feel about each other and what we're going to do about it. My sister, it's only now that I'm beginning to understand what you were trying to explain to me about how you just learned how to love since you began your relationship with Peter. Well, I'm going through the same experience with Jacques. The only love I knew was the love of my family and my friends. But this is a special feeling that's not easy to describe. All I know that when I met Jacques, suddenly I saw a man, not an expatriate—a man that I want to be with all the time, and spend the rest of my life with. You know what I mean? My sister, please try to understand; I'm counting on your support. You're the only one, except for Uncle Jeremiah, who might understand this relationship. Please, my sister, I need you. I love this man, and I want to be his wife. I know the whole thing seems incredible, but the reality of the situation is that what's happening between me and Jacques is real, it's serious, and cannot be stopped. It's as if we have known each other for several lifetimes. My sister, look, the feeling I have for this man is so powerful, that, just merely looking at him or being close to him as I sense the presence of his manhood, drives me out of my mind. I want Jacques, my sister; please, I need your support."

Bisi began to heave with laughter. "You have gone crazy, and you must be in love! Do you realize that the last thing you said didn't even make any sense? Anyway, any man that would make my sister feel the way she does and makes her talk nonsense, is the right man for her." Then, reaching over and putting her arms around my shoulders, Bisi continued, "I'm happy for you, my sister. You have my full support."

"Oh, thank you, my sister!" I replied. "You're going to help make me the happiest woman on earth. Now, listen, my sister, there's a reason Jacques wants us to get married as soon as possible, and I agree with him: Aside from us being so madly in love with each other, his father wants him to come to France so they can discuss some business, and he wants to be able to introduce me as his wife. That way, his father will realize that I'm also a part of the family. The other reason he wants us to get married as soon as possible is that he is tired of people thinking that I'm a prostitute when we're together."

"I don't blame him," Bisi replied. "By the way, does Jacques know that if he wants to marry you he'll have to go through all the native ceremonies?"

"I tell you, my sister, sometimes, the man thinks like a Nigerian. He himself brought up the subject. He said he wouldn't marry me any other way but the native way. I tell you, my sister, Jacques is out of this world."

Bisi banged once on the edge of the bar with her fist. "Good. First, we have to think of the best way for him to ask for your hand in marriage. Don't forget he's not an ordinary Nigerian man; he's an expatriate, and our people don't look kindly on mixed marriages. So, expect a tough fight ahead of you. But, don't worry—we'll come up with a good idea."

"I know, I know, with very careful planning we should be able to pull it off."

Bisi bobbed her head and looked away pensively. "Oh, yes, it's going to be a tough fight." Then, giving me several quick taps on my thigh, "Don't worry, I'll do everything in my power to help. All I want to know now is, are you really ready to take on your family and the world?"

"Yes, my sister, I'm ready for any trouble ahead; Jacques is worth it."

"Good. Let's drink to that!"

At this point, Bisi's serious countenance began to change. A smile formed across her face. Cocking her head to one side she observed me as though seeing me for the first time. "My, my my! My sister has fallen in love. Yes, let the celebration begin! Bartender!" she called out,

"Where are you?"

With that, Bisi slid from her stool and walked over to where the bartender was. "Hey, bartender, I called you four times to come over and serve us. You just looked at me each time. So, it's not because you didn't see me and my sister sitting over there. What seems to be the problem?"

"Problem?" The bartender glared at Bisi. "You be dee problem. Now, take you business to anoda hotel. Dis is a brand new hotel an' we wano keep it clean."

What I understood from what the bartender said took my breath away. I placed my hand on my chest and gasped for air, shaking my head in disbelief. I knew Bisi's temper and knew she took no nonsense from anyone. There would be trouble. I could not see her eyes from where I sat, but by the way the bartender was looking at her, I suspected that her eyes had conveyed to him that he was in a dangerous position. The smirk on his face transformed itself quickly to a face that was confronted by a leopard or tiger about to go for the kill.

"Repeat what you just said." Bisi stood, legs astride, hands on her hips.

Although the fear in the bartender's eyes was obvious, he stood his ground. "You hear what I say. Go look for business in anoda hote—"

The bartender's words were cut short by Bisi's hand which reached out quickly like a fighter's Sunday punch, then closed in tightly about the bartender's windpipe. "I will teach you a lesson you will never forget as long as you live, you bloody fool!"

With that, Bisi pulled the now helpless man over the counter onto the floor, still clutching his neck as firmly as she could. Then, with knees astride, hovering over the prostrate man's chest, she doubled the pressure using both hands. The expatriate who had been sitting at the bar, rushed to the bartender's aid. He dropped to his knees as he attempted to remove Bisi's deadly grip from the bartender's neck. "Madam, madam, you'll kill him, you'll kill him!" he shouted, as he struggled in vain.

"That's exactly what I'm trying to do. I want to teach him a lesson," Bisi replied, grunting as she intensified her grip.

"But madam, he'll never learn the lesson once he's dead. Please madam, for God's sake let go," the expatriate insisted, still trying to pull Bisi away.

I rushed over to the bar and began pulling Bisi's shoulders from behind. "Please, my sister, stop, stop, stop! In the name of your father and your mother, you'll kill the man! All the gods help us! Look at his face, he may be dead already."

Suddenly, the expatriate rose to his feet and addressed me. "I'm going to get the security people. You must talk her out of it, and quickly!"

"My sister, my sister," I said, dropping to my knees beside the bartender as I tried to use persuasion on Bisi. "Listen to me. Think of what will happen if you kill this man. Do you want to sacrifice everything to face a firing squad? Think about me, about your family and Peter. What for? For this worthless man? Is that what you want? Please, my sister, use your head! Think about it, this man is not worth it; there's too much to lose."

Just as swiftly as she had pounced on the bartender, Bisi released her grip on the man, walked over calmly to where we had been sitting, picked up our handbags and proceeded to take a seat at one of the tables inside the bar area, her eyes fixed on the bartender's inert body. I had no idea what to do. All I knew was that I did not want the bartender to die. I began alternating several slaps on the bartender's face and a few push-downs on his chest. "Hey! bartender common, wake up, wake up, wake up!" I repeated over and over.

"My sister," I heard Bisi call out. I turned to look at her without stopping my self-invented procedure. "Is he dead?" she asked, almost scornfully.

I looked down at the bartender's face. To my amazement, his eyes were blinking weakly, as his chest began to rise and fall. I beamed back the answer to Bisi's question. "My sister, my sister, you didn't kill him, he's alive!"

"Come here, come here, my sister, hurry," Bisi demanded, searching in her handbag.

I gave the bartender a couple of reassuring pats on his arm. "Stay awake, you hear? Help day come. You'll be all right. I'll be right back." I then rushed to toward Bisi.

"Hurry!" Bisi said. "Take this card. It has Police Commissioner Adekanye's home telephone on it. Hurry, call him and tell him what happened, and tell him to come over right away because I may be in big trouble. Hurry, use the bartender's telephone over there at the bar. The commissioner lives around the corner from here. Tell him I said he should come in his pajamas if he has to because there's no time to waste."

As I talked with the police commissioner on the phone, two uniformed security men carrying first aid kits rushed in, followed by a well-dressed man along with the expatriate who had summoned them. The security men immediately went to work on the bartender.

"Tank God, dee man is alive," one of the security men said as he knelt down beside the bartender.

"Yes, he look as if he not hurt too bad. I tink he jus' pass out das all."

The well-dressed man went directly up to Bisi, and I wondered how he knew who the culprit was. "Good evening, madam. I'm dee managa. What happened?"

"The fellow who went to get you, he saw and heard everything. Didn't he tell you what happened?" Bisi snapped.

"Yes, madam, he tol' me what happened, but I wano hear your side, madam."

"Look, I sent for the police commissioner. My sister just talked with him on the telephone. He'll be here any minute now and I'm not saying anything until he arrives."

"Commissioner Olu Adekanye is a friend of yours, madam?"

"Yes. I see the bartender is all right. I wanted to give him something to remember for the rest of his life. The audacity of him, calling me and my sister prostitutes!"

"Das what he called you, madam?"

"Yes. At least that's what he thought we were," Bisi replied. Then, the manager turned to address the security men hovering over the bartender. "He awright?"

One of the security men replied, "He awright, sa. He's jus' a little sore around dee neck." He gestured. "We'll take him to dee hospital for some rest. Dey'll keep him jus' one day das all."

"Madam, I'm so sorry dat stupid man talk to you two big women like dat. You and your sista come with me to the VIP lounge an' have your drinks dere while you're waitin' for dee commissioner. You can have dinner too if you wan', an' everytin' will be on the house. O.K. madam? Dat stupid man! If he had died, it wouldaf served him right. He don' know, but when he leave dee hospital, he has no job here. When dee commissioner come, I will tell him dere's no more trouble, because dee bartender is sacked; and we don' know where he come from, because dis hotel don't hire people like dat."

15

The Messengers

"Finally. Do you believe this?" Bisi said breathlessly, as we finally rushed onto the plane to find somewhere, anywhere to sit, "Here it is 12:28, and we had tickets to board the 9:15 flight."

"My sister," I replied, "whose fault is that, eh? When we queued up for boarding passes and I saw how one latecomer dashed* the boarding pass attendant so he could put his name on the 9:15 roster, I wanted to do the same thing, but you wouldn't let me. Remember?"

"Awright, awright, I'm tired, and my feet hurt from these heels I have on," Bisi said, as she kicked her shoes off. "Maybe if I can just close my eyes for a minute..."

"You do that, but don't sleep too soundly. You know it's a short flight to Port-Harcourt, and if you don't feel the bumpity, bumpity on the transport lorry from Port-Harcourt to Owerri, you might get some more sleep."

"Hm..., I doubt it, my sister, not after what I heard about travelling on those transport lorries. Unless you're a baby, how can you sleep when passengers are on top of each other like sardines? I'm not travelling on any lorry. We're taking a taxi to your uncle's house."

"It's really not that bad," I replied.

"I say, no lorry, awright? I just want to close my eyes for a few minutes."

The newly built airport in Owerri was not yet in oper-

---

*dash—to bribe or tip

ation, hence the flight to Port-Harcourt, from where we chartered a taxi to Owerri. I glanced at my watch when we landed and said to Bisi, "Thank goodness it's Saturday. There won't be any traffic at this time of the day in Owerri, and my uncle and his family should be home."

It was about 5:00 P.M. when our taxi rolled into the small government housing community for civil servants.

"Do they know we're coming?" Bisi asked.

"Yes, but they don't know why. So you hold on to Jacques' letter, since you're going to do all the talking. And don't forget, you must say that Jacques and I have been dating from the time I started working in Lagos. You know, they won't understand me marrying a man, especially not a foreigner, three days after I met him."

"True. Just as I didn't like it myself when you broke the news to me. You see, we Africans might—and I stress '*might*'—accept that sort of thing if it's possible to check the man's family background. In Jacques' case, since he's from another country, the elders will not be able to check his pedigree; and for that reason alone, they might refuse to have the marriage take place."

"Remember how we've decided to take care of that?" I interjected quickly.

"Yes, but having his employer and a few colleagues testify on his behalf is not quite the same. It's just a chance we'll have to take. What will happen? We can't tell. All we can do is try everything possible."

"And after I win Uncle Jeremiah over to my side, I—"

Bisi interrupted me. "Are you sure your uncle will approve this marriage?"

"Well, he has never failed me yet. He always told me that he loves me so much that whatever makes me happy would make him happy too. You know, he's like my father now since both my parents are dead. Yes, I'm sure Uncle Jeremiah will stick by me no matter what."

"Hm, I wish I had someone like that, that I could swear by. I guess I will soon when I take that old woman's advice and make up with my family."

"Until that happens, you have me, my sister." I said quickly.

"I know, my sister. I just wanted to hear you say it. And as for me, I don't have to tell you what I would do for you. I love you so much."

"I love you too, my sister, and would also do anything for you," I replied.

After the initial joyous reunion with Uncle Jeremiah and his family, coupled with a hearty meal of gari and okra soup, Bisi announced to the family as we relaxed in the livingroom just why we had made the trip.

"Now," Bisi began, "I know that what I'm about to say is going to come as a shock to you. But please, listen and try to understand."

"If Grace wasn't here with you, I'd have thought that you're about to give us some bad news about her," Uncle Jeremiah said quickly.

"No, no, no. Thank God for that. The way I look at it, it's good news, because it will bring my sister, Grace, much happiness. But at the same time, the news will really be an eye-opener to all of you, and you may not like it."

Uncle Jeremiah turned to his wife, Aunt Ada. "You see why I don't read those foreign suspense novels the children bring home from the bookstore? What do you think she's talking about?"

Aunt Ada replied, "Be patient, my husband. Let Bisi say what she has to say the best way she can."

Uncle Jeremiah nodded, stretched out his legs in

front of him, crossed his ankles; and leaned back in his lounge chair. "Go on, Bisi," he gestured.

Bisi continued, "Since my sister Grace has been in Lagos, she has been seeing a very nice gentleman who happens to be an expatriate—"

"Oh no!" Uncle Jeremiah exclaimed, rubbing his entire head with both hands. "I can guess what's coming next."

"Please, my husband, let her finish," Aunt Ada said calmly.

"As I was saying, he's an extremely nice man, and he wants to marry Grace, and has asked me to deliver this letter."

Uncle Jeremiah extended his hand slowly, took the letter, and proceeded to open it as he glanced suspiciously at Bisi and me. Then, he looked at the sender's section of the letter and asked, "And how do you pronounce his name?"

"Mr. Jacques Pialoux-low-low-Pialoux. Mr. Pialoux wants to know what he should do next," Bisi replied.

There was total silence while Uncle Jeremiah read the letter completely. When he came to the end, he wiped his mouth with the palm of his hand and cleared his throat. "But why did Mr. Pialoux not come to speak for himself and meet with us face to face?"

"Sir, I suppose he needs to know that he will be accepted first as an expatriate before trying to gain acceptance as a potential husband. He also thinks the elders might need time to get used to the idea of an expatriate asking for the hand of an African girl in marriage."

Uncle Jeremiah bent his head to one side and shrugged his shoulders simultaneously. "Well, he does have a point there."

Bisi continued, "Another consideration he's asking

for is that the process should go very quickly. He has to travel to France on some family business and he wants to introduce Grace to his father as his wife."

"Wait just a minute! This man is moving too fast! Is that how they do things in his country?" Uncle Jeremiah looked offended. "Doesn't he realize that we have such a thing as 'native custom'?"

"Oh yes, he does, sir," Bisi replied quickly. "He knows all about that. He has been in Nigeria for some time now, and he himself said he would marry Grace no other way. As for the rush about the wedding, he also knows it's not done that way, but he's asking for special consideration since he has to leave so soon, and time is of the essence."

Uncle Jeremiah nodded, but no one spoke for some time. There was no sign of the children who had remained outdoors, since they had been told that the business at hand was for adults only. Eyes downcast, Aunt Ada's body shook nervously as she waited for her husband to say something. Then she broke the silence, "Our Grace to marry an Oyimbo? Strange thing! I can't imagine it."

Uncle Jeremiah looked at me for the first time since he started reading Jacques' letter. "Grace, my daughter, it's obvious this expatriate wants you, and according to him, has fallen in love with you and wants to marry you. But do you want him, do you love him? Is this what you want?"

"Yes, Uncle, very much, Uncle," I said with the emotion of someone who is begging a killer for mercy. "Uncle, when Jacques came into my life, I saw a man, not an expatriate, but a good, considerate man, one who will protect and take care of his family, and most of all, a man who truly loves me. And now, I love him deeply, and I don't think I can live without him."

As I spoke, Uncle Jeremiah changed his position in

his chair. He was sitting up now with his elbow on his lap, his hand supporting his chin, and his eyes full of wonderment and admiration.

"Case closed," he said, clapping his hands. "As for me, I don't like the idea at all, but I want your happiness, my daughter. If this is what will make you happy, I'll do what I can to support you. However, both of you must remember that I am only one person, and we must present this unusual situation to the rest of the family for their consideration and approval."

"As for me," Aunt Ada said, "I go along with whichever side my husband takes."

Uncle Jeremiah then made a generous suggestion. "Let's have our own little celebration with some palm wine and cola nut. And after that, I'll call for a meeting of the elders here in Owerri tonight, since the matter is an urgent one, to have the letter read to them. So, by tomorrow afternoon, when both of you leave for the village in Uzoakoli, you'd have a better idea of the reactions of the elders when you present the matter to the rest of the family in the village. After that, when you return to Lagos, you'd have a good idea where Mr. Pialoux stands, and what exactly to say to him."

Within two hours, the Nwokeji and the Nwachuku family members began to converge in Chief Nwokeji's compound on the outskirts of Owerri township. Members who owned automobiles picked up members who did not. At times, a caravan of cars could be seen trailing into the compound; at other times, one or two lone cars entered unceremoniously. Bisi and I had arrived much earlier to assist in the preparation for the meeting. The floodlights were in place, since the darkness of the skies was already upon us. Chairs and benches were arranged neatly in the middle of the compound. Facing the chairs and benches, was one especially decorated cane chair reserved for Chief Patrick Nwokeji, the eldest uncle on my father's side, who was also our family chief elder around Owerri province. Chairs on either side of Chief Nwokeji's chair were reserved for two junior chiefs. Also in this special section was a small table draped with a white tablecloth with a bottle of Johnny Walker whiskey on it, and a small white plate containing four whole cola nuts. Bisi and I sat in the front row between Uncle Jeremiah and Aunt Ada.

Finally, it was time for the meeting to commence. There were twelve elders present, with their wives. My uncle, Chief Nwokeji, who was a retired attorney, rose to speak. He was a tall impressive looking man of about sixty-five.

"Ladies and gentlemen, I'm sure we're all aware of the reason we have gathered here tonight. Our brother, Jeremiah Nwachuku, informed me that he managed to visit each one of you early this evening, and gave each one of you a copy of this letter to read; the reason was to let you have some time, no matter how little, to consider this serious issue before this meeting starts. We will conduct all meetings concerning this issue in English throughout all our proceedings and ceremonies. You see, the woman who brought this message from Lagos is a Yoruba woman and does not speak our language, and it's important that she understands clearly what to report back to the man who sent this letter. Also, from time to time, some English-speaking people may be attending our proceedings. I must warn you also, that since this is an unusual case, there may be instances when things will not be done in the usual fashion. Another issue before us which our brother, Nwachuku, wants to bring to our attention is that the man who wrote us this letter has a deadline to meet. In other words, he wants to marry our daughter by a certain date, because he has to travel out of the country on some family business and would like to take his new bride with him, if we approve the marriage. There you have it. When we begin deliberations, these are the things you must consider. Now, let us begin."

Chief Patrick Nwokeji sat down, retrieved a large white handkerchief from his chieftaincy attire and wiped his damp forehead and his mouth. Then he continued the proceedings, still sitting.

"Stand up, my daughter so everyone can see you," he said, pointing at Bisi. Bisi complied, curtsying as she turned around to face the other elders. "Now, ladies and gentlemen, this is the young lady who brought us the letter; her name is Bisi Ladipo. There are several issues involved here, and the most important one is the fact that the man who wants to marry our daughter is an expatriate."

"Why is dee man not here facing us with his request? Why is he sending a messenger to us?" an elder asked.

"Good question, my brother," answered Chief Patrick Nwokeji, "but the man has answered that question cleverly in his letter. He stated basically that we may have the need to first address the issue of his being white; and that when we get to the point where the fact that he's white ceases to become an issue, he will then appear before us and plead for our daughter's hand in marriage like any other man. Now, let's hear other comments."

For the first few minutes, the evening air carried the soft murmurings which rose from the small group. Then, one by one, each elder stood to air his views:

"Disis entirely new to us; the fact dat dee man is white complicates mattas. I need more time to tink about dis. I understand his reasoning why he's not here, but it's difficult for me not to consida his color, especially in his absence. He should have come."

"I agree with my broda. Dee man should have come and talk to us face to face. How can we tell what kind of a man he is when we can't look straight in his eyes? There's a lot dat a man's eyes can reveal about him. Yes, he should have come. It's ridiculous deciding on a man who is not standing in front of us."

"As for me, I don't care wheda he is here or not; a white man should not be marrying a native girl. Where will our young men go to find wives if white men start coming here and marrying our women? I say 'no'; our daughta should marry her countryman."

"I go with you, my broda. We have to marry our own kind. What is wrong with dis young generation anyway? Disis an issue dat would not even enta our mind during our time. I'm telling you, dis world has turned upside down."

"All dese eligible bachelors in dee village, an' our daughta has to go an' pick a white man. I don't like it oh!"

"We all know dat times have changed, so what I want to do is pose dis question to everybody here. Should we derefore remain where we are, or change with dee times?"

"My broda, if we change with dee times, what will happen to our cherished culture? Wouldn't it den disappear forever?"

"I tink dat what we have to ask ourselves is wheda what we do, or dee decisions we make, will enhance our culture or destroy it. In dis case, what harm will be done if dis marriage takes place? We'll learn from dis man's culture, an' he will learn from us. Like dee saying goes, 'we're not losing a daughta, we're gaining a son.' An' in dis case, dee son we're gaining is special, because he's so different."

"I go along with dat, my brother. So, let dee man

come an' talk to us face to face, an' we find out more about him, den, let us give him dee same consideration we'd give a man from our village."

"Dee most important ting we have to consider here is wheda dis man can make our daughta happy. Miss Ladipo, who brought us dis letta, said dat our daughta an' dis man were seeing each oda for quite some time; which means dat she knows him very well by now; an' she must like him very much an' believe he can make her happy, odawise, dis letta wouldn't be brought to us in dee first place. So, as we try to come to a decision afta we've met dee man, let us put dis into consideration."

"But, my broda, do you really tink dat two people who are so different could like each oda an' have a successful marriage?"

"Have we tought about dee children dat will result from such a marriage? I tink we should. Don't children of dis nature have a hard time in dis world? We also want our grandchildren to be happy."

The comments and arguments continued for about one hour, after which Chief Patrick Nwokeji said, "All your comments are well taken, and I would advise you to continue to think about all the issues raised here this evening. In the meantime, I will ask Miss Lapido to go back to Lagos and tell Mr. Pialoux that the request he put before us in his letter should come from his mouth, so we can look in his eyes, listen to him, and learn more about him. We will also like to see and hear from respectable people here in Nigeria who know him. Then, we will have good reasons to either accept or reject him." And to Bisi, he said, "Did you hear what I said?"

"Yes, sir," Bisi replied, rising, with hands behind her back.

Chief Nwokeji continued, "Tell Mr. Pialoux that we're

inviting him to bring his request to us in person, and since he wants these proceedings to happen as soon as possible, tell him that we will be prepared to meet with him next week Saturday. We, the elders, will have a private deliberation when this meeting is over. After that, Grace's uncle, Jeremiah Nwachuku, will give you the time and place of the meeting. He will also give you instructions for Mr. Pialoux, regarding how he should prepare for the meeting—what he should bring, things like that. You understand?"

"Yes, sir," Bisi replied. "Thank you, sir. I will give him the message, sir."

"That's it then. This meeting is adjourned, but we elders are going to hold another private meeting inside the house," Chief Patrick Nwokeji said, rising. Then, recognizing my presence for the first time throughout the whole evening, he walked up to me and said, "My daughter, take Miss Ladipo in the house and join my wife and all the other wives for a nice late supper."

"Yes, uncle. Thank you, uncle," I replied.

I felt slighted and hurt that I had been ignored throughout the meeting and had not been asked for any input, since the entire meeting was about my life. I posed the question to Uncle Jeremiah on our arrival home that night.

"My daughter," Uncle Jeremiah said, in answer to the question, "you mustn't feel slighted. You were not even supposed to be present at the meeting. When a man asks for permission to marry a young woman, that woman is usually never present when that happens. That's the reason nothing was said to you. It was even more polite of the elders to have ignored your presence rather than ask you to leave the meeting."

That night, Bisi and I waited until everyone in the

house had fallen asleep, and in the privacy of our room, we celebrated our partial victory. We decided that the situation looked hopeful, since the elders considered Jacques' request important enough to summon him to a meeting the very next Saturday. As Bisi sipped champagne and I drank a Sprite, Bisi gave me even more reason to be hopeful.

"My sister," she began after taking her first sip, "do you remember at the meeting when Chief Patrick Nwokeji told me that Uncle Jeremiah would give me a message for Jacques, as to what he should do and what he should bring to the meeting next Saturday?"

"I remember," I nodded.

"Well, I have more good news."

The excitement was too much for me to handle. I jumped to my feet, and literally began hopping as high as I could, since I couldn't scream for fear that I would awaken everybody in the house. "What is it, what is it? Oh my dear mother, the good spirits and the gods!" I responded nervously.

"Your Uncle Jeremiah said that the private talk he had with you after our arrival from the airport had given him a good idea of the type of person Jacques is, and his background; so he was able to plead Jacques' case on a personal level. He stressed also to the elders, the importance of shortening the length of time it normally takes for an approval of a marriage request and the other ceremonies that follow, since Jacques needs it all to be finished before he travels. Your Uncle said his efforts paid off, because after he had explained the situation to the elders, they asked him to send a message to Jacques, advising him to come prepared just in case his request is approved."

"So, it's all because of Uncle Jeremiah things are

moving this fast?" I asked.

"Of course!" Bisi replied, "You're lucky you have someone like Uncle Jeremiah on your side, otherwise your folks wouldn't have even given a letter from an expatriate a second thought, let alone consider the possibility of a marriage."

"So, you think there's hope for Jacques and me then?"

"I think so," Bisi replied.

I became hysterical. I threw myself on the bed and began throwing punches at the pillows. Suddenly, I felt Bisi's hands tugging at my lappa which I had tied over my nightgown.

"Grace, common, common, control yourself now. There's more; your uncle told me more!"

"Go ahead, I'll try to calm down," I said, as I reached for my glass of Sprite, took a sip, and sat on the edge of the bed. "Go ahead. Tell me what else he said."

"Do you understand what the elders meant when they said Jacques should come prepared when we arrive here next Saturday?"

"Not quite. Come prepared, how?" I replied.

"There's so many things that will be expected of Jacques just in case the bridal ceremony and a wedding do take place."

"What kind of preparation?" I asked impatiently.

"Well, for one thing, since Jacques has no family here in Nigeria, he will need to bring witnesses to testify on his behalf."

I wanted to scream, but I stifled it by cupping my mouth with the palm of my hand.

Bisi continued. "They also want him to bring the price for the dowry, and other expenses, because, if the marriage is approved, the wedding will take place the following day—next Sunday; which means that everybody who will be accompanying Jacques should come prepared for a possible wedding. Is this hopeful news, or what?"

I couldn't help letting out a scream; however, it was a weak and very much controlled scream. I was mindful that I must not cause the whole household to jump out of their beds and investigate what was happening to me. Therefore, instead of really letting myself go, I opted for an *Igbe-gbe-gbe* dance. I danced until Bisi demanded that we get some sleep in preparation for our trip to Uzoakoli early the following morning. Bisi was right. There was a second mission to be accomplished—disseminating all pertinent information regarding Jacques' request to my siblings in the village. I discontinued my dance and managed to settle down for the night.

Uncle Jeremiah, Bisi, and I started the journey to my village the following morning. Uncle Jeremiah's car advanced rapidly towards Uzoakoli, its headlights illuminating the darkness as though hundreds of kerosene lamps had been placed on both sides of the road. The cocks had not begun crowing when we pulled over and parked by the pathway that led into my family compound. With Uncle Jeremiah leading the way, we walked, single file, toward the main entrance of the compound. Eyes downcast, I trailed behind pensively, absorbed in thoughts of how this news was going to be presented to my siblings, how it would be received, and how, ultimately, my future would be affected. I envisioned a whole lifetime with Jacques, growing old together. There would be many children and several grandchildren. Suddenly, Uncle Jeremiah's voice brought me back to the moment.

"Look," he said, "I can see the children moving about in the compound, and daylight is only just breaking. It's as if they know they're about to have visitors."

I shook my head to erase my delightful daydream. Then I glanced at my watch. "Five-thirty," I said. "This is the approximate time I told them to expect us."

Uncle Jeremiah turned his head quickly. "You mean they know we're coming?"

"Oh, Uncle, I'm sorry, I thought I told you," I offered quickly. "Soon after our arrival from Lagos, I asked your neighbour, Mr. Owba, if he would allow me to send his houseboy to Uzoakoli to deliver a letter to my siblings at my compound."

"Is that so? And he allowed you to do that?"

"Mh-hm!" I replied. "He was even the one who came up with the idea of preparing my siblings for our visit. You see, I had told him the whole story, and after the initial shock and even a strong disapproval of the intended marriage, he volunteered to help out in any way he could."

Uncle Jeremiah laughed. "Good old Mr. Owba! That's just like him. He's a strange fellow, that one. He talks on both sides of his mouth! He's the kindest man you ever want to meet but never knows where he stands on any issue." Then, he added, pointing toward the compound, "Look, the children have seen us. Brace yourselves now, they're coming full speed at us. Don't get knocked down!"

That was precisely what occurred, except that the knockdown was far from being violent. As my siblings converged upon me with cries of, "Our big sister has arrived," "Welcome, Big Sister," I was gently rendered horizontally on the ground.

Later, after a robust breakfast of fried beef liver with onions, dundu* and dodo, we sat in a circle underneath the renowned pear tree and the family meeting began.

*dundu—fried yam

Chukuemeka sat between Uncle Jeremiah and Bisi and I was flanked by my siblings.

"I think I should open the meeting," Uncle Jeremiah began, as he searched the eyes of each of my siblings. "You received a letter from your sister informing you about the man who wants to marry her, right?"

My siblings leaned tenderly toward me. "Yes, yes, an' we so happy for our big sista!" Chukuemeka said, while the others bobbed their heads in agreement.

Uncle Jeremiah continued. "Your sister must have also explained everything that's been going on, and how the elders back in Owerri are considering the matter. Am I correct?"

"Yes, our sista told us, but she forgot to tell us what village dee man come from an' whether we know dee family, because we wan' our sista to marry a man from a good family," Chukuemeka replied.

Once again, my other siblings leaned even closer toward me, smiling broadly, and again bobbing their heads in agreement.

"Awright, I'll let your sister take over from here," Uncle Jeremiah said.

I took a deep breath, cleared my throat, and tried to begin, but my voice quivered. I thought if I spoke rapidly I would not appear nervous. "But you see, this man doesn't come from any village; as a matter of fact he's not even a Nigerian, he's an expatriate, a Frenchman." I paused to observe how this revelation had been received. The affectionate smiles had suddenly been transformed into eye-bulging stares. My siblings seemed to have stopped breathing.

I began my explanation quickly, "I completely understand how the fact that the man is an expatriate would come as a shock to you. Believe me, before I met this man, I would be shocked, too, if I were in your position. You know that I too always believed such a relationship was out of the question. But when I met Mr. Pialoux, I learned something entirely new from him, from my heart, and from my emotions. I learned about the existence of different types of love. One is, let's say, the type of love I have for you, for our uncle here, and for Bisi. Another type is the one that overpowers you with such intensity that it's what's within this human being that counts, and not who he is or where he comes from."

My siblings quickly directed their gaze at Chukuemeka as if asking for clarification of what I had just said. In response, Chukuemeka shifted from side to side, brought his right fist to his mouth as he cleared his throat, and said, "Dis...is what our sista is trying to say: She's saying dat our tradition tells us who we should marry an' who we should not marry. But, when people leave dere village an' go into the world an' mix with people who are different from dem, sometimes dis will happen; just like what happened with our sista."

Uncle Jeremiah, Bisi, and I nodded simultaneously. My siblings stared at us. Chukuemeka continued with more self-confidence; however, the faces that stared back at him were contorted into woeful stares of confusion and disbelief. I saw also, looks of disappointment.

For a fleeting moment, I fell into a melancholy state of mind. I wanted to add to what Chukuemeka had said, but I knew that if I had tried saying anything at this point, my voice would have cracked and I would have probably been sending out ambiguous signals.

Uncle Jeremiah came to my rescue. "Look," he addressed my siblings, "your reactions are perfectly normal. I don't believe that there was any relative or friend of your sister's that didn't react the same way when he or she heard the news. Take me, for instance; when I read the man's letter, I thought he and your sister had actually lost their minds. But then, after that big shock, I gave the matter a lot of thought. I tried to understand what both of them had to say about it, putting aside our tradition for a moment. And guess what? I learned something, too. I learned for the first time that what should matter here is whether the man is a good man, a respectable man, a man who really loves your sister and will care for her and protect her like a man should protect his woman."

The tears that blinded me as Uncle Jeremiah spoke now came flooding down my cheeks. Justine, who was sitting next to me, rose to wipe my tears with the edge of her lappa.

Uncle Jeremiah continued. "And we have heard very good things about this man. That's the reason the elders are inviting him to come to Owerri, to stand before them face to face and let the request to marry your sister come right out of his mouth. Mind you, when the elders read the man's request in a letter, they didn't like it at all. So, you're not alone; the whole thing is strange to everybody. Then, we all started to look at it differently, and decided to give the man a chance. We want to look at the man like we would look at any other man in the village, and not like an expatriate. And that's what I'm begging you to do."

I felt the urge to jump up and embrace my uncle for what I perceived to be an excellent explanation. Suddenly, my siblings rose silently as if they had been prompted, and surrounded me, each one touching a different part of my body. Then, as they caressed me, they were saying the words I'd hoped to hear:

"You our big sista; you have more wisdom."

"If you say dis man is dee bess man for you, we believe you."

"If you say dee man is a good good man, an' he love you an' will take care of you an' protect you, we believe you."

"If dis...is dee man you love an' dee one you want to marry, we give you our blessin, an' pray for dee blessin of our moda an' our fada in dee grave."

16

White Chief

The following Saturday had just dawned when Jacques and I arrived at the gates of the compound of Chief Patrick Nwokeji. We had chartered a taxi all the way from Port-Harcourt to Owerri. The other three chartered taxis that had left ahead of us carried those who had come from Lagos as Jacques' witnesses, should Jacques' request to marry me be approved. As our taxi slowed to maneuver the turn into the chief's compound, we were suddenly flanked by several village children who began screeching at the top of their lungs, *"Ony'ocha! Ony'ocha! Ony'ocha! Ony'ocha biala*! Ony'ocha biala!"* Inside the compound, when the taxi driver parked the car, Jacques hurried out of the taxi and over to my side to assist me out. As he did that, the children became more frenetic, and went wild with their chant of *"Ony'cha biala."* Then, they switched to pidgin English, *"Ony'ocha, Ony'cha,* bend your head, make we touch your hair."

Jacques was amused by the children's request. "I certainly will not," he said sternly. "I'll not allow you to touch my hair! I washed it this morning. Look at your hands! You'll get my hair all dirty."

"Awu—uu, Ony'ocha," the children insisted, brushing their hands against their clothing, "Look, our hand day clean now. We no go doti your hair. We beg you, make we touch your hair."

*ony'ocha biala—white man has come

The commotion brought Chief Patrick Nwokeji, his family, and guests to Jacques' rescue.

"Leave this compound now now. Go, go, go, go," the chief ordered the children, clapping his hands; and the children scrambled as though they were running from a cheetah.

Soon after our arrival, we were informed that Jacques' witnesses and friends from Lagos had already arrived, and had been informed that they would be needed for the morning meeting to testify on Jacques' behalf, and at the night meeting, to stand as witnesses at the Bride Price ceremony if Jacques' request to marry me was approved. Although I was not supposed to be present at this initial stage, I had asked Uncle Jeremiah if I could attend if I could make myself inconspicuous.

"How'd you do that?" he had asked.

"Well, Uncle, since all the attention will be focused on Jacques, I will dress up like one of the wives with my face partly covered, and no one will notice me."

Uncle Jeremiah had found the idea quite humorous and ingenious. "Why do you want to be there anyway?" he asked.

"Uncle, think about it, I'm seeing this aspect of our tradition at work for the first time and I don't want to miss any of it if I can help it. Uncle, think of it—a white man going through such a unique ceremony. How often does that happen? And it's all about my own wedding!"

"You have a point there," Uncle Jeremiah had replied.

It was now time for the meeting to begin, and the elders and family members took their assigned places. Finally, once again, the meeting was called to order by the eldest chief, Chief Patrick Nwokeji.

After welcoming all present and explaining why the meeting had been requested, Chief Nwokeji began.

"Would you introduce the visitor to us, Brother Nwachuku?"

"Yes, Chief," Uncle Jeremiah replied, bowing his head slightly at the chief and turning to the audience. "Ladies and gentlemen, I want you to meet Mr. Jacques Pialoux from Lagos. He's the man whose letter Miss Ladipo delivered to us last week." And beckoning to Jacques, Uncle Jeremiah gestured, "Mr. Pialoux, will you please stand?" With that, Uncle Jeremiah sat down.

Jacques rose, standing erect with hands behind his back.

"Mr. Pialoux," Chief Patrick Nwokeji said, "I understand you have a request to ask of us."

"Yes, sir; I have, sir. I have come here very humbly, sir, to ask for the hand of your niece, and daughter, Grace Nwokeji, in marriage. I love her very much, sir, and will continue to love her and give her the best care and protection possible until I take my last breath."

"Where are you originally from, Mr. Pialoux?"

"You can call me Jacques, sir. I'm the one who should pay you and every elder here my greatest respect. I'm from France, sir."

"What did you do in France before you came to Nigeria?"

"I'm an engineer by trade sir, so, I was working as an engineer."

"What area of engineering is that?"

"Civil engineering, sir."

"What made you decide to come to Nigeria to work?"

"I was working in Saudi Arabia, sir, when I heard about the vacancy for an engineering position in Lagos and I applied for it."

"A man of the world, eh? You must have travelled to many countries."

"I have, sir."

"How long have you been in Nigeria?"

"Three years, sir."

"What is the name of the company you work for?"

"Benamou Nigeria Limited."

"If we want to ask the company some questions about you, how can we locate them?"

"The Headquarters is in France, and there are branches in Kano and Makurdi here in Nigeria. There are also other overseas branches located in Switzerland and Germany. I will give you all those addresses, sir. And by the way, sir, the chairman of the Lagos branch where I work has accompanied me here and will be one of my witnesses."

Chief Nwokeji nodded, leaned back in his seat, and looked about at the other elders, "Gentlemen, he's all yours."

"Mr. Pialoux, I mean, Jacques," one of the other elders began, "You say you want to marry our daughta."

"Yes, sir."

"You may not see anytin wrong wit' dat, but, all of us here do. In oda words, you are a white man, an' your calture is very different from ours, and you're askin' us for permission to marry one of our daughtas, a native girl. You see, Jacques, we see dis as a big problem, because, it goes against our calture. You have notin' in common with our daughta."

"I understand what you're saying sir, but you see, sir, Grace and I don't see the differences between us as hurdles that we cannot handle. We realize our differences, but it has not mattered to us and has not prevented us from loving and respecting each other. As a matter of fact, we find the differences extremely attractive, and we're able to learn new things from each other. And most importantly, sir, we see ourselves as simply a woman and a man who are very much in love with each other, caring, cherishing and respecting each other as human beings."

"Tank you Jacques," the elder replied, and looking about him he said, "I'm finished for now; another elder can take over."

Another elder began. "Jacques, how long have you known our daughta, Grace?"

"A few months. But when I first laid eyes on her I knew immediately she was the woman I'd want to be my wife."

I couldn't believe Jacques had decided to tell the truth. We had agreed that it would be best to pretend that Jacques and I had known each other much longer. He was supposed to say that we had known each other for at least two years.

My heart sank when I heard Jacques say, "A few months." I was sure he had lost his case. I clasped my hands tightly on my lap and prayed silently to the gods. I continued listening.

"So you believe dat love will see you through dis marriage eh? What about dee problems you'd encounter with people from her calture who oppose dis type of relationship? How would you deal wit' dat? You have admitted dat you're a worldly man. How are you going to deal with all the prejudice dat would be directed towards our daughta when you take her to oda places away from Africa? Surely, you're aware of what goes on in the world, in terms of prejudice, hatred, discrimination, an' so forth an' so forth, aren't you?"

"I am sir."

The elder continued. "When our daughta accompanies you on trips to various countries, I'm sure dat she would sometimes find herself in one of dose dangerous, embarrassing, or precarious situations which would cause her much pain and anguish. What den?"

"Sir, I think that people will always be prejudiced in one form or another regardless of their race or culture. We simply have to use our common sense in the way we live our lives, and that's how I would live my life with Grace. I would never place her in an uncomfortable or dangerous situation; that would be my responsibility as her husband. I would protect her with every power within me. My philosophy is this, sir: a person is responsible for his or her own happiness, and if one is intelligent and mature, one would not place oneself in situations that would cause any danger or anguish. So, if Grace becomes my wife, I would for example, choose where we live very carefully, and make it my duty to ensure that we live a safe and happy life."

The elder beamed as he replied, "Tank you, Jacques."

Another elder took over. "Jacques, how long do you intend to remain in Nigeria?"

"I was actually preparing to leave Nigeria when I met Grace; but after we met, I changed my mind about leaving any time soon. I love her very much, sir."

"Does dat mean dat when you marry our daughta you could leave Nigeria any time an' take our daughta away from us?"

"Sir, if you allow Grace to become my wife, I would never have her do anything she doesn't want to do. She will live wherever she wants to live. If she wants to live in Europe with me, that's where we would make our home. And if she wants to live in Nigeria, I would be happy to live here in Nigeria permanently. Also, no matter how great the distance, I would see to it that you see Grace as often as possible."

The questions continued until all the elders had had

the opportunity to speak. The last elder to speak cleared his throat loudly, pressed his lips together, and leaned back in his chair, "I've heard what my brodas have said, an' I've heard Mr. Pialoux, I mean, Jacques. I wanted to speak last so I could give dis matta more thought an' listen to what all my oda brodas have to say. I'm glad I did dat because I learned a lot just by listening to everybody. So, since we still have until tonight to give our answer to Jacques, I suggest dat we adjourn dee meeting, an' wait until den to come up with our decision. As for me, I need some more time to consider everything I've heard so far."

The other elders mumbled their assent.

Then Chief Patrick Nwokeji spoke. "Jacques, you've heard my brothers. Get some rest, and we'll get together again tonight, and give you a reply. You explained in your letter why you wish this matter to be treated with urgency, and we understand; and we're trying very hard to move things along quickly. I hope you realize that this is a precedent for us. We're not in the habit of rushing the reply to marriage requests, and I hope you understand and appreciate that."

"I do, sir, and I thank you from the bottom of my heart," Jacques replied.

Chief Nwokeji continued, "We've also taken into consideration the distance from here to Lagos; so we'll give you an answer one way or the other as quickly as possible so that you don't have to travel back and forth too many times to attend different meetings and ceremonies."

"I appreciate that, sir," Jacques replied, bowing his head.

The chief continued, "Now, after this meeting, when you get together with your host, brother Nwachuku, he will explain to you what may happen tonight, and what you might need to bring with you."

"Yes sir. Thank you sir," Jacques said, bowing his head once again. Then, he added, "May I say one more thing sir?"

"Go right ahead, Jacques," Chief Patrick Nwokeji replied.

Jacques then turned sideways, in order to obtain good eye contact with each elder. "I only want to thank you and all the elders for your graciousness toward me and for giving me such kind consideration. I want to also thank you for honoring my other request, to go through the proceedings as quickly as possible because of my forthcoming travel plans. I do understand that proceedings such as this and the reply to a wedding request such as mine, would usually take several weeks, or even months. So, I thank you all from the bottom of my heart for your cooperation. I only hope that I may become a member of such a fine family someday. Thank you again."

"That's all right, Jacques," the chief replied. "And by the way, I noticed that all your witnesses are here. Very good. We'll need only their presence or what they have to say about your character at subsequent meetings. We'll let them know. The meeting is adjourned."

Soon after the meeting, our prospective wedding group began the journey back to Owerri township to await the evening meeting. Jacques and I rode back with Uncle Jeremiah and his wife. Bisi rode with her boyfriend, Peter Feizlmayr; Jacques' employer, Robert Benamou, rode in a chartered taxi. It was not long into the start of the journey that Jacques began shooting questions at Uncle Jeremiah.

"What did the chief mean," Jacques began, "when he

said I should come prepared with things to do and bring to the meeting tonight?"

"He means that if they give their approval tonight, the Bride Price ceremony would begin immediately and you have to be prepared."

Jacques' eyes gleamed with excitement. "Is that really what he meant?"

"Hm-hm. You know, you made a very good impression on the elders. The plan was to summon your witnesses to testify on your behalf, but you were doing just fine by yourself."

Jacques grinned broadly.

"I think you won their hearts, and I think your request will be approved. Shhhhh!" Uncle Jeremiah added, placing his forefinger over his lips, "But never say I told you so."

"What about the elders who oppose the relationship?"

"I think they've been won over by the ones who support it."

There was a hint of doubt in Jacques' eyes. "I hope you're right," he said, uncertainly.

"You see, this is what normally would take place: Normally, even when a family likes their daughter's suitor, he's never told right away that his request would be approved. He's kept in suspense until the last moment."

"What happens when a suitor comes prepared, bringing the Bride Price, and whatever else he's supposed to bring, but then is rejected; what does he do then?"

"He goes back where he came from, and saves what he brought for his next bride-to-be. That's just the chance the man has to take. If he comes from a long distance away, and the request is approved and he did not come prepared, that's when the ceremonies are postponed to a later date. I must say, the elders try to be reasonable."

"That's interesting! The whole thing is so exciting, it's all worth the trouble." Jacques said.

"That's the spirit!" Uncle Jeremiah said, flashing a broad smile.

Jacques was almost jumping out of his seat. "Tell me, tell me, what else should I bring with me tonight to the meeting?"

"Now, let's see." Uncle Jeremiah thought for a few seconds. "You have already brought your witnesses from Lagos. So, that's all set. I hope you brought a lot of money, because you will be asked to pay for all expenses from the time your request is approved."

"That's not an issue; I'm prepared for that; and if I happen to need more money, I'm sure my witnesses will come through for me."

"Good. First, you will be asked to pay a certain amount of money for the dowry; then, there's the menstruation money, a—"

"What's the menstruation money?" Jacques interrupted.

"This is money that is given to the bride's mother for having prepared her daughter for motherhood."

Jacques turned to look at me. "Interesting!"

Uncle Jeremiah continued, "Then, there's money for the bride's family in the village; there's money for the bride's compound; there's money for the bride's village; then, of course, you will be expected to pay for all the food and drinks to last for several days. You see, sometimes, marriage celebrations continue for a whole week; sometimes longer, depending on how long the food and drinks last."

Jacques chuckled, "I like that. Well, for this wedding, I would make sure that the villagers continue to celebrate long after we've gone back to Lagos. It's the least I could do for the opportunity and consideration given me to marry one of their own." And Jacques took my hand and squeezed it.

Our car whisked by small, sleepy villages along Aba Road and the four of us talked and laughed heartily, as we envisioned a "once in a lifetime" Bride Price ceremony and wedding celebration.

As we drew near Owerri township, I suddenly felt exhausted, as if I had been sitting in one of those social science classes in the village for hours on end without any breaks for lunch or recess. I must have been dozing off.

"Are you that tired?" Jacques said, putting his arm about my shoulder, and pulling me closer to him.

"Not really," I replied. "I learned somewhere that one learns more by listening. So, sometimes, I prefer to close my mouth and listen."

I knew that Jacques was enjoying the question/answer session. "What else should I know if I'm approved?"

"Oh yes," Uncle Jeremiah replied after a brief pause. "It's customary for the intended groom to be dressed in native attire for the Bride Price ceremony and for the actual wedding ceremony."

"Great! What do I do now? That means we have to go shopping on our way to your house, right? We don't have much time."

"Not so." Uncle Jeremiah shook his head. "Those are special outfits, and they're usually custom made. It's not easy to find the right type of materials and the right tailor; and as you say, time is against us."

"So, what do I do?"

"You borrow outfits from me; one for the possible

Bride Price ceremony tonight, and the other will be a regular chieftaincy outfit for the wedding ceremony."

"Did you hear that, Grace?" Jacques said, nudging me. "When we walk down the aisle, I'll be your chief."

Uncle Jeremiah and I laughed quietly.

"What's so funny?" Jacques asked, raising his eyebrows.

"You forgot quickly didn't you? We'll not be walking down any aisle," I said. "Remember? The wedding ceremony will take place in a village compound. Remember?"

Jacques slapped his forehead with the palm of his hand. "That's right! What's the matter with me? I did forget. Anyway, it doesn't matter; I'm ready to do whatever I'm asked to do."

"Good. That's the spirit! You see, Grace," Uncle Jeremiah said with a quick glance at me, "the elders saw this quality in him. He's eager and willing to do anything just to marry you. The man loves you, my daughter. That's one of the reasons we all fell in love with him." Then, keeping his eyes on the road, Uncle Jeremiah thought of something else. "Oh, you'll like this: be prepared to sit on the floor throughout the Bride Price ceremony, since that ceremony is always done in the traditional fashion. The elders, family members, and your witnesses will all be sitting on the floor, in a circle inside a mud hut as the ceremony takes place."

Jacques looked up at the roof of the car. "I love it!" Then, bending forward, he asked Uncle Jeremiah again, "So you really think a wedding is definitely going to take place?"

"Of course, even the biggest fool could tell. Also, I've seen this sort of thing happen so many times. Elders and families always seem to have a sixth sense about a prospective suitor."

"What do you mean?"

"They can sort of tell at the first meeting with a suitor, whether he's the right man for their daughter. If they get the feeling that he's not, they wouldn't even bother to ask him to come back for a second meeting."

Jacques nodded slowly. "Oh, now I see what you're saying."

Uncle Jeremiah continued, "So, you see, when they ask someone to come back, it's almost always certain that there will be a wedding. And as I said before, tradition dictates that the prospective groom has to go through rigorous examination and questioning, to force him to remember always that his wife is special to her family and her village, and that the marriage is not to be taken lightly."

"Uncle, tell us exactly what goes on at the Bride Price ceremony. I'm also curious about that," I said.

Uncle Jeremiah obliged. "Awright. Well, when the relatives of both the suitor and the bride-to-be are gathered at the bride's compound, they will all be told when to start entering the ceremonial hut. In your case, Grace, since your parents are deceased, the ceremony will take place at Chief Patrick Nwokeji's compound, the one we have just left, and he will stand in place of your parents. And since Jacques has no family here in Nigeria, he will be supported by the witnesses who came with him from Lagos. They are important during both the Bride Price ceremony and the wedding ceremony. Speaking about witnesses from Lagos; Grace, my daughter, I'm so glad you invited Bola Balogun and his wife to participate in all this."

"You see why I fell in love with her and want to marry her?" Jacques pulled me even closer to him and kissed me on my cheek. "Aside from her beauty and class, she has a good heart. I have not heard her say an unkind word about Bola, even after he threw her out of his house."

"I'm proud of you, my daughter," Uncle Jeremiah said. "We're all proud of you. Anybody else would have stopped talking to Bola and would have ostracized him forever. When you wrote and told me about what happened, I was shocked. Bola and I have been friends for years. I didn't think he would do that to my own niece."

"Uncle, that's history," I replied. "I don't think about it anymore; I forgave him a long time ago. So—since it appears tomorrow is going to be my wedding day—let's not talk about unpleasant things! Go ahead, tell us more. What happens next once everyone is inside the ceremonial hut?"

"Yes, I'm talking about the Bride Price ceremony now. Everyone will be seated on the floor in a semicircle, including the chief; and in front of him will be a small plate containing some *oji igbo* and a bottle of whiskey. And stacked up beside the bottle of whiskey will be the envelopes for the different moneys that will be asked of Jacques. The chief would start the meeting by welcoming everyone present, and then saying something like this: 'I believe there is a young man here who requires something of us.'

"Then, one of Jacques' witnesses, maybe even someone like Bola Balogun, would say something like this: 'Honorable Chief, elders, ladies and gentlemen, I, Bola Balogun and my wife Helen Balogun; Mr. Peter Feizlmayr, a close friend of Jacques; Robert Benamou, Jacques' employer, and a close friend of your daughter, Grace; are all here this evening to bear witness before you that Jacques Pialoux is a good man, an honorable and highly respected man of the community. He is here this evening to request your daughter, Grace Nwokeji's hand in marriage.'

"Then, the chief would say something like this: 'Can you tell us more about Jacques and why you think he's worthy of our daughter?'

"Then, someone like Jacques' employer would continue with something like, 'My name is Robert Benamou, Jacques Pialoux's employer. I have employed Jacques at my company for the past five years, and it has been through his hard work and loyalty that the company has been doing so well in Nigeria; that's why he's now our vice president and director. He is one of the most responsible, reliable, and decent human beings I have ever met. Most of all, he loves your daughter very much; and there's no doubt in my mind that he will continue to love her, treasure her, and protect her for the rest of his life.'

"Then, the chief's reply might be, 'Thank you, Mr. Feizlmayr. Jacques, do you have anything to say?'

"And Jacques would reply, 'Only that I would like to marry your daughter more than anything in the world because I love her so much. I would do whatever is required of me if only I'm given permission to marry her.'

"The chief will then ask Jacques for money for the different things required, starting from the dowry money to money to cover all of the food and drinks that will last for a possible week of celebrations. The moneys are all put in their respective envelopes. Then the chief would have someone open the bottle of whiskey and pour some in a glass for him to perform the libation."

"What is that?" Jacques asked.

"Libation is when you pour a liquid, such as liquor, on the ground or floor as a religious rite to appease one's deceased relatives or certain gods or spirits. And of course, as the chief pours the whiskey gently on the ground or on the floor, he asks the spirits to bless and protect the prospective bride and groom and bring them happiness, children, etc. After the libation, the chief breaks the *oji igbo* into small pieces, throws a few down at the doorway. Then he will take a piece for himself, and pass the plate around for each person present to help him or herself. To end the celebration, everyone congratulates Jacques. And after that, participants in the Bride Price ceremony file into the compound to a small feast prepared by the eldest chief's wife."

"If all these things happen tonight, what then?" Jacques questioned.

"Well, since we're moving more rapidly than usual because you have asked us to do so, the wedding could take place tomorrow."

Jacques and I turned and embraced each other, rocking back and forth for a few seconds.

"Awright, awright, stop that and pay attention, you lovebirds," Uncle Jeremiah ribbed. "Tomorrow is Sunday, right?"

"Mm-hm," Jacques and I mumbled simultaneously, still in a close embrace.

"Before the morning breaks, every one of us at the Bride Price ceremony would then travel to Uzoakoli, Grace's village. For the purpose of the traditional ceremony, me and you, Jacques, and all your male witnesses, including the elders, would remain at the compound of Chief Ebenezer Owba, another member of our family who lives in Uzoakoli. We will pretend that this is your family compound, Jacques, where you were raised. Then, Grace, together with all the wives of the elders, including the female guests from Lagos, will all stay at her compound. When all of us are where we're supposed to be, in keeping with the tradition, a group of us men will walk down with you to the bride's compound to ask for her whereabouts. We would do this several times, and each time, we will be told that no one by that name lives there. Then we would return to your compound and wait for the wedding ceremonies to begin. And Jacques, let me warn you; there'll be a lot of play-acting taking place as the ceremonies progress. So, all you have to do is just go along with whatever is taking place."

"Wo-oh!" I said, placing both hands on my head, "Jacques, what an education this is all going to be for both of us."

"Yes, it's all going to be like something out of a movie! But, what I can't wait to do is get into my chieftaincy attire."

"Mm-hm," I grunted, as I bent forward and tapped Uncle Jeremiah on his shoulder, "Uncle, you know what he means, don't you?"

"What?" Uncle Jeremiah looked puzzled.

"He can't wait to be the only white chief most of the people have ever seen or heard of."

"How did you figure that out?" Jacques shook his head in wonder. Then, tapping Uncle Jeremiah on his shoulder, he said, "I told you she's a bright young woman!"

17

The Wedding

Although the darkness of the Sunday dawn still hovered over the misty clouds, the entire length and breadth of Uzoakoli had sprung to life. News of an extraordinary wedding which was to take place that morning, had spread quickly. A white man was about to marry a village girl! All destinations seemed to be leading to either the groom's compound, or the bride's. People came from neighbouring villages and from other sections of Nigeria. Cars bearing the license plates of other states were already pulling into both compounds, while those making the journey on foot, had begun their trek to the festive compound.

From my compound, came the delightful sounds of drums, singing, clapping, and dancing by young, beautiful, and colorfully-dressed women of the village. Meanwhile, information about the goings-on at the groom's compound also reached us. It was reported to us in my compound that all the men, with the exception of the other two expatriates who were present, were dressed in ceremonial attire in readiness for the wedding ceremonies to begin; that the "white chief" or groom stood majestically in the middle of the compound, flanked by Uncle Jeremiah, Bola Balogun, Peter Feizlmayr, Robert Benamou, the elders, my male siblings—Chukuemeka, Obi, Ofor, Chike, Isaac—and dozens of male guests from the village; that the groom presented the perfect picture of an Igbo chief on his wedding day, dressed in the ceremonial attire worn by the chiefs of that region; that on his feet he wore soft brown Italian loafers; and included in his ceremonial attire, was a hand-carved walking stick with a gold, lion-head shaped handle. We were also told that farther inside the compound could be seen men from the village surrounding six large smoky grills, where a cow, two goats, two sheep, and a lamb were already being roasted; that, earlier on, and in keeping with tradition, the groom had already been subjected to a confrontation by young bell-ringing village boys. (It was a tradition for the boys to ring their bells as loudly as they could and challenge the groom as he strolled with his entourage along a footpath.)

Feigning anger, the groom would say, "Would you stop ringing those horrible bells. I'm about to go deaf."

However, the more the groom demanded that they stop, the louder the boys rang the bells, while one of them would scream at the top of his voice, "We will continue to ring our bells until you give us some money." The groom would then respond by retrieving money from the deep pockets of his attire and handing it over to the boy. However, that would not stop the boys from ringing the bell. After this scenario had been repeated about three times, the leader of the boys would then say, "We will stop ringing the bell only if you promise us that you will not marry our sister."

Feigning sadness, the groom would reply, "Please, I really want to marry your sister. Tell me what to do so I can marry her."

"We want more money," another boy would respond loudly, "or you cannot marry our sister."

Even after the boys would be offered more money, they would continue with their bell ringing.

"What else should I do?" the groom would ask, feigning frustration and bewilderment.

"We'll stop ringing the bells after you have repaired the 'bridge' over which our sister must cross to come to you."

"Lead me then to the 'bridge,'" the groom would reply, stamping his walking stick forcefully on the ground. "My men are carrying the 'tools' that we need to repair the bridge.'"

At the site of the "bridge," about three of the groom's men would immediately drop the tool box on the ground, remove some of the tools, and give one to each man. All the men would then get busy "repairing the bridge."

When the "work" is completed, the groom would then say, "The 'bridge' is mended. Now, will I be able to marry your sister?"

"You can, if you can find her," one of the boys would say. "We heard that she is missing. But, don't you worry. We will help you find her. Go back to your compound and wait for us to get back to you."

While all this play-acting took place, at my compound, the women of my village had dressed me up for my wedding and prepared me for the walk to the groom's compound. I was wearing red george* over a white lace blouse with minute gold studs in the center of intricate floral patterns. Spread out like a blossoming flower, a stiff, pink satin scarf was skillfully entwined around my head. On my neck were strands of thin gold chains and long coral beads; and dangling from my ears were long, wide, gold leaf-shaped earrings. In one hand I clutched a small, folded, pink umbrella, covered with white floral designs.

As I emerged from my hut, I was flanked by the young, beautiful, singing and dancing girls, and other

*george—an expensive and unique cotton lace fabric

women who had gathered at the compound. Soon, we began to advance onto the main road leading to the groom's compound. Walking beside me on one side was an attractive, colorfully clad young woman holding a bright yellow umbrella over my head to protect me from the morning sun. On my other side was Bisi Ladipo, dressed in a white cotton lace lappa over a matching buba and a gele of gray and white satin, which matched her leather pumps and handbag. Behind the umbrella girl walked Helen Balogun, in a pale blue organza dress that draped down to the calves of her legs. She also wore a white, wide-brimmed straw hat, white low-heeled pumps, and held a small matching clutch bag. Immediately behind me were my female siblings, Patricia and Comfort, who were surrounded by all the wives of the elders. I had been told that my male siblings, Chukuemeka, Obi, Ofor, Chike, and Isaac, were already at the groom's compound.

My procession moved on slowly to allow the singing and dancing girls to perform intricate ceremonial movements for the spectators who had lined the road. Finally, we reached the footpath that led into the groom's compound. Still singing and dancing, my procession waited at the gates for our cue to enter the compound. I craned my neck to steal a glimpse of my white chief, and there he was standing majestically in the middle of the compound looking more regal than had been described to me. The dozen-or-so men, including the other chiefs who surrounded him, could pass as the subjects of the chief himself. The white chief stood out like a tiger surrounded by each of the other animals in his jungle. As I continued to observe Jacques, I became even more proud of him, and I loved him all the more for his willingness to do whatever it took to marry me. And at that moment, I wished that I was in his arms, engaged in a passionate embrace and kiss.... It was my umbrella girl who got me out of my daydream.

"Madam," she said, "Chief Nwokeji day wave for us to come inside dee compound."

As we pressed on into the compound, the women in my procession and the spectators who lined the street, including the guests who had already jammed the compound, began calling out my name, clapping their hands, and hopping or swaying to the frenzied beat of the drums at one end of the compound. Finally, the groom's group and my group stood facing each other, with Chief Patrick Nwokeji standing between us. Jacques and I smiled at each other as we let our eyes say how much we loved and wanted each other, since we could not touch or speak with each other at this point. Uncle Jeremiah then came forward holding a tray containing a bottle of Johnny Walker whiskey, a plate of *oji igbo*,* and a plate of *okwa ose*.†

"Yes," the chief said, picking up the *oji* and holding it up for all to see, "we have some *oji*." He then broke it up into small pieces, placed them back in the plate and held up one small piece. Then he began to pray: "We thank you, all you good spirits of our dead, to have allowed us to live to see this day on which our beloved daughter is getting married. We thank you also to have brought us a fine young man as a son-in-law, and for the wisdom to accept him with open arms. Please, we beg of you, let them have a happy marriage, a happy life, and lots of children. And tomorrow, when they leave Uzoakoli to go back to Lagos, please go with them, and guide them throughout their journey, and don't let any evil befall them. Amen."

*oji igbo—cola nut which is unique to the Igbo tribe
†okwa ose—tiny, hot, black seeds that are usually eaten with the ogi igbo

"Amen" could be heard reverberating from the compound to the street. The rest of the *oji* was then distributed among the elders and my family members.

Next, the chief picked up the plate of *okwa ose* and said, "And all you spirits, I ask that whoever chews this *okwa ose* will enjoy it and not choke from it. Amen."

And another thunderous "Amen" resounded.

Again, the chief distributed the *okwa ose* among the elders and my family members, after which he picked up the bottle of whiskey and began the libation. At the end of the libation and more prayers, the chief took my hand and gave it to Jacques, who received it eagerly with both of his hands, as though he had just been given a unique and precious gift. Cupping both our hands in his, the chief said, "My family and I are very happy to give you, on this day, our loving daughter, to be your wife. And by the way," the chief quickly added, "I was told that you brought two gold rings, one for yourself and one for your wife. We don't have that tradition, but we'll allow you to put the rings on each other's fingers. The only thing we won't allow you to do is kiss each other in front of everyone here, as you do in your country." And most of the guests found the chief's remark amusing.

After Jacques and I put the rings on each other's finger, Chief Patrick Nwokeji announced to the crowd, "This woman is now this man's wife." On that announcement, screams and shouts of joy exploded in the air, while the drummers banged their drums frantically to the accompaniment of the other musicians. In the meantime, Jacques and I could not resist embracing each other, although that was not considered acceptable behavior. We lingered in the embrace with tears in our eyes and were pleasantly surprised that no one attempted to pull us apart. Instead, the celebrations began in earnest. The compound, footpaths and the immediate roads had been transformed into ballrooms. Both the young and the old began dancing feverishly to the exhilarating sound of the music. As some danced, others made their way to grills that displayed now ready-to-eat meats. Also displayed on small tables pulled together to make one long, wide table, were calabashes filled with palm wine, various sorts of imported whiskey, wine, beer, and soft drinks.

However, in spite of all the grandeur, the feast, and the jubilation, my husband and I wanted nothing more than to be alone together. When we approached Chief Nwokeji for permission to leave the celebration in order to get some rest and prepare for an early morning trip back to Lagos, we were astonished that he went along with our wishes; so, Jacques and I slipped off unnoticed to my now deserted compound.

As we left for Lagos the following morning, we observed that the number of guests and spectators lingering along the roads and footpaths leading to Chief Nwokeji's compound had virtually doubled. The music and dancing had reached delirium proportion, and we were assured that the celebration would continue for the rest of the week.

18
Recantation

The 1:55 Nigeria Airways DC-10 was to be three hours late departing from Port-Harcourt to Lagos. According to airline officials, the plane had not left Lagos due to mechanical problems. As to be expected, almost every passenger waiting for that flight displayed some impatience and displeasure about the news of the delay. Some people paced the floor, mumbling obscenities; some stumbled aimlessly in and out of the airport, puffing more cigarettes than necessary; and others were engaged in combative question-and-answer sessions with airline officials:

"Why you don't use more planes? Why is jus' one plane going and coming, going and coming?"

"Because Lagos to Port-Harcourt is not far; it takes only forty-five minutes and we have only three flights a day. So, there's no need to use more planes. Normally, the plane never has any trouble. It's only dis one time when dere's trouble."

Jacques and I did not consider the delay to be an inconvenience. After all, we were newlyweds and revelled in our time together, regardless of the circumstance. We found it to our advantage that most of the passengers were preoccupied in making themselves comfortable for the next three hours. As a result, Jacques and I took our own advantage of the situation and found an unoccupied bench for two in a secluded section of the airport, where we sat, bemused with each other's company, until we were alerted to board the late arriving plane.

It was not until we were on the plane that I realized I had not had a full night's sleep since that Saturday night at Uncle Jeremiah's house. Consequently, after boarding the plane, I fell asleep immediately, my head resting comfortably on my new husband's shoulder. Suddenly, I was awakened by a nudge to my ribs. I raised my head lazily and looked over at Jacques, but he had also fallen asleep. I snuggled against him and went back to sleep, convinced that I was imagining things. Again, I felt another nudge to my side; and again, I looked at Jacques. He was still drowsing. Then, this time, I felt a thump in the middle of my head. Startled out of my sleep, I looked about me to investigate what might have fallen on my head. Jacques still had not awakened; he was actually snoring lightly. I turned to look at the passenger sitting on the other side of me and her austere-looking eyes blazed with fury.

"Yes, that was me trying to get your attention."

"Why? What's wrong?" I replied, "Please, I'm really exhausted, let me get some sleep; I'll talk with you later."

"No, no, no, no, you have to wake up and listen to me. I see you heading toward the path of destruction. It's my duty as an older African woman with more experience than you, to save you."

I was convinced the woman was crazy. I looked to see whether Jacques was finally awake and was paying attention; but he had not been disturbed.

"What destruction?" I replied. "What are you talking about? Look, you don't even know who I am; so what is this about destruction? I beg you, let me get some rest!" I turned my back on the woman, slid my arm under Jacques', and attempted to resume my sleep.

The woman was persistent. She tugged at my sleeve. "Look, take it from me; later on, when you get to be my age, it will be too late. Come to your senses."

I was beginning to lose my patience. "Look," I said, "I don't know what your problem is, but if you don't leave me alone, I will find a seat somewhere else." With that, I turned my back on her once again and closed my eyes. I was afraid to go to sleep now, since I was convinced the woman belonged in an asylum and might be dangerous. I did not want to awaken Jacques to alert him to what was going on for fear that it might enrage the woman; I got the feeling that she wanted her words to be confidential between both of us. So, I braced myself in anticipation of another verbal assault.

While I waited, I wondered why the woman thought that she was older than I. I was sure that she did not look a day older than me, except that she was dressed like a very wealthy woman, or perhaps was the wife of some politician. It was now apparent that this woman's behavior was incongruous with her appearance. She was stunningly dressed in a lace buba, the holes of which were intricately covered in gold embroidery. Spread out like the wings of a bird, was her gele of the same lace, cocked on her head like a bowler hat. Her opulent looking jewelry glittered each time she moved.

Since it now seemed unlikely that I could go back to sleep, I decided to get to the bottom of this once and for all. It did not matter to me now whether the woman was insane, wealthy, the wife of a politician, or was older than I. I removed my arm gently from Jacques' and turned to face her.

"I wish you'd tell me what you're talking about," I said, trying to appear calm although I was extremely irritated. "If you keep on beating about the bush, we'll be in Lagos before you come to the point."

The woman sat up, moved to the edge of her seat and

twisted her body around to face me. She spoke rapidly. "You cheeky devil! You've lost all the respect you have been taught growing up African. Who do you think you're talking to? Don't you have any respect for your elders or for yourself? That's exactly why I woke you up; to drive into your thick skull that you must have some respect, at least for yourself. Look at you! Instead of settling down with a nice African man, you're running around selling your body and soul to expatria—."

I interrupted sternly. "Look, you're picking on the wrong woman. First of all, I'm not as young and inexperienced as you think, and I'm certainly not the type of woman you think I am, and for your information, this man sitting besi—"

"Shut up, and listen to me, and stop covering up what you're doing," she cut in.

"That's it!" I said, elbowing Jacques. "Jacques, wake up and get the flight attendant. We need to sit somewhere else. This woman is a well-dressed lunatic."

Startled, Jacques shot up in his seat and brushed his mouth with the back of his hand. "What's going on?"

Before I had a chance to respond to Jacques' question and explain how the confrontation had started, the woman sprang at me like a cat after a mouse. "Who are you calling a lunatic, eh, eh, eh?" the woman said. She grabbed me by my hair and pulled me off my seat.

Jacques struggled to pry the woman away from me. "What's going on?" he repeated.

She finally released me and lunged at Jacques, who managed to overpower her by holding tightly onto her wrists. Soon, we were surrounded by flight attendants and passengers, all trying to stop the altercation the best way they could. Finally, a female flight attendant managed to calm the woman down, while other crew members led

Jacques and me toward the captain's cockpit to tell our side of what had happened. Soon after, we were seated elsewhere, while the crew members restrained the woman and listened to her grievances.

Later, as Jacques was examining my upper body to ensure that I had not sustained any injuries from the woman's attack, I heard a voice call out softly, "Excuse me, Mrs. Pialoux?"

I looked up to find a male crew member in full uniform, complete with a cap. "I'm dee captain," he said, "I want you to know dat we had radioed dee police authorities about dee trouble on board dee aircraft, an' we were told dat upon landing, statements would be taken from you and dee woman who attacked you; and dat will be done before dee other passengers are allowed to disembark. However, after we spoke with dee woman and she learned dat you're husband and wife, she became remorseful and she asked me to apologize to both of you. She also gave me dis envelope to give to you, madam. I also told her about your celebrations dat took place only yestaday, which was dee reason you were so tired on dee plane and did not want to be disturbed. Here, madam, take dee envelope. Dis... is her way of saying dat she is sorry for her misunderstanding. Take it, madam."

I looked at Jacques, and he responded, shrugging his shoulders, "It's up to you."

I hesitated for a moment. Then, I reasoned that if I did not take the envelope, I was in essence saying that I was still angry and would never forgive the woman for what happened. So, I took the envelope.

"Good," the captain said, "Madam, you've done dee right ting. Now, dis... is what ah wanno know. Should I cancel dee alert call to dee controls at Ikeja Airport and say everytin' has been settled, and no charges will be filed?"

I nodded. "Yes, do that; say all is settled."

"Good," the captain replied. "One more thing! The woman wants to know if she could come over and shake your hands and congratulate both of you."

"That's fine with us," Jacques and I said almost simultaneously.

Then, I added, "Tell her it's all over with and I've forgiven her."

"Good enough," the pilot replied, and left quickly.

Later, as our taxi rolled out of Ikeja Airport, inching its way in the "go slow," I rested my head on my husband's shoulder. We were in traffic for what seemed like an eternity. Yet, we remained awake and very much alert to the happenings on the roads—the street vendors vying for attention and squabbling over potential buyers; passengers at bus stops, climbing over each other to get on the already congested public buses; the fistfights erupting here and there amidst small groups of people. Finally, Jacques interrupted my entertainment. "You haven't opened the envelope to see what's in it," he said. "Aren't you curious?"

"Not really," I replied. "It must be money, and it really doesn't matter how much. The idea is, it's a peace offering, and it's the thought that counts."

"I know, I know, but I'm curious even if you're not. Open it," Jacques replied.

Reluctantly, I tore the envelope open. Jacques observed my movements impatiently and saw the amount before I did.

He whistled loudly, and then exclaimed, "Five thousand naira!"

"What?" I replied, bringing the cheque closer to my eyes. "Jacques, you're right. It is five thousand naira!"

"Well, it's all yours. You can make it the first deposit in your own personal bank account in France when we go there."

"Why am I depositing the money in France, when I've never been there before and I don't even live there?"

"That's part of my plan for us. Of course you'd have to agree to it. Eventually, we'll be settling down in France; but what I didn't tell you is that, at the same time that I got that call from my father to come home to talk about the family business, I was also asked by my company to direct the branch in Paris!"

"So, you've been promoted? Congratulations, my husband!" I said with an embrace and a kiss.

"I didn't want to bring all this out before the elders, because I thought they had enough to deal with already. For them, it was difficult enough just getting used to the idea that I'm white."

"True."

"All right, my dear wife, now that you know all this, would you settle down in France with me?"

"My dear husband, what a question!" I replied.

Jacques quickly embraced me. "I love you more than anything," he said in my ear. "You're mine forever and ever."

My face pressed firmly on Jacques' chest, I whispered, "I love you even more than that."

*   *   *

But that part of my life soon disappeared, like the painting of Badagary Beach which hung on the wall of my hotel room where I had fled from my homecoming party in search of solitude. I counted on my fingers how long

Jacques and I had been married, and came up with eight years. The first six were ecstatic and glorious; however, by the end of the sixth year, Jacques began to voice his dissatisfaction with me, our marriage, and our life together. First, he complained that I had lost the "bush woman" qualities he had fallen in love with—my love for the simple things in life; and the joy I used to have in waiting on him hand and foot, rather than having him come home in my absence and prepare his own meal, or warm up some leftovers. He knew he was also expected to help with things pertaining to housekeeping, such as doing the dishes and waxing the floors, or vacuuming. He brooded over the children that we did not have after medical tests results confirmed that I was sterile. He also complained that I had become self-conscious, cynical, defensive, truculent, materialistic, and too worldly for his liking.

During those years, I found myself spending each day either shopping or window-shopping, and then lunching with my neighbor, Madam Callamand, to whom I had poured out my marital problems. Soon, I was beginning to prefer my adventures with her rather than staying home to prepare my husband's meals.

In the last two years of our marriage, Jacques hardly spoke to me and whenever he did speak, it was to outline my faults. Finally, I admitted to him that he was right on all counts, pleaded for forgiveness, and promised to change things around. As for the issue of children, I also stressed that I would be willing for us to adopt as many children as he wanted. But, my pleas had come too late, and they fell on deaf ears. Jacques began staying away from home most nights, until he finally moved out of the house. And when he finally asked me for a divorce, it did not come as a complete surprise.

Even a generous divorce settlement—a huge house

and a large bank account—did not ease the pain of losing my husband. However, Jacques continued to show interest in my welfare and would telephone frequently to insure that I was comfortable. Although it was an extremely thin thread that held us together after our divorce, it was nevertheless my desire to remain in France permanently rather than return to Nigeria. I fantasized that living in France would afford me ample opportunity to carry on my private campaign to try to recover my husband. I treasured Jacques' telephone calls and never failed to ask him to reconsider his devastating decision; but, he stood firm. He made it clear that he could never be happy with me again, regardless of what I was prepared to do. Finally, one day, I received what I thought was one of Jacques' occasional telephone calls. I was thrilled to hear his voice and when I embarked on one of my usual pleas for forgiveness, he stopped me abruptly to break the news about his upcoming wedding to a young Haitian woman.

My heart sank as I listened. I thought I was going to have a seizure. I found it difficult to breathe for the next few seconds.

I thought that as long as he remained single, there was a chance of us getting back together. But a marriage to another woman was like my death sentence.

"Are you there?" Jacques asked, obviously concerned.

"Ye...s," I replied, struggling to catch my breath, "Con-gra-tula-tions! When is the wedding taking place?" I added, my voice cracking.

"This coming Saturday," he replied.

I could think of nothing else to say, and when I dropped the receiver after that conversation with Jacques, I decided that the wedding day of my former husband would find me on a jet plane to London, en route to Nigeria. My family and friends in Nigeria of course had no idea Jacques and I had been having marital problems; I did not want them to worry. My letters had been full of lies about how well things were going. Now, I worried about how to explain my divorce from Jacques, to my family.

I had never learned to sleep my worries away in times like this. Perhaps my insomnia had turned out to be a blessing. It had given me the opportunity to devise a most ingenious explanation for the breakup of my marriage, and to inform people of Jacques' new marriage. The manner in which the presentation was to be given, as well as its timing, would have to be planned carefully. The day-dream had even altered my defeatist attitude about the way I was handling the loss of my husband. I now was aware of what my first order of business should be: I must make the final decision to let go of Jacques, to reach deep down into my inner core for the strength to go on with my life, and to find some consolation in all of this. A miracle had taken place. I felt an extraordinary peace and serenity spreading through every fibre of my being. Suddenly, I was not afraid to face anyone, even my family, regarding my failed marriage. I was prepared to be truthful in the way I would describe what had happened if anyone was interested in knowing.

What I wanted to do at that very moment, was to rush back to my "welcome home party" at Bola Balogun's house and join in the celebrations. This time, it would indeed be joyful dancing to celebrate the beginning of a new life, and the realization that after all, I had so much to be thankful for.

Getting ready to leave my hotel room for the Baloguns', I thought about my beautiful and comfortable house in France, and how lucky I was to have an abundance of the things that gave me pleasure. I also realized that there was still continuity regarding the most significant components of my life. I was free to visit Nigeria whenever I so desired, to experience my roots and to cherish my family and friends. And there was every evidence that I had not been abandoned by the watchful eyes and strong arms of the spirits of my ancestors and the gods of my people. How else could this miracle have happened?

More importantly—I had no regrets for having gotten off the village mat.